About the Author

Alan Liptrot was born quite a while ago in Barnsley, Yorkshire. After living in various parts of the country and the world, he has come home to Barnsley, like an elephant returning to his birthplace. He is currently on a diet.

Dogmeat Dave's Bag

Alan Liptrot

Dogmeat Dave's Bag

Olympia Publishers
London

www.olympiapublishers.com
OLYMPIA PAPERBACK EDITION

A CIP catalogue record for this title is
available from the British Library.

ISBN: 978-1-80074-802-6

This is a work of fiction.
Names, characters, places and incidents originate from the writer's
imagination. Any resemblance to actual persons, living or dead, is
purely coincidental.

First Published in 2022

Olympia Publishers
Tallis House
2 Tallis Street
London
EC4Y 0AB

Printed in Great Britain

Dedication

For my sister, Patricia and my brother, David.

Acknowledgements

Thank you to Jay Prydderch for providing inspiration and encouragement.

Chapter 1

Dogmeat Dave was in one of his moods again, his bitterness oozing like Coca Cola from a shaken bottle. He'd never been the same since the accident and you just couldn't talk to him when he was like this, nevertheless, Mo, the youngest amongst us was trying his best. 'You've been married, haven't you, Dave?'

'Yeah, I was married for a while. What about it?'

'What went wrong?' asked Mo.

'I lost my wife,' Dave spat.

'That's not entirely true, is it, Dogmeat?' I interjected.

'Okay,' said Dave, 'I woke up one morning and she'd gone. I fuckin' misplaced her then, is that better? It'll happen to you eventually; everybody ends up in a single bed, love.'

I liked Mo. During the six or seven years he'd worked with me, he'd never been a bit of trouble, but we were feeling the pinch at the moment. I'd been knocked for a few thousand quid on an extension we'd built and hadn't had the funds to pay him for a few weeks now, and the guilt was causing me sleepless nights. The only solvent one amongst us was Jimmy Onion, who had a well paid, salaried job in Sheffield. No one knew quite what he did for a living, we just knew he was minted. Mo and I were finding it hard to justify our weekly get together, but who amongst us was going to call time on a tradition which had survived industrial disputes and marriages?

This was supposed to be a pleasant, Saturday lunchtime, drink, same time, same pub, same table, but sometimes it just seemed like a chore. I fully appreciated that Dogmeat Dave had been dealt a bad hand, but he hadn't handled it with any grace. The accident had happened many years ago now and, if anything, he was getting worse. His moods were up and down like a bride's nightie. It's true, life is full of uncertainties, and we are all at the mercy of the fickle finger of fate, but how you handle it is the mark of a man. Dogmeat detested being a wheelchair user and we'd learned to lift our drinks as he approached, because without fail he would ram the chair into the table, and anyone who wasn't in the know would lose their beer.

The Railway Inn, once, long ago, flourished as an important cog in the local economy, a landmark where people gathered for a final tipple before moving on to the station next door. Alas, the track had been removed in the 1950s after over a hundred years of service and the route had become part of the Trans Pennine Trail, a coast-to-coast route for walkers and cyclists. Now, the station had gone, leaving successive owners having to generate new sources of income. Some were successful, but sadly it had proved too big a challenge for most. Walt, the present incumbent tried his best to attract custom. Quiz nights, raffles, karaoke, open mike evenings, pie nights and local promising bands were just part of his strategy. Not all his ideas were good ones, in fact some were downright bizarre. On the whole though, he'd stuck to the task admirably and the business was holding its own.

The car park in front was surrounded by a low brick wall with a separate entrance and exit. It was considerably larger than it needed to be, a consequence of its illustrious past. At the far end stood a food trailer, with "Bobby Burgers" emblazoned on all sides. It was a large pub with high ceilings and ornate cornices, albeit a little yellowed, but the story of its history was there if you cared to look for it. The facade was much the same as it would have been seventy years ago, although time had taken its toll. The paintwork was dry and flaking and pigeons lined up on the overgrown gutters waiting to pounce upon a morsel of burger bun.

'I'm off for a Woodbine.' Dogmeat wheeled off, heading outside for a smoke. I heard him shouting at the youngsters who were leaning against the rail in the sunshine enjoying a pint. 'Get off the fuckin' ramp, will you?'

'He's getting worse,' said Jimmy Onion, looking over his glasses which were perched on the end of his nose.

'Just leave him alone,' I said, 'he'll come round.'

My best mate, Bert the greyhound, lay on the sticky carpet at my feet. If anyone complained to Walt about the dog being in the pub, they would be out on their ear. He'd tell them that Bert was an assistance dog. Truth is, Bert only ever assisted me in sinking a few jars, but Walt knew which side his bread was buttered. He wasn't going to turn away his regulars for a stranger who would probably never show his face again, anyway, Bert had become a fixture in the pub, a canine celebrity. Walt's fortunes had improved with the building of a new office block next door, but some of the gobshites who came in left a lot to be desired. Dogmeat hated the way they started every sentence with "so" and was often inclined to make his feelings known to all and sundry. When he returned, reeking of tobacco smoke, I steered the conversation to old times, when myself, Jimmy Onion and Dave had been at school together. We often reminisced about supposedly better days, a safe place to be when Dogmeat was on one.

'Remember when you fell in the canal, Dogmeat?' I asked.

'Oh yes, mi mam was always telling me not to play by the old canal. It was only a foot deep, but I went headfirst and soaked missen from head to toe. If she had ever found out, she'd have given me a right twatting. Good job it had been a sunny day so I could dry out a bit before I went home. I had to sneak my undercrackers into the airing cupboard cos they were never going to dry under my trousers. I can still recall that feeling of them up the crack of my arse to this day. Makes me shudder.'

'Did you ever do anything like that, Jimmy?' Mo was always fascinated by these stories.

'Did he fuck,' said Dogmeat. 'He was too careful.'

'I had my moments,' said Jimmy Onion.

'Like what?' Dogmeat never really liked Jimmy Onion, he merely tolerated him.

'I crossed the canal on that huge pipe with spikes on.'

'That's cos we made you do it.'

'I did it though, didn't I?'

'The point is,' insisted Dogmeat. 'You wouldn't have done if we weren't there.'

'Of course I wouldn't. Why would I? Do you imagine that I'd be walking on the canal bank alone and thought, Oh, there's a dangerous looking pipe with spikes sticking out all over it. I must scrabble across it?'

'I went over that pipe,' I said.

'I know you did Johnboy, we all did. That's why Jimmy Onion came over, cos we'd have left him behind. He was bricking it, shaking like a shitting dog.'

'It's a bypass now,' I said.

'What is, bro?' Mo asked.

'The canal. It was disused when we used to mess around, forty years ago. They filled it in and made a road.'

'Shame,' said Dogmeat. 'They ripped up the fuckin' railway lines as well. That put paid to the jobs that depended on it.'

'There was the old farm further along as well,' I said.

'That's right. It's still there,' said Jimmy Onion. 'Derelict now of course.'

'It was derelict when we were kids,' Dogmeat said. 'We played war games in the old buildings, remember?'

'We used to imagine those rusting containers were Chieftain Tanks,' I said.

'And a suitably shaped branch was a Tommy Gun,' added Jimmy Onion.

'Get the beer in, Jimmy,' said Dogmeat Dave. 'It's got to be your round.'

'Again?' he said.

'Aye, it's your turn,' I said. I wasn't sure, but Jimmy was flush, so I went along with it.

'Pint of Guinness, two pints of John's and pint of Fosters.' Jimmy Onion shouted his order across to the bar. Walt was good to us. He didn't provide a table service for everyone.

'Can you remember that old well, smack bang in the middle of the yard?' I asked.

'They capped it off for safety,' Jimmy Onion said.

'Bone dry, it was,' said Dogmeat. 'But fuckin' deep, just the same.'

'How do you know how deep it is?' Jimmy said.

'Everyone knows it's over one hundred feet deep,' Dogmeat insisted. 'It's common knowledge.'

'You don't know that, you're just saying.'

'I'm telling ya,' said Dogmeat angrily. Here we go again. 'It's over one hundred feet deep.'

'Okay, okay,' said Jimmy Onion. 'Keep your hair on.'

'There you go, lads.' Walt had come over with the beer and a bowl of water for Bert, who jumped up and gratefully lapped at the steel dish, splashing water over Walt's latest idea to attract custom, a treadmill which he'd placed right next to our table. It was part of the mini gym he'd installed, and mini was the appropriate word. One treadmill, one spinner and weights that only came out on request, or some joey would throw them through the window after a skinful. A gym in a pub eh, the fuckin' imbecile. I think he'd attracted three members so far, not forgetting the young bulls that held the Stella Olympics from time to time. Entry fee, five pints. Dogmeat Dave would fuck them off in no uncertain terms if they tried to do it when he was around.

'Hey, Walt,' I said. 'How deep is that well in the old farm?'

'Mighty deep,' answered Walt.

'There you go,' said Dogmeat. 'I told you.' As Walt retreated.

'Walt doesn't know,' said Jimmy Onion. 'He's not from round here, he's only saying what he thinks will make you happy.'

'I bet you a hundred quid.' Dogmeat was at it again. He was ready to bet on anything. He once bet on the number of seconds it would take for a fly to leave the adjacent window sill. It took a while for the fly to take off, but it was probably trying to extract its feet from the syrupy mixture of beer and dust that coated the paintwork.

'It's all well and good betting, Dave,' offered Mo, 'but how are you going to prove it?'

'I'll fuckin' measure it.'

'How are you going to do that?'

'I'll sort something, don't you worry your pretty head,' said Dogmeat.

'Fair enough,' said Jimmy Onion, the only one of us who

could afford to accept the bet, 'I'll take the wager. I say the well is less than one hundred feet deep, but I don't see how you're going to prove it. It'll be sealed for sure, to start with.'

Although the farmyard wasn't visible from the path we would pass it every time we ventured to the pub via the Trans Pennine Trail. When the weather was suitable, we used the trail as a convenient shortcut from the part of town we lived in, half a mile or so distant. So, that's how it all began, a dispute over a well, and to be fair, we hadn't been near the place for years and years. It might not even be there any more. It was all Dogmeat's fault, he had a habit of dragging me into things, things which very rarely had a satisfactory outcome.

'Listen up,' shouted Walt over the din. 'It's quiz time. Only ten questions, two pints to the winner.'

'He's never done this before on a Saturday,' Mo said, as Walt weaved amongst the tables handing out paper and pens.

'Are you in, lads?' Walt didn't wait for an answer, he placed a sheet of paper and a pen on the table. 'I want that pen back mind.'

'What are you playing at, Walt. It's Saturday afternoon. It's sacrilege,' I said.

'Market research,' Walt said. 'Bear with me on this one.'

'How much?' I asked.

'That's the best thing about it, Johnboy,' Walt said. 'It's free.'

'Two pints is no good to us,' said Dogmeat. 'There's four of us.'

'Tell you what,' said Walt. 'Seeing as it's you, you can have four halves if you win.'

'Sound, bro,' said Mo, not grasping what Walt had said. Walt smiled and moved on to the next table.

Dogmeat put Mo in charge of writing the answers as Walt

moved to the end of the room and began his experiment.

'Question one – What is the capital of Turkey?

'Istanbul,' whispered Dogmeat.

'No it's not,' said Jimmy Onion. 'It's Ankara.'

'Is it fuck,' said Dogmeat, louder.

'What am I putting?' asked Mo, all of a fluster.

'It's Ankara,' I said. Dogmeat shot me an accusing glance.

'Question two – Which sport takes place at Happy Valley?'

'Don't argue with me over this one,' Dogmeat said. 'It's horse racing.' We fell silent and Mo wrote down the answer.

'Question three – In which year did Queen Elizabeth the first die?'

'1603,' said Jimmy Onion.

'You're going to have to make it easier than this,' someone shouted. 'Haven't you got any football questions?'

'Question four – Which poem, written by Alexander Pope, is the source of the famous quotation, "To err is human, to forgive divine, and a little learning is a dangerous thing"?'

'Aw, fuck off will ya.' A beermat flew towards Walt and set the precedent. A barrage followed, causing the quiz to be abandoned. Looks like Walt had overestimated his Saturday clientele.

Dogmeat slid the pen into his pocket. 'He'll not be needing that again.'

'I was enjoying that,' Jimmy Onion moaned.

'Aye, you would do, you fuckin' nerd,' Dogmeat replied.

Now, you're probably wondering how Dogmeat and Jimmy acquired their names. Well, Dave once did a short stint in a pet food factory and Jimmy Onion, real name Charles Newton, had an onion shaped head. At high school, he liked to show off his masculinity by sporting a few wisps of blonde hair on his chin.

He had slightly more on his head, but not much. Now he has hardly any at all. This all added to the onion like appearance, which was even more authentic when we made him cry, not that onions cry of course, but you can see where we were coming from on this one. He hated the name and still does today, that's why it stuck. As for me and Mo, we're just John Barratt, Johnboy to my friends, and my enemies too, and Mo, Mohammed Kashani. Nothing complicated about that.

The following Saturday found us, once again in The Railway Inn at our usual table. Bert was on the treadmill with his lead tied to the framework. I set him off slowly and gradually increased the pace until he was setting a brisk pace. I think he was enjoying himself, but who knows what was going on in his head, if anything at all. He just looked straight ahead and kept on keeping on. Dogmeat had disappeared. I thought he had gone out for a smoke, but he'd been gone quite a while. I assumed he had gone to the bookies. Jimmy Onion had, as always, his face in *The Times*. Mo and I had endured a bad week at work, no money again for either of us and my debt to Mo was increasing exponentially. If it wasn't for his father's help, he'd be in shit creek by now and I felt bad about it. Before I left home today, my wife Sally had given me a lecture on economics, a surly lesson on the basic concept of "money in, money out", and how one had to always be greater than the other. She questioned how I could have the barefaced cheek to spend money on beer when she was going out to work to keep food on the table blah, blah, blah. I took it on the chin and left for the pub. The lecture was becoming as much of a routine as the actual drinking session. I'll just say one thing here and now, I very rarely went home drunk. It was more of a social gathering than a binge. Fifty odd years of life and almost twenty-five years of unholy union had brought me to this point, and I wondered what was the point of it all. I stared, unseeing, toward the bar area. If I understood the reason why… why any of us are here and for what purpose, I'd get my head down and apply myself for the common good, but as far as I could see, it was all a fuckin' joke. What was it all about? Where did I come from? Where was I going? Should I take sandwiches? Because, when you take away fucking and fighting, there's not a lot left is there?

Dogmeat brought me back to the present with a bang as he slammed a pair of bolt cutters down on the table, making the beer glasses jump. We all instinctively dove in to save the pints. Some things are precious.

'What the fuck, Dogmeat?' I said, trying to avoid the tsunami of beer and lager that was heading my way. 'What you doing, man? And what you got there?'

'I've just been up the ironmongers.' He held out his hand in presentation, leading our eyes to the bolt cutters.

'Why do you have those, er… pruners on the table?' Jimmy Onion wasn't very good with tools, he'd probably never handled one in his life.

'They're not pruners you bonehead,' said Dogmeat disparagingly. 'They're fuckin' bolt cutters.'

'Why do you have bolt cutters on the table then?'

'That cover on the well is going to be fastened down, isn't it? These are going to get us in there.' The rest of us had forgotten about the well, but we should have known that Dogmeat never gave up on a bet. 'I also have here,' he said, 'a roll of twine fifty metres long, that's… a lot of feet.'

'Just over one hundred and sixty-four.' Jimmy Onion wasn't going to pass up on a chance to show that he had a brain the size of a genetically engineered pumpkin.

'Exactly,' said Dogmeat, with emphasis on the middle syllable, 'we'll lower this twine down the well, see when it hits the bottom, mark the twine, pull it up and measure it with this.' He pulled a tape measure from his pocket.

'How will you know when it hits the bottom, Dave?'

'Good question, Mo, my son,' said Dogmeat, 'I'm going to tie the bolt cutters on the end... weight you see... gravity.'

'Does it really matter?' asked Jimmy Onion dismissively.

'Course it fuckin' matters, we have a hundred notes on it don't we?'

We were distracted by a young couple who'd just walked in. The girl was wearing a white tee shirt and pale blue, tight jeans. The boy was tall and slim. You could see he was proud to be seen out with his lass.

'Cast yer eyes on that eh?' Dogmeat followed the couple with his eyes. 'What yer reckon, Johnboy?'

'Eight,' I said. We always marked the girls out of ten.

'Mo?'

'Seven.'

'Only seven? Them fuckin' wranglers must be sprayed on.' To Dogmeat, all types of jeans were wranglers.

'She's nice all right, but she's got a big conk.'

'What you doing looking at her face, you idjit? I'm giving her a well-deserved eight point five. What about you Jimmy?' Dogmeat always asked him, but he knew he wouldn't join in.

'I think you ought to have more respect. It'd serve you right if her boyfriend heard you.'

'I'm not worried about that scrawny bastard,' Dogmeat growled.

'Oh dear,' sighed Jimmy Onion.

We were full of ale, and spirits were high as we shouted our goodbyes to Walt and the other regulars. Taking our usual route, we crossed the car park and exited the car park in the corner by the burger van and on to the trail. Although the weather was good, the track was quiet, just the odd runner or cyclist passed us by. The old farm wasn't visible from the trail, due to a small hillock, and the dirt track up to it was accessed behind a small, decrepit, flat-roofed square construction, which I assumed was once something to do with the railway. We had to trample down a few plants to create a way for Dogmeat to get through. At one point, we had to lift him and the wheelchair over some stubborn roots. By the time we had placed him on the even, dirt track beyond the bushes, Jimmy Onion and I were exhausted, bent double, hands on our knees, blowing out of our arses. Dogmeat was okay though, he must have felt like the fuckin' king of Siam perched up there on his chair. It hadn't rained for a while, so once we got past this section we could make good progress, and Dogmeat could make his way along on the track under his own steam. Bert looked to be enjoying this new route and he darted left and right, sniffing out the territory. The landscape was quite open here as we passed through what was a field of crops. It was however, a public footpath, even though it was seldom used. Wind turbines rotated slowly on the horizon off to our right. The sun was just strong enough to make the walk a pleasant experience.

When Dogmeat had produced the bolt cutters, I felt much like Jimmy Onion. It was a stupid idea, but now, with the alcohol coursing through my veins, I felt like a little kid again. Even Jimmy Onion was giggling like a ten-year-old as we made our way up the slight incline. We reached the top and the farmyard lay below us. Pressing on, we arrived at the forgotten enclosure and entered. I stopped and looked around, pondering on the ghosts of past souls who would have, many years ago, inhabited this place, including our childhood selves. Inexplicably, a dark feeling crept over me.

'We shouldn't be here, Johnboy?' I looked at Jimmy Onion, his mood had changed too.

'Come on then.' Dogmeat had gone on ahead. 'Don't just fuckin' stand there, you balloons.' He'd spied the covered well in the centre of the dusty yard and was making a bee line for it. Mo wasn't far behind him. Jimmy Onion and I slowly made our way over and joined them around the well, which had been capped at ground level with a rusty iron sheet.

'I don't think we'll be needing your bolt cutters,' I said, pointing at four large padlocks, which had been smashed and discarded a few feet away from the plate, 'someone has beaten us to it.'

'Makes no sense,' Mo said.

'It would appear there are other idiots abroad,' said Jimmy Onion.

'It'll just be kids messing around,' Dogmeat assured us. 'They've saved us a job. Come on drag the plate out of the way, let me get my hundred quid.'

'Wait a minute.' I didn't want them moving anything until I'd got Bert on his lead and secured him to a decaying iron framework away from the well. He looked at me quizzically as I tied him up and went over to the others.

'I'd give you a hand if I could, lads,' Dogmeat was loving it, seeing us bust a gut for his hundred quid. 'That'll do,' he said, when the plate was nearly off. 'Tie this on.' He handed the bolt cutters and the twine to Mo.

'Be careful, Mo,' I said, as he shuffled on his stomach nearer to the edge of the abyss. 'We don't want any disasters.' He peered

23

down into the darkness, just his head over the hole. I moved round and grabbed his ankles, just to be on the safe side. Bert was staring at us, wondering what the fuck we were playing at. 'Can you see anything, Mo?' I asked.

'I wish we'd brought a light,' said Mo. 'Give me a minute for my eyes to get used to it.' His voice echoed inside the well.

'You don't need to get used to it,' Dogmeat barked. 'Just lower the bolt cutters down the well until they stop, or not.'

'There's already a rope hanging down here,' Mo said. 'It's tied to an old ring near the top here.'

'Pull it up,' said Dogmeat. 'See what it is.'

'There's something on the end of it.' Mo pulled at the rope while I clung to him. 'It's a bag.'

Chapter 2

Mo hauled the bag, still attached to the rope, out of the hole. It was a black leather holdall with long looping handles. We looked at each other, then at the bag, which was in good condition and had collected no dust. I deduced that it had been placed in the well quite recently, and that disturbed me a little. I glanced around the derelict buildings expecting to see prying eyes but saw only the crumbling masonry.

'Knock about, Mo, open it up then,' Dogmeat said impatiently. Mo moved the bag away from the edge of the well and pulled at the zip fastener. It moved easily along its runner. He eased the sides apart to reveal... banknotes, lots of them. We stared, slack jawed for what seemed an eternity. My heart was racing, I looked around again.

'Put it back. Let's get away from here,' Jimmy Onion said.

'Fuck off. Finders keepers,' said Dogmeat.

'We're going to create a world of trouble for ourselves. The kind of people who put this here aren't going to be angels, and they're going to be really, really annoyed when they come back for it and find it's missing, and anyway it's probably drug money or worse.'

' Don't be such a pussy, Jimmy,' said Dogmeat. 'Nobody is going to know who's taken it, as long as we play it smart. What do you think, Johnboy?'

'I know where Jimmy is coming from on this, but to be honest, I need the money. Mo needs the money. I haven't paid him for weeks.' It was all well and good for Jimmy Onion to take the moral high ground, but he was comfortably off. It's always been easy for people with money to preach morals to the less well off, the worst kind being the ones who were once in my position themselves. No, fuck it, we were keeping it. If Jimmy didn't want a cut, then so be it.

'What about you?' Dogmeat turned to Mo. 'Put it back or keep it?'

'Well, I am a bit short at the moment, bro, I…'

'That's it then.' Dogmeat didn't wait for Mo to finish. 'Three to one,' he said to Jimmy Onion. 'I love democracy, don't you?'

'This isn't democracy,' said Jimmy Onion. 'It's lunacy. What if someone is watching us? What if these people are killers? We'll be looking over our shoulders for ever.'

'What if, what if?' said Dogmeat mockingly. 'What if my aunt had a pair of bollocks? She'd be my uncle. Pick up that bag Johnboy, we're off… sharpish.'

We slid the steel plate back in place before I released Bert, then I grabbed hold of the bag, zipped it closed and lifted it. It was reassuringly heavy as I began to walk away. The others followed me out of the yard and down the dirt track. We argued all the way back, but the decision had been made. I kept scanning the area, half expecting to be jumped. When we reached the trail, we looked left and right before helping Dogmeat back on to the tarmac. One solitary cyclist passed us, but I don't think he even noticed the bag. He was too busy setting a personal best.

'Slow down you fuckin' dick,' Dogmeat called after him, but he was gone.

We reached our neighbourhood and Jimmy Onion peeled off towards his home without a word. With Jimmy gone, the atmosphere lifted and we chatted. Sally would be out at this time, so we agreed to go to my house, which was the nearest, and investigate the bag further.

We filed into my house via the back door, checking to see if any of the neighbours were watching. Bert went straight to his water bowl then collapsed into his bed whilst the rest of us gathered around the kitchen table. I cleared the detritus and unzipped the bag, shook the contents out onto the pine surface and gazed at the pile of filthy lucre, all the time wondering if Jimmy Onion hadn't been right. There was a lot of dosh there, somebody was going to be right pissed off. It was in separate packs held together with elastic bands, which we counted to be, more or less one thousand pounds per pack. We sorted them into groups of ten packs, then counted the packs.

'Wow,' gasped Mo breathlessly, gazing at the two hundred and fifty wads lying on the table. Two hundred and fifty grand, give or take.'

'Sixty-two thousand, five hundred each,' I said after I'd retrieved a calculator from a drawer. 'That's right,' I said double checking. 'Two hundred and fifty thousand divided by four.'

'It'll be more than that,' said Dogmeat. 'Jimmy Onion said he wasn't interested, so fuck him.'

'He might change his mind when we tell him how much it is.' The faintest of trembles in Mo's voice betrayed his state of mind.

'We've hit the jackpot, boys,' said Dogmeat, elated. 'Our fuckin' boat has finally come in.'

'So what we gonna do with it?' I asked.

'You keep it here, Johnboy, until the dust settles.'

'I can't have it here,' I protested. 'Sally is sure to find it.'

'Not if you use your noggin,' said Dogmeat. 'Put it somewhere out of the way.'

'You take it, Mo,' I said.

'I wouldn't have anywhere safe to put it, bro.'

'Don't be such a fuckin' pussy,' Dogmeat said. 'Anyway, I don't think we should be carting it around the streets, do you? They could be looking for it right now.'

'That's what worries me,' I said.

'I have to get off now, Johnboy,' said Dogmeat, bringing the debate to an end, so we packed the money back into the bag and Dogmeat turned to leave.

'Be careful with my bag, Johnboy,' he said.

'Your bag?' I said. 'How come it's yours all of a sudden?'

Dogmeat stopped and spun his wheelchair around. 'It was my idea to go to the well, wasn't it?'

'Yes, to find out how deep it was,' I protested. 'You didn't know the bag was there.'

'That's irrelevant, Johnboy,' Dogmeat said. 'If it wasn't for me, that money wouldn't be sitting on your kitchen table, but don't worry, lads, you'll get your cut.'

'Fair enough,' I said, knowing better than to argue with him. All I wanted was for Mo and I to get a share, and if that was what was going to happen I wasn't fussed whose bag it was. If Dogmeat wanted to call it his bag, fine, no problem.

Dogmeat swore as he negotiated the threshold at the bottom of the doorway. Mo and I looked at each other, smiled and shared a high five. Our troubles were over… we believed.

Mo departed shortly after, and I had become the guardian of the bag. I couldn't let Sally see it, fuck me, I couldn't let anyone see it. I had to hide it before she got back. I took it upstairs and pulled down the loft ladder with the next to useless pole, that put me in a state of peril with every use. This wasn't the time to be knocked out by a rapidly descending lump of steel. Up in the loft,

28

I sat on the board by the water tanks, my eyes searching for a secure spot, but I had a change of heart. The loft is the first place anyone was going to look wasn't it? So I came back down and struggled with the ladder. It wouldn't go up again, it kept sticking. 'For fucks sake,' I screamed. 'Get up there.' The shouting did the trick and it finally slid back into position. By this time, I was sweating like a fat lad in a pie shop. I'd spent too much time in the loft, so I swiftly went out of the back door to the garden shed, which was well hidden amongst the untended foliage, I wasn't much of a gardener. I'd only had the bag a short time, but I was overwhelmed with paranoia. Was someone watching us when we took it? Was someone watching me right now? I cleared a space beneath a bench, placed the bag there and covered it over with junk, then I uncovered it again and stuffed some old copies of the *Green 'Un* sports paper on top of the money, before rezipping and stuffing it back in under the bench. Surely, no one would think to look there, especially Sally, who hadn't been near the shed apart from one time, years ago, when she opened the door, looked in and tutted. Back in the kitchen, I tried to calm myself with a cup of tea, then I went and had a shower. I stood under the flow of water for a long time, trying to wash away the anxiety, wondering just what on earth we'd done. The buzz of the alcohol had worn off now, leaving that familiar down which so often occurred after the session. Why hadn't I listened to Jimmy Onion?

That night, sleep didn't come easily, truth be told, it didn't come at all. My head was playing a video over and over in a never-ending loop. Mice were chewing away at the bag in the shed and it must have been about four thirty when I gently slid out of bed, dressed and went out to the shed. There's nothing like the smell of a fresh summer night, but I was in no mood to enjoy it. Bert came out with me and sniffed around the garden. As quietly as possible, I retrieved the bag from below the bench and took it indoors. To my surprise, there were no signs of teeth marks, rodent or otherwise. I crept back upstairs and placed it in a cupboard in the small bedroom that I used as an office.

'Where have you been?' Sally asked, drowsily.

'Just needed a bit of air, love.' That answer seemed to suffice. She went back to sleep. I didn't.

Sally and I persisted with the ritual that is Sunday dinner. When our marriage was in the flush of youth, we enjoyed preparing and eating the meal together, nowadays we usually sat in silence, unless she had a gripe she wanted to get off her chest. This was the new norm and I fuckin' hated it. I think we both realised that the relationship was down the pan, but which one of us was going to be brave enough to blow the final whistle? I suppose that when this breaking of the bread together ended, so would our marriage. It would be like the last supper as I was about to be crucified financially. Love brought us together, but money kept us together. The non-payers had put me on my arse, making me a much less attractive proposition. And to think, I had once fought for her. As a young woman, she had been quite something, cute, with all the right bumps in all the right places, and credit to her she'd looked after herself over the years. A local thug, Andy Warburton, had the hots for her around about the same time as I did. Inevitably, we ended up fighting and I received a good hiding, but Sally, who was always behind the underdog, took up with me instead of Warburton. Sometimes, I wish I'd been a better fighter.

'What were you up to last night?' I thought she'd been half asleep and it wouldn't have registered, but I should have known better. She never missed a trick.

'Like I said, I needed a bit of air. I didn't feel very well.'

'You shouldn't go out drinking then, should you?'

'It wasn't the drink; I didn't have much.'

'It's not just that though, is it?' She was on a roll now. 'We can't really afford it can we?'

'Ah well.' I sighed and waited for more.

'Ah well, ah well now is it?' Every statement a question. 'It's about time you faced up to your responsibilities.'

'Aw fuck it.' I clattered the cutlery hard down on to the plate, splashing thick, brown gravy on to my clean, white tee shirt. 'For fuck's sake,' I said. 'Come on, Bert, we're going for a walk.'

'And it's about time you tidied up after yourself, you're a disgrace.' I felt like a chastised teenager.

Monday came around and I felt better about life. No one had bothered me or come near the house. I hadn't had any unexpected phone calls and Sally was none the wiser. The sun was shining, and Mo and I were working locally. We'd already completed the garden walls behind the bungalow, and we had now turned our attention to the erection of new porch. I hate asking for money, and I had intended to secure a deposit for this job, but Mr Dawson, the owner, had dragged his feet and we just kind of carried on with the work. Time had drifted and I was into the builders' merchant for quite a sum already. I wasn't too worried though, I had the bag at home. I just hoped the house didn't burn down in my absence.

'What you going to do with your cut, bro?' asked Mo.

'I'm not sure, but it's a nice problem to have. First thing is to sort you out, Mo, I really appreciate your patience on this one.' And I did. 'Then I might fuck off on holiday somewhere.'

'Where you fancying?'

'Anywhere that Sally's not.' I laughed, but I was serious. I needed some time away from her. She was slowly eroding my life force. To be honest, a separate break could do us both a lot of good. 'What about you, Mo?' I was enjoying the speculation. 'Got plans?'

'The pram filler is on its way, isn't it? I suppose that will take up a huge chunk of it, then I'll sort out my family.'

'Yeah, of course. Good luck to you, Mo. If anyone deserves a break, it's you.' I ran a line of mortar ready for the next course using the last of it from the board. 'Gobbo,' I shouted, in the traditional Yorkshire way. Mo emptied the contents of the wheelbarrow on to the board and went off to start the mixer again. I smiled.

Snap time came around and I settled myself on a stack of bricks ready to enjoy a couple of cheese and beetroot butties. Mo joined me and Bert sat right in front of me, full of concentration, waiting for any offering that came. I always brought a few dog biscuits and a water bowl for him. He was quite partial to a hide chew, which kept him out of my face while I had my sandwiches. I threw one on to the lawn and he rapidly followed it. Mr Dawson came around the corner with two mugs. 'Tea up, lads, that'll be three pounds twenty,' he said with a straight face. I looked at him and he burst into laughter. 'Nearly had you there, didn't I?' he said.

'You did that,' I said. 'About the money, Mr Dawson...'

'Is that the phone ringing?' He cupped his hand against his ear and beat a hasty retreat back around the corner before I could say any more.

'Phone, my arse,' I said.

After work, I wandered into the garden away from Sally and called Jimmy Onion. I hadn't spoken to him since we parted in bad spirit on the trail on Saturday, and I was hoping that when I told him just how much money had been in the bag, he would have second thoughts about pulling out of the deal. He was having none of it, he simply kept repeating that it wasn't our money and how it was unethical to even think about keeping it. I tried my utmost to convince him that it was okay to put ourselves first for a change, to treat ourselves, but my words fell on stony ground. Even worse, he wasn't going to turn a blind eye. If we didn't tell the police, he would. I pleaded with him. I reminded him that Mo was soon to be a father, that I owed a lot of money to a lot of people and Dogmeat was chomping at the bit to waste a shitload of wonga in the bookies, but he was adamant. 'You have to do the right thing, Johnboy,' he said.

'If we don't keep it, bad people are going to get their hands on it,' I said, trying to sway him.

'I don't care, it's not our money.' Jimmy's mind was set.

'You are fuckin' joking?' I'd called Dogmeat to tell him what Jimmy Onion had said. He didn't react well. 'No way am I passing up on this opportunity,' he said. 'He can fuck right off. I started at the bottom and worked my down. I've made a lot of bad decisions and had some bad luck on top of that. This time, the gift horse is keeping his lips tightly sealed and I suggest Jimmy does the same too, the fuckin' bozo.'

'What can we do?' I asked. 'He's going to tell the police. He's got us by the bollocks mate.' As sad as it made me, I couldn't see any way out of this. Life had raised me up to a great height and body slammed me right back down to earth. In an instant, I was broke again.

'I don't know, Johnboy.' I could hear the anger in Dogmeat's voice. I couldn't see him, but I just knew he was shaking. 'I'll think of something,' he said. 'There has to be a way around this, let me think.'

'Do you think we'll get a reward if we hand it in to the police?' I asked forlornly.

'Will we fuck,' said Dogmeat. 'And if we do, it'll be three bob and a blackie's egg and we'll never hear anything about it again.' He reflected my own feelings about South Yorkshire Police. The miners' strike and Hillsborough had left a nasty taste around these parts. 'How does Mo feel about this?' Dogmeat added.

'Mo thinks he's on for a big pay day. He knows Jimmy is against it all, but I haven't told him that he's going to bubble us if we don't hand it in. He'll be devastated.'

'Leave it until Saturday, give him time to ponder,' said Dogmeat. 'And we'll talk to him when he's had a beer or two, see what we can do.'

'I suppose that's all we can hope for,' I said. We bid our goodbyes and hung up. I pictured Dogmeat violently snapping shut his antiquated flip phone and throwing it across the room. He would be livid, good thing he lived alone. I stood there by the shed, numbed. All that money was in the bag, in my house and it was looking like it was worth jack shit. I turned my head skyward. 'Dear Lord.' I said. 'In my lifetime, I've very rarely asked you for anything, but for fuck's sake, could you just take your foot of my neck for a while?' Bert had been watching me. He barked once. 'Sorry Bert,' I said. 'It's way past your dinner time isn't it?' He wagged his tail as I moved towards the back door of the house. 'You don't know how lucky you are, dog.'

Sally was waiting for me in the kitchen. 'You're taking a lot of air of late,' she said with just the right amount of venom in her voice. She must have been on a course for this sort of thing, if not, she ought to be running the fuckin' class.

'I'm not hurting anyone am I?' I took Bert's bowl out of the cupboard and half filled it with mixer, opened a tin of Chappie and piled it on the mixer. He was into it before it hit the floor.

'You think more of that dog than me.'

'Don't be daft,' I said, even though she had hit the nail on the head. She had stated the blindingly obvious, but I kept my powder dry. Bert didn't bend my ear every time I walked through the door. Bert didn't make me feel like I was walking on broken glass.

'Look at that.' She threw an open envelope on the table. I could see it was from British Gas without having to look inside, another fuckin' bill. It looked like she had ripped it open with her teeth. 'And that.' Another one hit the table and slid towards me, council tax. 'And that.' Fuckin' hell, she was in the zone now. This one was the water bill, closely followed by the electric bill. She must have been saving these up for this performance. She looked at me, waiting for me to say something, but what could I say? I didn't have the money to settle the accounts.

'We've got a job nearing completion in the next day or so,' I said. 'I'm going to sort it soon as I get paid.'

'You should have been a rear gunner,' she spat. 'Because you're always gunner do summat, gunner do this, gunner do that. I've had it up to here.' I had to hold back an inappropriate chuckle, she looked like she was saluting me when her hand snapped up to her forehead. 'We can't carry on like this,' she continued.

'Can't disagree on that one,' I mumbled.

'Disagree?' She strung the word out for maximum effect. It was as if I'd pissed in her corn flakes. 'You are the original Johnny Opposite. You always disagree with me.'

'No I don't,' I protested.

'There you go again,' she said triumphantly. 'Doing it again.'

Chapter 3

'I have a horse for you, Johnboy,' said Dogmeat. 'Absolutely nailed on, dead cert.'

'No way,' I said. I'd followed his tips before. Yeah, one or two came in occasionally, but generally they were a complete waste of time and money. Every winner he had made him forget about his long list of failures. There were times when I pointed out the error of his ways, tried to help him, and there were an equal number of times he'd told me to fuck off, so I'd stopped doing it.

'You'll be sorry. Wearing an even number as well.' Dogmeat had a thing about even numbers. He hated odd numbers, especially three.

'Thanks, but no thanks,' I said.

'Here.' Dogmeat pushed a grubby piece of paper over the table. 'Take this, you might change your mind. Last race, evening meeting at Donny.' I humoured him by pushing it into my pocket.

'What about you, Mo?' asked Dogmeat. 'Interested?'

'I'm all right, Dave,' Mo replied. Dogmeat never pressed Mo as he did with me, and he wouldn't even bother offering the tip to Jimmy Onion who had yet to join us because he had some business to attend to, so to accommodate him we were out a little later than usual.

'Jimmy's late,' Mo said.

'Fuckin' typical,' said Dogmeat. 'Jimmy Onion alters the time of the sesh, then doesn't turn up.'

'Don't worry, he'll be here,' I said.

'Hey, Mo.' Dogmeat jabbed his elbow towards Mo, causing him to spill a little of his drink. 'Would you tackle that one?'

'Bit too old for me, Dave, but I'll give her a six for effort.'

'Johnboy?'

'Six point five. She's looked after herself by the look of it, kept herself smart, eh?'

'She's a fine-looking woman, but she's definitely on the turn. Yeah, I think six point five is about right,' said Dogmeat.

Bert had stayed at home with Sally for this one, it could sometimes be a bit too rowdy for him in The Railway later on. She reckoned she had no time for him, but she loved him to bits really, as I did. They'd be cuddled up on the settee by now, watching an old film. When I was home, he wasn't allowed on the furniture. I'm surprised I was to be fair, but I once went home early and caught them. Sally had been asleep and feigned outrage when she woke and found Bert next to her. 'Get off the sofa, you bloody thing,' she shouted, but I knew the score.

'When Jimmy Onion gets here,' I said, mostly for the benefit of Dogmeat, 'just play it cool, don't go at it like a bull in a china shop.'

'I know, I know,' Dogmeat said. 'I'm not a fuckin' idjit.' He was far from an idiot, but the problem was that he couldn't control his temper. Sometimes, I felt like a fire fighter, keeping an eye on the smouldering embers before he combusted, out of control, and when that happened, the slightest breeze would fan the flames. If we were going to have any success with Jimmy Onion, a modicum of self-control would have to be exercised, but it wasn't in Dogmeat's DNA.

'He's here now,' I said. 'Remember, stay calm.' Jimmy Onion ambled over and took his regular seat. 'How's it going,

Jimmy? Eh, Mo, be a good lad and get Jimmy a pint, will ya?' I thrust a note into Mo's hand.

'Get a round in while you're at it,' said Dogmeat, draining his glass. I looked at Dogmeat and pushed more money into Mo's hand, money I could ill afford to spend. If Sally saw this, she'd go apeshit. Dogmeat gave me a cheeky smile and winked.

'Sorry I'm late,' said Jimmy Onion.

'Ah, don't worry about it, love.' Dogmeat smiled. For the moment, he was trying.

When Mo returned with the drinks, I broached the subject. 'About the bag,' I said. 'We've been talking.'

'You don't waste time. I've only just walked through the door,' said Jimmy Onion.

'Sorry Jimmy,' I said. 'But we really do need that money. I've got bills flying in from all angles.'

'And I'm fuckin' skint.' Dogmeat's smile had disappeared. I raised a palm to soothe him.

'I fully understand your situation,' said Jimmy Onion. 'But you're asking me to break the law.'

'No, we're not, Jimmy,' I said. 'There's nothing on the news about a robbery. No one is looking for us. It's just a huge piece of luck we've had, isn't it?'

'Are you trying to tell me that the money doesn't belong to anyone? A gift from the gods, eh?' Jimmy said. 'Of course the money belongs to someone. Of course, someone is looking for us. They just don't know who we are yet... and when they do, we're looking at a lot of trouble.'

Right on cue, two strangers appeared at the bar. Big, ugly, tattoos, you know the type, bent noses and more hair on a gooseberry. They looked around, locking on to people's faces and they seemed to spend an eternity scrutinising my face. I stared back and swallowed hard. I realised, inexplicably, that I was holding my breath. I released it, involuntarily puffing out my cheeks. They must have seen my guilt. Eventually, they turned, leaning over the bar in the direction of Walt. They were asking questions, weren't they?

'What did I tell you?' whispered Jimmy Onion.

'Shhhh, for fuck's sake, don't attract attention.' Dogmeat elbowed Jimmy in the ribs. 'Go and get beer,' he said to me. 'See if you can find out what they want.'

'I've got beer,' I said. 'Wouldn't that look suspicious if I went to get a round in when our glasses are full? Anyway, I'm going nowhere near them.'

'Go and *pretend* to get beer then, you fuckin' jellyfish.'

'You go,' I suggested to Dogmeat.

'I'm not going to hear anything from the wheelchair, am I?' He held his arms apart to illustrate his incapacity. 'If you wanted someone to go and sniff their bollocks, I'm your man.'

As it happened, it didn't matter. The gorillas were making their way out and we breathed easily again. Mo looked at me questioningly, looking for guidance. He was rattled but I was just as perturbed as he was.

'Well, if that doesn't tell you what to do.' I'm sure I detected a slight shake in Jimmy Onion's voice. 'Nothing will.'

'Fuck 'em,' said Dogmeat with bravado. 'Eh, Walt, come over here a minute, will you?'

'What can I do for you, Dave?' Walt asked as he closed in on us.

'What did those blokes want?'

'Who?'

'The two big lads,' said Dogmeat.

'Oh, them. They were trying to get me to have new double-glazed windows, but there's nowt wrong with the windows I've got is there? They said it would make the place warmer, cut my heating bills etc. I told them that we very rarely have the heating on, so off they went.'

'That's what they were looking around at,' I said. 'At the fuckin' windows.' I felt the blood returning to my limbs.

'What's wrong with you lot?' Walt asked. 'You look pale.'

'Aw, it's something and nothing, Walt.' I said.

'If you don't want to tell me I'll get back to my duties then,' Walt said, a little miffed. He turned and left us.

'We're in the clear, boys,' Dogmeat said.

'No, we're not. We need to hand the bag in.' Jimmy Onion was back at it again. 'Just think about it, how are you going to spend that much cash? You could only spend it in small amounts, there'd be no benefit. And how do we know it's not counterfeit?'

'I don't give a fuck if it's real or not,' Dogmeat said. 'I can think of lots of ways to spend it, and I'm going to enjoy it.'

'We have to go to the police.'

'Fuck that for a game of dominoes,' Dogmeat said.

'Then you have to put it back where you found it,' Jimmy Onion insisted.

'What you mean by *you*,' said Dogmeat. 'Us, we. You're just as much part of this as we are.'

'All right, all right. We should return it. But, make no mistake, if we don't put it back I'm going to the police.'

'I've told my dad that he won't have to bail me out much longer,' Mo said. 'But that shook me up a bit.'

'Maybe Jimmy's right,' I chipped in. 'Is it worth it?'

'What's up with you? Scared off by a couple of poxy double-glazing salesmen. I'm going for a woodbine.' Dave pushed away, out into the car park.

Maybe Dogmeat was right, maybe Jimmy Onion was right. I tried to clear my head enough to consider my choices. The money would allow me to get back on my feet. I could pay Mo, pay my bills and get Sally off my back. On the other hand, if we put the bag back, I'd have no money, but I wouldn't have to look over my shoulder for the rest of my life. It was a no win situation, but I knew in my heart of hearts that I wanted the money. It didn't matter now anyway, because Jimmy Onion had laid down the rules. The three of us were quiet, turning over the quandary in our heads. Boy, I was depressed.

Jimmy Onion broke the silence. 'I'm going.'

'No,' I said. 'Don't go, Jimmy, stay and have a wet.'

'I think it's best. Call me when you've made a decision.' He quickly finished his Guinness, stood up and left.

'I think we've lost the money,' I said, turning to Mo. We have no choice but to put it back,' I said dolefully.

'I don't know what I'm going say to my dad, bro. You know, that money would have made a big difference, but que sera, we move on.'

We were interrupted by a commotion emanating from the car park. People began running out to see what was happening. Mo and I followed. Two teenage girls were screaming, 'Let him go, leave him.' We looked over to where the row was coming from and saw Dogmeat's left arm wrapped around the neck of Bob the burger man. God knows how, but he had managed to get him in a headlock with his left arm and was punching him repeatedly with his right hand.

'Who's the fuckin' spud now, eh?' Dogmeat was saying. 'You fuckin' burger flipping, char boy.' I ran to separate them and managed to free Bob. His face was a mass of blood.

'What you playing at, Dogmeat?' I asked.

'You will notice,' he said, 'that this wanker has left his van. I'm not on the inside. He came out to attack me.'

'I didn't attack him,' Bob said through his busted lips. 'I came out to talk to him and he grabbed me.'

'You thought I was an easy target, but you got a surprise, didn't you?'

'I didn't, I'm not like that.' Someone handed a tea towel to Bob to help stem the blood flow.

'How did it come to this?' I asked.

'He called me a spud,' Dogmeat said.

'I didn't, he misheard. I wouldn't do that to a...'

'Bollocks,' Dogmeat blurted. 'My legs don't work, but there's nowt wrong with my ears, old cock.' He turned to his audience and moving his hands in a circular motion, performed an elaborate bow from his chair. 'Extra ketchup on your burgers today, girls and boys,' he shouted. 'I'm off home, see ya. And by the way, your burgers are fuckin' shite.' With that, he rolled out of the car park and on to the trail. We made sure Bob was okay before we returned to our table by the treadmill.

It was just myself and Mo now. Earlier, I'd bought a round of drinks for four of us. Now we were down to two and I was going to lose out, but never mind, eh? The session was still young, and I was going to have a good drink come what may. I needed to leave this reality for a while, be in a better place, somewhere I didn't have to think. I wasn't in the habit of getting blind drunk, but I craved the few hours of peace it would bring. I knew I'd have to pay the price tomorrow, but so be it. There's down and there's fuckin' down and I was down amongst the dead men. I finished my pint and ordered a double Jack Daniel's with ice, no mixer. Mo stuck with the ale, but after a while opted to leave early too. My company must have been riveting. There's

42

no sadder sight than a lonely man staring into his glass.

I don't know how long I was in there, or how much I had drunk, but the sun was sinking over the horizon by the time I rose from my seat. To be fair, Walt would happily have kept serving me, but we both knew that I'd had enough. I staggered out to the car park, but instead of turning right on to the trail, I went over the car park and left in the direction of the high street. I concentrated on trying to keep a straight line. I felt like bursting into song, but I didn't. This was grand, taking in the air. In my mind, I was strutting, but I must have looked a knobhead, weaving my way along the pavement, constantly making adjustments to keep on the right course. Luckily, most of the shops were closed and the town was mostly empty. I never gave Sally a thought, but just imagine if this had got back to her. She would have a field day. Heading further along the pavement, I met another pisshead coming the other way.

'Scuse me, pal,' he slurred. 'I'm a stranger round here. Do you know where the King's Head is?'

'Yeah,' I said. 'Just up from the King's Bollocks,' I said without breaking my stride.

'Dickhead,' he shouted, as we passed. I stopped outside a shop selling electrical goods. The large TV in the window was showing highlights of the test match. I stared, mesmerised, watching the ball skim across the outfield to the boundary. When the ball skipped over the rope, I signalled a four, just like Dicky Bird, then moved on, singing 'I don't like cricket... I love it.' I jumped the bollards as I entered the pedestrian precinct and found myself outside a betting shop. Something must have sparked in my head because I remembered Dogmeat's tip and fumbled in my pocket for crumpled note he'd handed me. Only a few stragglers remained as I approached the counter at the end of the shop.

'Am I in time for the last race at Doncaster?' I asked.

'Just,' said a young man.

I shoved the dogeared paper towards him along with a twenty-pound note.

'Last race at Donny,' I said, pointing at the note.

'I know… you said. Do you want it to win or each way?'

'Course I want it to win. Why else would I put fuckin' money on it?' He snatched the money away and issued a betting slip. I paused, looking at the slip of paper he'd given me.

'Get out the way then.' Behind me, a man was also keen to place his bet on the last race, before it was too late.

'Sorry, mate.' I made way for him and moved toward the front of the shop. There was a toilet near the door, so I thought I'd make use of the facilities while I had the chance. I had one on the tailboard, for sure. It was a small room with just one toilet and a small corner wash basin. I dropped my pants to my ankles, sat down… and drifted off.

I thought I'd slept for just a few minutes, but after I'd wiped my arse, opened the toilet door and stepped out into the shop area, everyone had gone. My head was banging, and it took me a moment to come to terms with where exactly I was. As the truth dawned, I momentarily wondered if my horse had won. Everyone had gone, I'd been locked in. I tried the front door, but of course, it was locked. It looked out to the street and that too was deserted. It was proper night now, dark. I heard the alarm make one beep, then five seconds later another. I went to the back of the shop and tried the door behind the counter. Locked, why would it be otherwise? I looked in drawers behind the counter, maybe I could find the key. Bingo, a brass key on a company keyring nestled in the corner.

'Beep.'

The key fitted the lock and turned. I swung the door inwards

44

only to find another obstacle, a barred, iron gate that was locked too. I rattled it a little, but it was secure, so I gave up on the rear door. I felt for my phone, then remembered that we had all agreed never to bring our mobiles to the pub. Jimmy Onion said they were antisocial, but it was all right for him to stick his face in the newspaper.

'Beep.'

I went back to the front window to see if anyone was passing, but everyone was at home watching telly. I shoved and pulled at the door, but it wouldn't budge. I banged on the window in vain. No one could hear me.

'Beep.'

I wondered if Sally had noticed that I hadn't returned home, and if she even cared.

'Beep, beep, beep.' Then it went off. It was deafening. My head couldn't take it. I went down on my knees in the centre of the floor, hands clamped against my ears. A red beam was sweeping around the place, so I sat on the floor against the wall and shut my eyes tight. All hell had broken loose. Eventually, the key holder arrived and let the police in. They pinned me to the floor and handcuffed my wrists behind my back.

I spent the rest of the night and a large part of the next morning in a cell, nursing a bad head, fitfully sleeping. I asked them to turn out the light, but they wouldn't entertain the idea. After much persuasion, telling and retelling of my story, they accepted that I was trying to break out and not in. In the end, they were laughing about it, but I didn't see the funny side. When I finally arrived home Sally didn't even ask where I'd been. She hadn't phoned the police, to report me missing, she had done fuck all and to be honest, I think she was disappointed when I walked in. Even Bert was indifferent to my homecoming. It goes without saying, Sunday dinner was off. I went to bed.

Chapter 4

'You wear pyjamas in bed, Mo?' I asked incredulously.'

'What's wrong with that, bro?'

'Nobody wears pjs these days. It's a thing of the past. I'm surprised you have a kid on the way. Right passion killers they are.'

'I've always done it, ever since I was a little lad.'

'Fair enough, for nippers, but not when you grow up. Never trust a man who gets dressed for bed,' I said. It was our last day at the bungalow. Just a few bits to finish and it was pay day, and not before time, especially now we had decided to return the bag. We only had to point the lead flashing, generally tidy things up and we'd be done.

'Most people wear them,' Mo said.

'Do they fuck,' I said.

'I bet if you did a survey, you'd find that they did.' Mr Dawson came into view, carrying a tray with coffee and biscuits. It was the first time the biscuits had surfaced in all the time we had worked here, but this was the last day, and I surmised that he thought there was no danger of us growing accustomed to the treat.

'Thanks very much,' I said. 'If you don't mind me asking, Mr Dawson, me and Mo are just having a discussion about nightwear.'

'Go on.' I could see that he was intrigued.

'Do you wear pyjamas in bed?'

'No,' said Mr Dawson. 'They make my bollocks sweat.'

'I rest my case,' I said as Mr Dawson shuffled off back inside.

'That's not exactly scientific, is it?'

'It's good enough for me. I read an article once that said sleeping buck naked increased your happiness levels.'

'It hasn't done much for you, bro.'

'Fair point, Mo, but just think how fuckin' miserable I'd be if I wore pyjamas.' I reached for the unopened packet of malted milk biscuits and noticed that the best before date had expired two years ago. Now I understood why he had brought out the whole packet. I had marvelled at his apparent generosity, but whatever we didn't eat could be going in the bin. I bit into one, it was okay. Mr Dawson would probably wait a few days to see if we didn't have the trots, then decide whether to bin them or crack on and eat them himself. We were test dummies.

It was beginning to spit with rain, so we put ourselves about a bit to finish before it came properly. Mo was singing. He was in good spirits considering what had happened of late.

I'd reversed my black pickup on to the brick-paved drive ready for loading. The rain was coming a little heavier now, but it didn't matter, we'd just about done.

'I've been thinking, Mo. If we do have to put the bag back, maybe we could sneak a couple of wads out for us, the three of us I mean, me, you and Dogmeat of course.' I dropped the last of the surplus bricks into the back of the truck. 'Not a lot like, not to be greedy, just to help us out a little, you know? We *have* been to a lot of trouble after all, haven't we?'

'Won't Jimmy know that we've had some?' Mo asked.

'Don't forget, he only glanced inside the bag back at the farm. He didn't come back to mine to count it did he? Anyway,

Jimmy can bollox. If it wasn't for him, we'd be rolling in it by now. I can't believe he's doing this to us, the selfish bastard.'

'He's a man of principle, bro, and we did tell him how much was in the bag.'

'He's not going to count it is he? He'll just be happy to see it returned.'

'I'm up for it if Dave is,' said Mo. 'But I wouldn't want to step on anyone's toes. I don't want to cheat anyone, apart from whoever put it in the well in the first place.'

'Whoever left the bag wouldn't think twice about doing what we're doing, so I wouldn't worry about it. I'll ring Dogmeat and see what he thinks.' I went to sit in the truck cab and made the call. He answered after a couple of rings. 'Eyup, Dogmeat, how's it hanging?'

'I'm good,' he said.

'About this money,' I continued. 'I think we know by now that we're going to have to put it back, but me and Mo thought it would be a good idea if us three took a little out for ourselves.'

'Don't do that for now, Johnboy. I'm working on a plan.'

'What you got in mind?' I asked.

'Can't talk right now, I'm busy. Catch you later.' With that he was gone. I was kind of happy that Dogmeat had an idea. I was clueless as to what he had up his sleeve, but maybe, just maybe, we could keep hold of the money. I say "kind of happy" because most of his ideas had a habit of going pear-shaped.

We finished loading. I smiled at Mo and rubbed my hands together. 'It's pay day,' I said. 'I'll be able to show my face in the builders' merchants again, eh?' I was overdue with the payments and they were ready to suspend my account, so I'd had to use other companies, ones that I used infrequently because they were so expensive. It compounded my problem, but I had no choice.

48

Anyway, I would have been too embarrassed to go into my regular place. I could feel the other builders whispering about me.

'Lovely,' Mo replied. 'My mortgage payment is coming out of the bank this week.'

I went into the new porch. 'Nice job,' I thought. It's good when you know you've done a good job. I rapped on the inner door. No answer. I banged harder and eventually I saw Mr Dawson through the frosted glass.

'Hold on a minute, I'm looking for the key.' I whistled to myself as I waited.

'Here it is.' The door swung open. 'What can I do for you?'

'We've finished, Mr Dawson, I hope you're pleased with it.'

'It's lovely thanks.' He looked at me waiting for something else.

'The job's complete,' I said.

'I know it is.'

'I wondered... err... if.' I hated asking for money, even when it was due to us. I sometimes emailed late payers and told them that an imaginary battle-axe in the office was giving me grief about the payment. 'Is there any chance of some money, Mr Dawson?' I'd never received the stage payments as he always found an excuse not to pay.

'As soon as I get it, I'll pass it on to you.' Alarm bells were ringing. I was becoming a little tired of working for nothing.

'What do you mean, don't you have it?'

'Yes, I've got it,' he said. 'It's just that it's tied up at the moment. You know how things are with this account and that.'

'I know I have to pay for all this.' I waved my hand around in Mr Dawson's new porch.

'It'll not be long, just be patient.'

'I can't be patient.' I don't very often lose my cool, but the red mist was descending. 'I need to fuckin' pay people. I have to pay Mo. I have to pay my fuckin' gas bill. I have to eat.'

'No need to swear.'

'No need to fuckin' swear, I'll…' He slammed the door in my face.

'Right,' I said as I marched back to the pickup and climbed in. 'Get in Mo.' Mo obliged. Bert was having a dump on the manicured lawn. I whistled him and he ran and jumped on Mo's knee.

'I think we all know where this is heading,' said Mo. As soon as the door was closed, I pushed the gear stick into reverse and raised the revs. The engine was roaring as I released the clutch. The pickup lurched backwards and rammed into the newly built porch, instantly demolishing it. 'Have that, you cunt,' I shouted. Mo was shaking, Bert was rolling around on the seat, but I don't think he was laughing. We set off down the drive, struggling to detach ourselves from the rubble, with most of Mr Dawson's porch in the back. We were never going to get any money now, but some people need a lesson. I was wild, fuck the consequences.

I dropped Mo at home and took the chance to check the damage. I knew something wasn't right because the indicator light in the cab was doing strange things. No wonder, the indicators and lights on the left side of the truck had gone. They were probably on Mr Dawson's drive. The tailgate was bruised and dented, so was I. This was going to cost a fortune to repair.

'See ya, Mo,' I said. 'Sorry about the money.'

'Que sera,' Mo said. 'See ya, bro.' Mo set off up the steps to his front door.

When I arrived home, I threw my sandwich box into the sink and lifted Bert's lead off the hook by the door. 'Come on, Bert, let's go for a walk.' We went out onto the trail but turned in the opposite direction to the farm and the money. I didn't want to think about it. I didn't want to think about anything, but the thoughts wouldn't leave my head. The lyric from Bill Withers' song was rattling around in there, "We all have pain, we all have sorrow". Fuckin' 'ell, he wasn't wrong there, was he? We walked a long way. I considered the option of just walking and walking, never turning back, but Bert would be wanting his dinner, so I mustered the will to do an about turn.

Back at the house, not unexpectedly, the police were waiting, inspecting the rear end of my pickup. I saw them before they saw me and had the inclination to turn away, but I knew I would have to face the music sooner or later. The older officer was scratching his chin and the other, a young lady who I remembered from the betting shop debacle, spotted my impending arrival and elbowed her colleague. They never took their eyes off me as I moved closer.

'Is this your vehicle, sir?' He had that arrogant half smile they so often wear, when they know they've got a squeeze on your gonads.

'Aye, it's mine. Do you wanna buy it?' I said. 'One careful owner.'

'It's you again,' said the female officer. She didn't look old enough to be out of school, never mind be a member of the local constabulary. She wasn't a bad looking lass to be fair, easily an eight. 'You're becoming a frequent flyer, a one-man crime wave,' she added.

'I didn't know it was a crime to get locked in a betting shop.'

'Quite,' said the older man. 'How did your vehicle sustain this damage?' Why couldn't he call it a pickup or a truck like everyone else, the fuckin' gobshite?

'A porch ran into the back of me. It was much too close.' I said, sarcastically. 'You know damn well how it happened.'

'We do, sir. We believe you drove your vehicle into Mr Dawson's porch.'

'Correction,' I said. 'I drove my vehicle into my porch, which happened to be attached to Mr Dawson's house.'

'Mr Dawson could have been seriously injured,' the young one said.

'Was he?' I asked.

'No he wasn't, but that's not the point.'

'Fuckin' shame about that then,' I said.

'Would you like to accompany us to the station to explain yourself, Mr Barratt?'

'Do I have a choice?'

'It would make things less complicated if you came with us, sir,' she said.

'Let me put the dog inside. Give me five minutes.' Sir, eh? I'd been fuckin' knighted. I took Bert inside and gave him his dinner, then wrote a note for Sally. "I have to go to the police station, don't know when I'll be back. I've fed Bert, don't fall for his bullshit".

I went outside and got into the back of the police car. What a day this was turning out to be.

'I think we need to talk.' I hadn't been in the door two nanoseconds and Sally wanted to talk. She hardly ever spoke to me, only to gripe, but now she wanted to talk and I was tired. The police wouldn't bring me home, so I had to walk in the pissing down rain. I was drenched and I just wanted a shower and bed.

'It's not working, is it?' Sally said.

'Not the washing machine again?' I'd only recently forked

out to have it repaired. 'You're overloading it and I've told you to use that cow dung stuff they advertise on telly.'

'Calgon.'

'That's the gear.'

'It's not the washing machine,' Sally said in frustration.

'What's not working then?' I asked, bemused.

'Our marriage,' she said. 'Our marriage isn't working.'

'Well, we've had it a while.'

'Is that supposed to be funny?' She wouldn't know funny if it walked up and bit her on the arse.

'What's wrong with it?' What a fuckin' idiot question that was. I should have asked what's right with it.

'Everything. You spend your time either in the pub or at the police station, you're up in the middle of the night doing, I don't know what, your office is a pigsty and you're not contributing.'

'Why don't you say the word… money. That's what's bugging you, isn't it? What happened to for richer or poorer and all that shit?'

'I'm not arguing,' she said. 'You're sleeping in the spare bedroom from now on.' She was arguing. The decibels were rising.

'Why should I sleep in the spare room, you sleep in the spare room.' Bert was on his bed, tilting his head to one side, looking from one to the other of us, trying to work out what was going on. He wasn't used to us talking to each other.

'I've moved your clothes in there now. Call it a trial separation if you like, until you come to your senses. You can use the bathroom after I've done with it.'

'Thanks a bunch,' I said. 'You're all heart. You call it a trial separation. I'll call it a fuckin' liberty, in my own house.'

'It's best all round,' Sally insisted.

'Best for who?'

'For both of us.' She left the room before I strangled her. I heard her tramping upstairs in a huff. I wanted a shower, but I thought she might be going to the bathroom. It's come to something when I'm scared to use my own bathroom, I thought.

'We'd be better off without her,' I said to Bert, in answer to his inquiring stare. 'Me and you would do just fine, wouldn't we mate? We could come and go as we please, eat what we wanted, when we wanted, without the unrelenting diatribe. Man, I could crash my truck as many times as I fuckin' liked. We could watch what we wanted on the telly instead of Emmerdale and Coronation fuckin' Street. Have you ever noticed, Bert?' I added. 'That no one on Coronation Street watches Coronation Street on their telly. That's cos it's fuckin' rubbish. They know that. We could watch as much football as we liked, no problem, eh?' I'm sure I saw Bert nod, before he rested his head back down on his bed and closed his eyes.

'You have a kip, old boy,' I said.

I remembered that I hadn't eaten so I looked in the fridge and found some eggs. We had bread, so there it was, an egg butty. I took out the vegetable oil and poured a good amount into the frying pan. You need plenty of oil in the pan if you're going to fry anything. Don't listen to all those medical experts, they know jack shit about what's good for you. I wiped a liberal amount of butter on the bread, no skimping, and butter mind, not that shite they pass off as spread. What the fuck is spread anyway? It could mean anything. I'd spotted half a growler in the fridge as well. That would do nicely while the eggs were frying. In my opinion, and not just mine, our local butcher made the best pork pies in Yorkshire. I put the growler on the kitchen table, the same table we'd counted the money on. The oil was hot, so I cracked two large eggs into the pan. The fat spat and fired everywhere; Sally would boil her piss if she'd seen it, but fuck her. They would only take a minute or two to cook, just enough time to down the growler. I sat in front of the pork pie and an irresistible wave of fatigue swept over me. It'd been a long day. I swear I'd only nodded for a moment.

Bert was pawing at my leg. The smoke alarm was going off something manic. The sight of the frying pan on fire snapped me fully awake.

'What the?' I jumped up. I was trying to remember what the procedure was for fat fires. I know you shouldn't throw water on them, but I couldn't remember what you should do. It was something to do with a towel wasn't it? If I'd pondered any longer, the whole fuckin' kitchen would have been ablaze, so I quickly opened the back door, picked up the pan and ran out with it. I should have gone a bit steadier because burning oil jumped out onto the floor. I threw the pan in the garden, along with my eggs, and ran back in. The cushion floor that we had laid for Christmas last year had patches of fire between the door and the cooker. It looked like a landing strip in a jungle clearing. I stamped out the flames, but the floor covering was ruined. More expense. I waited for Sally to come down and rebuke me, but it seemed she'd rather burn to death than see me again. I abandoned the idea of eating and crept off to my new bedroom.

Chapter 5

'You're kidding,' I said, in fake disbelief. After waiting over thirty minutes to speak to someone. As always, I'd had to endure the numbers game.

'For contents insurance, press one. For buildings insurance, press two, For landlords insurance, press three, For motor insurance, press four. For...'

I pressed four before it went on any longer.

'For car insurance, press one. For motorcycle insurance, press two. For motorhome insurance, press three. For commercial vehicle insurance, press four.'

I pressed four again. I'd been on my way to the body shop for an estimate. No, not the one that sells smelly soap and shampoo, the one that repairs cars that idiots like me have smashed up. I'd been sat in a lay-by for over an hour after I'd left early to avoid Sally. It was her day off and I had to use the bathroom before she needed it.

'For renewals press one, for new policies press two. To make changes to your policy, press three. For claims, press four.' Four again. I heard ringing. Thank fuck for that. It rang and rang... then went dead.

'Hello,' I said. 'Hello... hello... hello.' I was talking to myself. Some little fucker in the call centre had picked it up and hung up immediately, probably because it was break time. I had to go through the ordeal again. Eventually, I reached the same stage, and I heard the ringing again, then a voice. I felt deep, short-lived joy.

'Hello,' I said, but the voice just talked over me.

'All our operators are busy right now helping customers. Your call is important to us, so please hold and we'll be with you as soon as we can.'

'If my call was important, you'd answer the fuckin' phone,' I shouted.

'You are at position... six... in the queue.' A crackly version of Lionel Richie's "Hello" played on a continuous loop, to allay my mental torture.

'No Lionel,' I said. 'It's not you I'm looking for.'

The music stopped.

'You are at position... five... in the queue.' Lionel again.

I was almost comatose by the time I got to speak to a human, stated my policy number, postcode, date of birth and the colour of my fuckin' toilet roll. Then I received the answer I expected.

'We're waiting for the police report, but I wouldn't think your policy covers this incident,' said the soft-voiced lady on the end of the line. I had an inkling they'd find a way not to pay, but I had to make the effort.

'It could have been an accident,' I said. 'I could have slipped the truck into reverse by mistake.'

'Was it an accident?'

'No,' I confessed. It was futile trying to argue the toss, and anyway it would all be in the report. I wasn't getting anything and that was that.

'Will that be all, Mr Barratt?' My admission had brought the conversation to a swift conclusion.

'Yes, thanks, love'

'Bye, have a nice day,' she said. I hadn't had a nice day for a while. I placed my mobile on the seat beside me and fastened my seatbelt, but before I could fire the engine, the phone rang. It was Dogmeat.

'What you up to, Dogmeat?' I asked.

'I'm training for the Olympics, high jump. What do think I'm doing?'

'Yeah, course you are,' I said.

'What *you* doing?' Dogmeat enquired.

'I'm going to Martin's garage to get a price on this damage.'

'Any joy from the insurance?'

'No, self-inflicted. If Dawson hadn't phoned the police, I'd have been okay.'

'That's not good. You know, I'd help you out if I could.' Dogmeat said.

'I know you would.' And he would have.

'Well, that's exactly what I'm going to do.' He laughed.

'Have you won the lottery then?'

'No, have I fuck. I want you to call Jimmy Onion and tell him to meet us on the track on Saturday, before we go to the Railway.'

'Fair enough,' I said. 'But, why.'

'We're going to put the bag back. Don't forget to bring it.'

'Whatever you say, Dogmeat. But I thought you had a solution.'

'I have, don't worry. Gotta crack on now, see ya.'

'All right, tara, mate.'

I couldn't imagine what Dogmeat had in mind, but I did as he suggested and called Jimmy Onion. He didn't answer, so I left a message telling him the good news. Good news for Jimmy Onion, but not so good for me.

'How much?' I thought I'd misheard.

'Ball Park,' said the guy at the body shop. 'Two and a half to three thousand.'

'That's some ball park,' I said.

'That's what it is these days,' he laughed. 'Parts aren't cheap.'

'I thought it only needed a couple of lamps.'

'Tailgate's twisted, mate,' he said. 'If you opened it, I doubt you'd get it shut again. You may be better off scrapping it.'

'I can manage with it closed. Can you patch it up to make it road legal, until I get back on my feet? The insurance won't pay.'

'I suppose we could do that,' he said, rubbing his chin, 'but it would be a temporary job you understand? It's down to you to make sure your vehicle is roadworthy.'

I didn't have much of a choice, so I booked it in for the following Thursday, said my goodbyes, and left. I didn't want to get back home too early, so I parked in the library car park and sat there for a while wondering what to do. Then I thought, 'Fuck it, I'm going to the King's Head for a swift half to pass the time.'

It was still morning, so only three or four serious drinkers were in the pub, all regulars, all sat apart from each other at their own table. I ordered and paid for a pint of Fosters, leant on the bar and looked around. Yellowed wallpaper, beermats that had been on the table for months, only replaced when someone nervously ripped one apart, or used it to level up a table leg. The bench seat which ran around the perimeter hadn't been cleaned for years. No jukebox in here, no music. The punters needed to contemplate their lot without distractions. What a dive. I looked closely at one of them. Was it? Yes it was, it was Lobo.

'Hey, Lobo,' I called. 'Is that you?' He looked up and nodded. I hadn't seen him for twenty, maybe twenty-five years but he still had the distinctive weasel eyes. As I walked over I could see that life had taken its toll. 'Can I join you?' I asked.

'Can if you want,' he said, but I got the impression he'd rather be left alone. I sat down across from him. 'What you been up to all these years?'

'Who are you?' Lobo asked.

'It's me, Johnny Barratt, don't you remember? We used to go around together with the other lads back in the day. Remember the pub crawls?'

'Ah yes,' he said quietly.

'It's nice to see you, Lobo. How you keeping?

'I'm all right.'

'Are you married?' I asked.

'No.'

'Are you working?'

'No.'

'What do you with yourself?'

'I come in here.'

'Ah, great,' I said. This conversation was going nowhere fast. It was like looking into the future. Lobo was me in a year or two if I didn't sort myself out. It disturbed me, so I downed my pint and left him to it. Passing time is one thing but putting up with that shite is on a whole different level. I'd find something else to do.

I called at the cash point and withdrew one hundred pounds. I enjoyed the feel of cash in my pocket, however, the funds were getting low and I didn't take it for granted that the hole in the wall would deliver indefinitely. It was market day, so I took a leisurely walk amongst the traders. The fruit and veg seller was doing a brisk trade, as was the growler man, but most of the others were very quiet. Some of them were touting absolute junk, so it wasn't surprising they had no punters. I was unwittingly following the aroma of sizzling bacon which was wafting across the marketplace. As I turned at the corner at the end of the row of stalls, I saw the converted Transit van with its serving hatch propped open. Three or four people were waiting for food, some were walking away with a fist full of burger and others were scanning the menu. I joined the orderly queue and waited until it was my turn. Say what you will about the Brits. We're shit at a lot of things, but we know how to queue, and our serial killers are up there with the best too.

'Bacon and tomato butty please.'

'Coming right up,' said the cheerful young lass in the naked lady apron. 'Tea or coffee?'

'No thanks, love.'

'Are you keeping busy?' I asked.

'We're always busy. People like their snap, don't they?'

'They do that, love,' I said, nodding towards the Golightly family that were approaching.

She giggled. 'Two-fifty please,' she said. 'Brown sauce and ketchup are on the end there.' She passed the sarnie through the hatch along with a paper serviette. I ate it as I strolled out of the market, the butty, not the serviette. A dollop of tinned tomato squirted out and dropped on to my jeans, but I didn't mind. It was a good butty and she'd taken the time to cut off the rind. Some of the offerings you got were chewy as fuck. You'd take a bite and the whole filling would slide out in one go, stuck together with a length of stringy fat. Aye, she'd put some love into this one. Two-fifty though, there must be plenty of profit in that. I know they have to pay to stand in the market, but the cost of the sandwich itself didn't amount to much.

I'd stayed out as long as I could bear, but I couldn't mooch around all day. I had to go back sooner or later, so I made my way to the car park. When I got to the truck, a traffic warden was sticking a ticket on my windscreen.

'What's that for?' I was fuckin' furious. 'It's a car park, isn't it?'

'You're right,' he said. 'It is a car park, but it's not a free car park.'

'Where does it say you have to pay?'

'There,' he said gleefully, pointing up at the "Pay and Display" sign I'd parked in front of.

'Why don't you get a fuckin' proper job?' I ripped the ticket from the windscreen and jumped into the truck.

'For fuck's sake,' I said, banging the steering wheel with the palms of my hand. 'When am I going to get a break?'

I arrived home to the monotonous hum of the vacuum cleaner sucking the life out of the carpets upstairs. I fuckin' hated that sound. Sally had used it as a weapon of mass guilt since the off. In the days before she went out to work, she'd wait until I got home to start cleaning, knowing I would have to join in or be branded as an absolute arsehole. Fair play to her though, she'd made a cracking job of the kitchen. The floor was gleaming, pity about the burn marks, and all the surfaces had been cleared, cleaned and polished, it looked mint. I hardly dare move in case I disturbed something. The Hoover stopped and I heard her bouncing down the stairs, look out. I suspected she'd been looking out of the window waiting for me.

'I've spent all day getting this house back to something like.' She was firm, but calm. 'I'm asking you now, to keep it like this. If you use something, put it back where you found it, if you dirty something, clean it... and try not to burn the bloody house down.' Happy that she'd had her say and I'd had the good sense to refrain from having the last word, she went into the front room to watch a rerun of Tipping Point.

I took my shoes off and, like a scolded schoolboy, I went up to my room. She'd been in here too. I couldn't find anything, but it was immaculate. I laid on the bed and stared at the ceiling, thinking about how shit my life was. I hoped Dogmeat's plan was going to come good. I allowed myself ten minutes shuteye, but I had paperwork to get out of the way and a couple of calls to make. The show must go on, so I roused myself, stretched, sending the light shade swinging, then went to my office. Sally had left no stone unturned in there either. The papers that had been strewn across my desk had been stacked neatly and the pens were back in the holder. The cough spots had disappeared from the computer screen and the place smelled fresh.

'Oh no!' The bag was gone, I searched around, she may have put it somewhere else, but it wasn't there. I went back into my bedroom, I couldn't find it there either. 'Sally,' I shouted, running down the stairs.

'What's wrong now?' She had her feet up on the settee, cup of tea in hand.

'The bag,' I gasped. 'The leather bag. Where is it?'

'I took some things to the charity shop.'

'You took the bag to a charity shop?'

Yes,' she said. 'I've never seen you use it, so I got rid of it. I looked in it and it was full of old newspapers. There's too much trash in this house.' I think she was referring to me with that jibe.

'Oh fuck.' What were the boys going to say? They wouldn't believe me. They were going to think I trousered the money myself. 'Which charity shop?'

'I can't remember,' she said scornfully. 'I called in a few of them, shared your junk out amongst them. God knows why they'd want that rubbish, but they took it… seemed glad of it.'

'Think,' I said. 'Which one did the bag go to?'

'I've just told you. I can't bloody remember, and don't tell *me* to think.' I looked at my watch and it was too late to go back into town. It was getting near closing time, so I'd have to wait until the morning.

I don't have to tell you that sleep was out of the question that night. The conversation I was going to have with Dogmeat churned around in my head. Jimmy Onion would think that I had concocted an idea to keep the money, he may decide to go ahead and inform the police. Mo would believe me, but a suspicious eye could be cast upon him by the other two. Would they think that Mo and I were in cahoots? What a mess. I had to get that bag back, come what may, preferably without the others knowing. I don't know why I'd landed the job of looking after it in the first place. No one had asked me, they just palmed it off on me.

Understandably, I was up and dressed early. I wanted to be outside the first charity shop as it opened. That first cup of coffee of the day is usually a thing of beauty, but today everything was bitter. I couldn't stomach breakfast, not even a slice of toast.

I'd had all night to formulate a plan. I was going to work my along the high street on one side, then work my way back down the other. I didn't know how many charity shops there were and if any were down the side streets, but I had to start somewhere.

The first one I came to was an animal rescue charity, and as soon as it opened I was in.

'You're keen,' said the mature gentleman whose neck I was breathing down.

'Do you have a leather bag?' I'd examined the goods on view and saw nothing that resembled my bag.

'Wait a minute, I'll have a look in the back.' He came out with a school satchel. 'This any good?'

'Is that all you've got?'

'"Fraid so,' he said.

It was the same story in the next two shops. The whole high street seemed to be made up of charity shops and bookies. I'd already spent well over an hour and got nowhere. I started back down the other side. The hospice shop was double fronted and quite busy. A spotty teenager welcomed me and asked what I needed.

'I'm after a leather bag, black. Do you have anything like that?'

'We did have up until about ten minutes ago.'

'Have you not got it now then?'

'No, I sold it.'

'Who to?'

'Just… a man.'

'What kind of a man?' I asked. 'I mean, what did he look like?'

'Stocky, bald. I didn't really take much notice.' I was in his face and my questions were making him feel uneasy. People were beginning to look at me.

'Which way did he go?'

'I don't know.' A stern looking lady was heading towards me, probably the manager, so I retreated before she could collar me.

I came out into the morning air, looking left and right, deciding what to do, which way to go. I could see the end of the street and there was nothing to make me think that the bloke who had my bag had gone that way, so I turned opposite, running frantically, bumping into indignant shoppers, all the time looking, looking, looking.

'Go steady,' said an old lady whose carrier bag I had knocked out of her hands. 'There's eggs in there.'

'Sorry, love,' I called back as I sped off.

I stopped to catch my breath. I didn't realise how out of shape I was, and I felt sick. If I wasn't careful, I was going to have a fuckin' heart attack. I drew oxygen into my bursting lungs and raised my head, then I saw him, on the bench outside Wetherspoons. He had the bag open, checking the contents. I eyed him up and down. He had a Barnsley FC tattoo on his forearm and a dotted line around his neck, with the words "cut here" at the front. He didn't look like the type of guy you could mess with.

'Is that your bag, mate?' I asked. He looked up to see the source of the voice, and it didn't worry him.

'Yes, what's it to you?'

'There's been a mistake,' I said. 'It's my bag. My wife took it to the charity shop by mistake.'

'It's mine now,' he said. 'What's so special about this bag? Go buy another one.'

'My dad left it to me,' I lied. 'Football memorabilia, programmes, sports papers, you know, just rubbish really, but it has sentimental value to me. It's just rubbish to anyone else.'

He took out the top *Green 'Un* and examined it. 'Some of these old football papers can be worth a lot of money,' he said, eying the dirty newspaper. I didn't want him to delve any deeper.

'Not this lot,' I said. 'It's only worth anything to me.'

'That's what you say.'

'Don't get me wrong. I'll buy it. How much did you pay for it?'

'Fiver,' he said.

'I'll double it, a tenner.'

'Two hundred quid.' He smiled as he said it.

'Ah, come on, it's not worth that much.'

'I'll keep it then.'

'I've only got…' I pulled money from my pocket. 'Hundred and twenty.' I showed him the notes.

'Cash point there,' he said, pointing at the bank across the road.'

'Okay, okay,' I relented. 'Wait here.'

'I'm going nowhere, pal.'

While I was withdrawing money, he was looking at the next paper. 'For fuck's sake hurry up,' I urged the machine. I snatched the money and returned.

'How much did you take out?' He asked.

'Hundred quid,' I said.

'The price is two hundred and twenty now.'

'You said two hundred.'

'Inflation,' he said. 'Take it or leave it.'

I slapped the money hard into his palm and picked up the bag. 'Cunt,' I said as I walked away.

Chapter 6

We met, as agreed, earlier than usual on Saturday morning. I felt uneasy clutching the bag to my chest as we waited for Dogmeat to arrive. Bert was on his lead today with Mo steering him. We couldn't do with him running wild, sniffing here, sniffing there, delaying us and causing a distraction.

'You're doing the right thing,' Jimmy Onion said, reading the concern written into my face.

'If you say so,' I replied. 'You know I'm financially embarrassed, don't you?'

'Things will pick up, Johnboy. When one door closes, another one opens, and doing it the honest way always feels better.'

'Yeah,' I said. 'And every silver lining has a cloud.'

'Here he is,' Mo said, spotting Dogmeat wheeling down the track.

'You're late,' said Jimmy Onion.

'Sorry boys, I was just digging out my old pool cue.' Dogmeat's cue was one of those that came in two parts and screwed together in the middle. He had it slung around the back of the chair like a quiver.

'Are we playing pool?' I marvelled how Dogmeat could think of playing games at a time like this.

'I thought we'd have a game, for a change, eh?'

'It's been a long time,' Mo said. 'We'll be a bit rusty.'

'Use it or lose it,' Dogmeat said as we moved off.

'Do you have any poo bags?' Mo asked, as Bert squatted on the path.

'No,' I said. 'He usually goes in the grass when he's off the lead.'.

'We can't just leave it here.'

'Why not?' Dogmeat asked.

'Because someone might tread in it,' said Jimmy Onion.

'They should watch where there going then,' was Dogmeat's reply.

'Boot it into the verge,' I said.

'These are my best trainers,' Mo objected.

I waited until Bert had finished and toed the turds off the path myself. 'All done,' I said. I didn't want to owe Mo a pair of trainers on top of everything else. The price of them was scandalous. In my day, before the marketing men had taken over the world, it was pumps or sneakers, available in black or white.

'How are you, Dave?' Jimmy Onion asked.

'Shite, same as usual.'

'Ah well,' said Jimmy Onion. 'I'm glad you're doing well. I have to say,' Jimmy Onion continued, 'how pleased I am that you've come to your senses about this money. I'd have much preferred that you hand it in, but if you feel you can't, I'm happy with this course of events. Life's full of compromises, isn't it?'

'The money would have been useful,' Dogmeat said, 'but you've got us by the nads, Jimmy, so we don't have much of a choice, do we? Unless you're going to have a last-minute change of heart. Why don't you leave it to us three and forget you ever saw the bag, and we'll never mention it again?'

'That's the problem, Dave. I couldn't just forget. It would be on my mind continually. Believe me, you'll thank me for this one day.'

'I don't think so,' Dogmeat said.

We came to the path by the flat-roofed building, lifted Dave over the rough area, and continued towards the farm. Our progress along the rarely-used track was unsurprisingly problem free. Once inside the compound, we moved to the centre and removed the heavy cover from the well head. I handed the bag to Mo, to tie on the end rope.

'No,' Dogmeat said. 'I think Jimmy should put it back, then he knows it's done.'

'I'm not very supple these days, Dave, it would be better if Mo did it.'

'I insist,' Dogmeat said firmly.

'Come on, Dave,' said Jimmy Onion. 'I'm more than happy for Mo to do it.'

'You're doing it, Jimmy.' Dogmeat said sternly.

'I'm going for a drain off while you two are arguing about it,' I said, strolling across the courtyard and entering a small building which held the remains of an elevated platform above my head. I assumed it must have once been used for storage, a barn type of place. I wasn't a farmer so I didn't ponder upon it for long. From my vantage point behind a small, barred opening, I could see and hear Jimmy and Dogmeat arguing. 'What fuckin' difference does it make who puts the bag back?'

'All right then,' said Jimmy Onion. 'If it's that important to you, I will.' Jimmy Onion had taken the bag and was unzipping it to check the contents. 'It's all there I assume?' he asked.

'Yes, it's all there,' Dogmeat said. 'What do you think we are, fuckin' liars?'

Jimmy Onion looked at Mo for confirmation.

'We haven't taken any,' Mo said. 'We were going to but we thought…'

'Too much information, Mo.' Dogmeat cut Mo short.

'Good,' said Jimmy, happy that the contents of the bag were intact before he resealed it and crept closer to the precipice.

I was pissing like a racehorse at this point. Whistling, which was a habit of mine during urination, I looked out at the three of them, wondering how Jimmy was so sure that we wouldn't return and take the bag later. Was that what Dogmeat had in mind when he said everything was under control? Was Jimmy going to make regular visits to check on it? If he was, he was doing it without me. I intended to make this the last time I came anywhere near this place... ever. As the thoughts coursed through my head, Dogmeat's strategy became clear, and before I could utter a word Dogmeat had removed the thick end of the pool cue from its holder and like Babe Ruth, had struck Jimmy Onion around the back of his head as he knelt at the edge of the well. I heard his skull crack before he slowly dropped into the abyss. Just as I was about to run across the yard to the boys, an unfamiliar voice stopped me in my tracks.

'Nice work.' A large man had entered the compound and was advancing towards the scene. I'm no firearms expert, but I know a gun when I see one, so I moved back to the opening in the wall, hoping that the man hadn't seen me.

'You've got something of mine,' he said. 'Move away from it.' He waved his pistol and Dogmeat and Mo moved away from the bag allowing the man to stand alongside the bag. I judged him to be in his forties, bull-necked, sunglasses even though the sky was overcast.

'I now have a problem,' Bullneck said.

'What's that then,' Dogmeat said, apparently still calm.

'You two. You're my problem. You've seen my face.'

'We won't say anything, bro,' Mo said, knowing where this

was about to go, as his favourite song said.

'You're wasting your time, Mo,' said Dogmeat. 'He intends to kill us.'

'Your pal's right,' Bullneck said. 'I'm sorry, but you have to go down. You do understand, don't you?'

'No, please,' Mo said. 'I'm about to become a father.'

I assessed my options. I had to do something, and quickly. He had his back to me as I moved stealthily across the dusty surface. Dogmeat saw me approaching but quickly averted his eyes so as not to give the game away. Mo, not so smart, clocked me and kept his eyes on me. Look away Mo, look away, but he didn't and Bullneck turned. I sprinted the last few yards and rammed my head into Bullneck's chest, knocking him backwards and down. The gun flew across the courtyard, Bullneck screamed as he was falling into the well, it was awful to hear.

'Well done, Johnboy,' Dogmeat said. 'I knew you'd bail us out.' I couldn't answer for shaking. 'Get the lid on, lads, let's get away from here sharpish.'

'What about Jimmy Onion?' Mo asked.

'No need to worry about him, he was dead before he hit the bottom,' Dogmeat said.

'And that bloke,' I said. 'Are we just going to leave him?'

'Fuck him, he was all for shooting us and pushing us down the hole. Besides, there's nothing we can do for him. Just get the fuckin' lid on will you?'

We did as Dogmeat instructed, but I felt uneasy about leaving the two of them down there in the dark. If Bullneck had survived the fall, he was in for a horrible death. It concerned me greatly, but I couldn't see an alternative, so we complied and placed the lid back over the well.

'Pick up that gun, Mo,' Dogmeat said. 'Be a good lad and

put my bag behind me will ya?' Mo silently did as he was bid.

Once again, we were back on the trail with the bag, nervously glancing in both directions, waiting for Bullneck's mates to show. I just wanted to go home and hide, but Dogmeat had other ideas.

'Take the money back to yours,' he said. 'Then come back to The Railway.'

'Surely we're not going drinking after this?' I said.

'We have to, Johnboy. How would it look if we didn't turn up on the very day that Jimmy Onion went missing?'

'I suppose you're right,' I conceded.

'You know I'm right. Take Mo with you. I'll see you in there later.' Dogmeat wheeled off and we turned in the opposite direction.

Dogmeat had already sunk a couple of pints by the time Mo and I settled down to our first.

'Where's Jimmy?' Walt had a tower of empty pint pots leading from his palm all the way over his shoulder.

'He's probably not well.' Dogmeat winked at me as he said it, the callous bastard.

'Let's hope he gets right soon,' Walt said as he walked away. 'I don't like losing a punter.'

Dogmeat didn't seem at all disturbed by the day's events, if anything, he was in better than usual form. 'Our share has just gone up boys,' he smiled. 'What's that now, eighty odd grand each?'

'Something like that,' Mo said. 'I must admit, that had crossed my mind, but I don't half feel guilty about it.'

'No need to feel guilty, Mo my old son. You know it's for the best.' Dogmeat took a huge slurp of his ale.

73

'What you going to do with your cut, Johnboy?' Dogmeat asked.

'I haven't given it much thought,' I said. 'Because a couple of hours ago, I was resigned to losing it. First thing though, is to sort out Mo. I owe him a fortune.'

'Oh, don't worry about that, bro,' Mo said. 'We've all got money now. What about you, Dave, a new motor?'

'No, don't forget it's cash and we're going to have to be very careful what we do with it. What I'd really like to do, is set up a little business, have a purpose in life. All I'm doing at the moment is treading water, passing time, vegetating. I need something worthwhile to do.'

'What kind of business?' I asked.

'I don't know,' Dogmeat said. 'Wringer out for a one-armed window cleaner or something.'

We were laughing now. We'd just murdered two men, one of which was our friend, and we were laughing. Maybe it was the ale, or just sheer relief at still being alive and breathing ourselves.

'Come on,' Dogmeat said. 'Let's have a couple of games of pool?'

'You're not going to use that cue, are you?' I asked.

'Course I am,' Dogmeat replied. 'What do you think I'm going to use, a fuckin' broom handle?'

'I know, but it's…'

'It's what?' Dogmeat said. 'It's a pool cue. Pound a game, winner stays on.'

We were in the habit of turning our chairs upside down and placing them on the table when we vacated it for a while. It was Walt's idea to do this, to avoid a repeat of the scene when a group of unsuspecting drinkers took our regular table, naturally believing it was available. When they wouldn't move at the first

74

request, Dogmeat grabbed the back of a chair and yanked it backwards, causing one of the guys to spill his beer. All hell kicked off and we were barred for a couple of weeks, before Walt decided that he liked our money and invited us back.

I was on first, and naturally, Dogmeat beat me. That was the first pound gone. Then Mo had a go and lost, then me, then Mo ad infinitum.

'Come on Dogmeat,' I said. 'Let's go back to our table after this one.'

'Just another couple of games,' he said.

'Two games and that's it,' I said.

A youngster stepped into Dogmeat's field of vision as he was lining up a shot, and placed a two pound coin on the edge of the pool table to indicate his intention to play.

'What the fuck's that?' asked Dogmeat.

'We want a game,' the youngster said. 'You've been hogging the table long enough.'

Dogmeat quickly made his way around the table to where the youngster was standing. 'You see this cue?' he asked.

'Yeah, course I do, I'm not blind.'

'I'm going to wrap it round your fuckin' neck if you don't pick up that coin,' Dogmeat threatened. The youngster looked into Dogmeat's eyes, saw that he meant it and put the coin back in his pocket.

'Good lad,' Dogmeat said. 'Now fuck off.'

We returned to our table, but not before Dogmeat had extended the two games to three, just to make the lads wait a little longer. It was nice to get back to the table and take the weight of my feet after prancing round that pool table, knocking balls about. However, it felt strange, the three of us and an empty seat and it worried me that any pangs of remorse I might have had,

had now left me. Surely, I should be feeling bad. Walt interrupted my thoughts when he laid three more pints on the table. We thanked him and he left, so we got down to quietly discussing what the future held for us.

'I'd love to get out of the building game,' I said.

'Me too,' Mo added.

'It'd be a novelty doing something you get paid for eh, Mo?' Dogmeat laughed, making me feel a little awkward.

'A fresh start,' I said. 'Something I enjoy doing.'

'I don't think there's much demand for ale testing,' said Dogmeat. 'Joking apart, what would you like to do?'

'I'm not sure, but it'll be something I get paid for up front. I'm sick of getting knocked.'

'What are you going to do, Mo, if Johnboy here quits the building trade?'

'I'll do whatever turns up, bro.' That was Mo in a nutshell. Easy going, easy to please. Not a bad bone in his body. Even Dogmeat liked him.

'You know where the money is don't you?' Dogmeat said.

'It's at my place. When are you coming round for it?' I asked.

'Not that money, you whopper. You can hold on to that for a while. I'm talking about making money.'

'Oh right,' I said. 'Where is it then, this money?'

'Food my friends. The big profits are in food, fast food.'

'I don't know about that, Dogmeat,' I said. 'That new restaurant on the high street was only open for five or six months before it went pop.'

'Not a restaurant, Johnboy. Mobile catering is where the money is.'

'What?' said Mo. 'You mean like Bob's Burger van in the car park.'

'Same idea, but if we can't do better than that, my prick's a bloater.' Dogmeat was becoming animated with the idea. 'I was thinking of a fuck off big one, like they have at the fair, with chips and things. Bob can't do chips. All he's got in that little van is a hotplate and a cooker.'

'He has a tea urn,' Mo said.

'That goes without saying. A tea urn is standard,' Dogmeat conceded.

'He's got a bain marie as well,' I said. 'You can see it at the front there. It says on it "Bain Marie" and some other stuff.'

'What the fuck's a bain marie?' Dogmeat asked.

'I don't know,' I said. 'But he's got one.'

'Whatever he's got,' Dogmeat said. 'He doesn't know how to use it judging by his food, it's shite. Not exactly Michelin star standard, is it?'

'Could be a great idea,' I said. 'I can see one small problem though.'

'What's that, Johnboy?'

'How are you going to get in and out the van with the wheelchair? How are you going to serve people?'

'That's where you lads come in,' Dogmeat said. He'd obviously given this some thought. 'You'd like to move into the catering business, wouldn't you, Mo?'

'Yeah, I suppose so,' Mo said, unconvinced.

'And what would my role be?' I asked.

'You and Mo would be the public face of the business, right at the coal face. You'd love it.'

'What would you do?' I asked.

'I'd be the mastermind behind it all, setting business strategy, marketing and buying. Those burgers don't just appear by themselves you know. Someone has to source them.'

'You can get them at the cash and carry down the road,' I said.

'It's not just burgers though, is it?' Dogmeat went on. 'There's baps.'

'You can buy them in the supermarket or at the bakers,' I said.

'Sausages,' Dogmeat said.

'Butchers.'

'I'll make your money grow, Johnboy. This would be just the beginning. In a couple of years, we could have fast food trailers all over South Yorkshire, maybe even farther afield. Who knows?'

'Where are you going put this burger van?' I asked.

'Let's get one thing straight from the start,' Dogmeat said. 'It wouldn't be a burger van. It would be a mobile catering trailer.'

'Where would you put this mobile catering trailer?'

'Here in the car park to start with,' Dogmeat said.

'But Bob's already claimed the car park,' Mo said.

'It's a big car park, there's room for another one at this end.'

'Bob's not going to like that,' I said.

'Fuck Bob,' said Dogmeat. 'We'll put him out of business in six weeks.'

'I don't think Walt would agree to another burger van in his car park,' I said.

'I keep telling you, it's not a fuckin' burger van. Don't worry about Walt, I've already had the nod from him.'

'You don't let the grass grow under your feet do you?' I said. I felt like we'd been groomed.

'No,' Dogmeat laughed. 'It's in my loft.'

'I'm not sure about this, Dogmeat,' I said. 'It's fraught with danger. We could lose money on it.'

'Come on, Johnboy. It wouldn't take all our money and we'd have a tidy sum left over. The best thing about this is that we can buy a second hand one with cash. You know, untraceable.'

'I suppose that's one thing,' I said.

'And with you and Mo's skills, we could buy one and renovate it if we wanted. We'd save money there. And just think,' Dogmeat added, 'No one would get their food until they'd paid for it. That's exactly the kind of business you were looking for isn't it?'

'There is that about it.' Dogmeat's last point was making me warm to the idea a little.

'And when we get established, we can employ a young lass with big tits to hang over the counter while we sit in here.' Dogmeat was really working on me now.

'Sounds good to me, bro,' said Mo.

'You see,' Dogmeat said. 'Mo knows a good idea when he sees one.'

'I don't know, Dogmeat,' I said. 'I'm no chef.'

'You'd learn, and Mo could handle all the exotic food. You'd make a great team.'

'I was born in Barnsley,' Mo said.

'It's in your blood, Mo,' Dogmeat said. 'Have a think about it lads while I go for a Woodbine.'

Chapter 7

Monday morning saw Mo and I cleaning gutters on an aging semi. We had a ladder apiece and starting at each end we worked our way to the centre, pulling out clumps of grass and mud. Hitting rock bottom workwise, gutter cleaning was all we could get at the moment. We had enough money to knock it on the head, but we had to keep up appearances as we still weren't absolutely sure whether Bullneck had been a lone ranger or part of a larger group, so we had to be watchful and keep the money under wraps for the time being.

'I'm not enjoying this, Mo,' I said. 'I'll be glad when we don't have to do it any more.'

'It's not so bad, bro.' As always, Mo was at peace with himself. 'Decent weather, good company.'

'What do you think about Dogmeat's idea?' I asked.

'Which one? He's full of ideas.'

'The burger van,' I said.

'I'd love to do that,' said Mo, enthusiastically.

'Really?' I said. 'The novelty might wear off pretty quickly you know, stuck inside a fuckin' burger van for hours on end. Mind you, it has to be better than this'.

'Dogmeat said we could employ somebody later on, if all goes well.'

'The young lass? You don't believe that do you?' I smirked, 'He's full of shit.' I scooped a piece of debris out of the gutter with my trowel and let it fall to the ground. Bert was in the wrong place at the wrong time and the soggy lump of mud hit him square on the head. He ran away quickly, turning his head from side to side to see who had attacked him. He never thought of looking up.

'Poor old Bert,' Mo said.

'Sorry, Bert.' I laughed. 'How many times have I told you not to walk under ladders? You think we should do it then, Mo?'

'I'd like to,' Mo said.

'Okay then,' I said. 'We'll do it. From this moment on, we are masters of our own sausage.'

The job didn't take long, so we were packed up and home sharpish. We'd been paid as well, which was a nice feeling, even though it wasn't much. I'd dropped Mo back at his and parked up behind my house. I unlocked the back door and swung it open. Bert rushed in ahead of me, straight to Sally.

'You're back early,' she said, stiffly.

'It wasn't much of a job,' I said. 'I thought you'd be at work.' Looking through to the front door, I saw two suitcases standing in the hall. The last thing I wanted was visitors, but it didn't take long for the penny to drop. They were our suitcases.

'Where are you going?' I asked.

'Does it matter?'

'Are you going to your mother's? I don't think she'll want you there, love. She's not the friendliest, is she?'

'Leave my mother out of this. I'm not going to mother's.'

'Where are you going then?' I asked again.

'I've told you, it doesn't matter. You don't need to know. I'll be back for the rest of my things later.'

A car pulled up in front of the house and Sally opened the door, picked up the two suitcases and struggled out. My instinct was to help her with the heavy luggage, but I let her sweat by herself. A man jumped out of the car, advanced up the path and took the cases with ease. It was Andy Warburton.

'All right, Johnboy,' he said, as casual as you like, considering he was stealing my wife.

'Fuck off,' I said.

'No need to be like that,' answered the school bully.

'You've gone right down market now haven't you, Sally?'

'Watch your mouth,' Warburton said. 'If you're not careful, we'll be looking at round two.'

'Anytime you like,' I said, with bravado. 'Only this time, the loser has to keep her.'

'That's what happened last time, you dork,' said Warburton. He was right and I felt foolish.

'Just fuck off then… and make sure you don't bring her back when you've had enough of her, cos believe me, you'll want to.'

They loaded the cases into the boot of the car and Sally opened the back door. I thought it strange that she was going to travel in the back, but that wasn't what was going to happen. She whistled and shouted Bert. In a flash, he had run and jumped into the car. He was fast when he wanted to be. I'm sure he thought he was going for a walk.

'No, Leave Bert here.' But it was too late. Sally was in the car, and they were off. I ran to the end of path. 'Don't take the fuckin' dog,' I shouted, but they were gone, leaving just me and a few bemused neighbours on the street. 'Get back in your houses,' I screamed at them. 'You fuckin' nosy bastards.' I went back into the hallway and rammed my fist into the art deco mirror that Sally loved so much. The mirror smashed, but my hand hurt like fuck. Furious didn't begin to describe my feelings. Andy fuckin' Warburton, what was she thinking? That eternal question that plagues jilted partners sprung to mind; how long had it been going on? If that bastard had been in my house, I'd kill him. I looked around the house for signs of him. I didn't exactly know what I was looking for, but my head was a shed. Of course, I found nothing to suggest he'd been here, no anomalous socks under the bed, no cigarette ends, nothing. I now had the house to myself and I felt forsaken and alone. Right there and then, I decided that I couldn't live alone, my life would be desolate without Bert. I had to get him back.

'Bert's been dognapped,' I blurted.

'What do you mean, Johnboy?' I was so glad that Dogmeat had answered his phone when I needed a shoulder to cry on, and I'm not ashamed to say there were real tears running down my cheek.

'They've taken him, the bastards have taken him. I came home and they took him.'

'Woah,' Dogmeat said. 'Slow down and explain yourself.'

'Sally has fucked off with Warburton and taken Bert.'

'You're kidding, Andy Warburton?'

'One and the same,' I said.

'He's a fuckin' crook,' Dogmeat proclaimed. 'Did you have any idea what was going on?

'We weren't getting on very well, but I didn't think she'd do this. I love that dog.'

'I never liked him. He was never any good, even at school he was an arsehole.' Dogmeat was saying all the right things.

'I know, and now he's got Bert.'

'Go and get him back then.'

'I don't know where he lives,' I blubbered.

'Steady down, Johnboy, we'll sort something out. Someone

will know where he lives.'

'You don't know what it's like, looking at that empty dog bed.' I could hardly breathe for grief.

'Listen to me, Johnboy,' Dogmeat said determinedly. 'We'll get him back, trust me.'

I'd left my truck at Dogmeat's and we were heading back to mine in his car. Dogmeat was driving with the hand attachments that were connected to the brake and accelerator, and Mo was in the back peering over our shoulders. We guessed that Sally would use the front door when she came for the rest of her belongings, so we parked far enough away that we could see the house, and still be inconspicuous. She'd probably need four or five trips for her fuckin' shoes alone, so we were confident we'd spot her sooner or later. As soon as I got Bert back, the locks would be changed, rapido.

'It's like a stake out,' Mo said.

'That's exactly what it is, Mo,' said Dogmeat.

'We need cardboard cups with coffee, and dark glasses, and pastrami on rye,' Mo said.

'What the fuck's pastrami on rye?' inquired Dogmeat.

'It's what Kojak and his mates used to eat when they were on a stake out... I think it was Kojak, or was it Magnum?'

'You've been watching too much ITV4, Mo,' I said. 'I can pop in and get you a coffee if you want.'

'Don't be fuckin' stupid, Johnboy,' Dogmeat said. 'You'll blow our cover.'

'We're not in New York, it's fuckin' Barnsley,' I said.

'People have eyes in Barnsley you know. If you go back in now and they come back, we've wasted our time. Just sit tight.' Dogmeat opened the glove box and pulled out a pack of cigarettes.

'You're not smoking in here are you?' I asked.

'I'm not getting the fuckin' wheelchair out again. I'm quite comfortable here. Who's car is it anyway?' Dogmeat lit the cigarette and let the window down.

'That stinks.' I pulled the lever on the passenger door to open it, but Dogmeat grabbed my arm before I could get out.

'Where are you going?'

'Outside, until you've finished,' I said.

'You can't get out, you'll be seen,' Dogmeat said. Mo was starting to cough in the back. 'Drop the windows if you don't like it.'

'Turn the ignition back on then, it's foggy in here,' I said, choking. With the window down, Mo hung his head out like a pet spaniel.

We waited, and waited for what seemed like hours. It had been in actual fact, two and half hours. My arse was getting numb, I was hungry and beginning to wonder if there wasn't a better way. Mo was complaining that he needed the toilet.

'It's a good job you didn't have that coffee, isn't it?' Dogmeat said.

'I could do with something to eat,' I said.

'You'll manage,' Dogmeat said. 'Have patience.'

'I can't hold on much longer,' Mo said.

'You'll not have to,' I said. 'They're here.'

'The cheeky bastard,' I said when I saw Warburton's BMW reverse onto my drive.

'I'm gonna kill the bastard,' I said, making for the door handle again.

'Hold your fire, Johnboy,' said Dogmeat. 'Take it easy. Think of Bert.'

Warburton got out of his BMW and went around the car to open the door for Sally.

'Look, she thinks she's fuckin' royalty now,' I said. 'Can you see Bert?'

'I don't think he's with them, Johnboy,' Dogmeat said.

I hated the thought of Warburton being in my house, and it took all my willpower to sit tight. However, we waited until Sally had gathered her belongings.

'I've paid for most of that stuff,' I complained, as they carried it out to the car.

'Chill, Johnboy,' Dogmeat said. 'You wouldn't look good in a dress. Let them take what they want.'

'They've got the fuckin' dog bed.' Dogmeat had to restrain me once again. My fists were clenched tight with fury.

'If you go on like that, you're not going to get Bert back, are you? Just cool your jets.'

We followed Warburton from a distance, always keeping two or three vehicles between us. Heading south towards Sheffield, we almost lost them on the recently remodelled motorway roundabout, the one where no fucker knows which lane to go in.

'A fuckin' five-year-old must have designed this,' Dogmeat grumbled. 'Fuck off, will yer,' he added as someone sounded their horn when we switched lanes.

After we'd negotiated the roundabout, we turned off the main drag and the roads became much quieter. The urban sprawl had given way to farmland making it more difficult to remain unnoticed. The road undulated, so at times we lost sight of Warburton, but when we rose to the crest again, we could see the black BMW. The only problem was that he could almost certainly see us too, but would he take any notice of a car he didn't know?

86

Probably not. I doubt whether he even looked in the mirror.

'Keep your distance,' I said.

'I know what I'm doing,' Dogmeat snarled.

'Just saying.'

'I'm fuckin' driving.'

'I need the toilet,' Mo said.

'Don't piss your pants in here,' said Dogmeat. 'It's like the fuckin' school trip.'

'On the school trip there'd have been a toilet on the bus,' Mo said, squirming on the back seat.

'You want me to have a shitter installed in my car now?'

'No, I just want you to stop so I can relieve myself.'

'We can't stop now, Mo,' I said. 'We'll lose them. Tie a knot in it or something.'

'If we'd have had that coffee I could have pissed in the cup,' said Mo.

'Lovely,' said Dogmeat.

The road continued like this for a further few miles, until we entered a small village and Warburton turned left at a crossroad by the post office.

'Fuck off,' Dogmeat replied.

The BMW turned left again into a recently built housing development, which an estate agent would probably label "executive homes", big, detached fuckers with double garages and four, five or even six bedrooms, and more bathrooms than you could shake a stick at.

'Nice round here innit?' Mo said.

'Aye,' Dogmeat said, 'He's done well for himself.'

'All from illegal activities, no doubt.' It hurt me to admit it, but I was jealous. There's no wonder Sally went off with him, but let her live her new life of luxury, I simply wanted Bert back home with his dad, where he belonged.

Warburton swung the car off the road and through some tall, iron gates which had opened automatically as he approached. We waited a minute or two after the gates had closed behind them and very slowly crept by. The BMW was sitting on the Indian stone, paved drive. Now we knew where he lived, more to the point, we knew where Bert was, but how were we going to get him out of there?

The next day, I was sitting in the front room nodding off, watching Bargain Hunt, when the doorbell sounded, causing me to jump and spill my can of Fosters. I knew I shouldn't drink on a school day, but what the fuck, I could do what I wanted now.

'What the fuck you doing here?' I said out loud. I'd opened the door and been surprised to see Warburton. Had he seen us following him?

'We've come for Sally's car. Can we have the keys please?' He was civil enough and I didn't want to rock the boat, so I went along with his request.

'Are you okay?' he asked. He sounded genuinely concerned.

'Bearing up,' I said. 'What about you?'

'I'm good,' he answered. 'Hey, you don't know Billy Liddell by any chance do you?'

'Can't say I do, never heard of him. Who is he anyway?'

'Just a mate of mine who's gone missing,' he said. 'It's not important.'

'Sorry, I can't help you.' I handed over the keys. Sally, who had hung back in the parking area had begun shrieking and I knew why, so I slammed the door on Warburton. It was evident that she'd clocked the damage I'd done to her car with my lump hammer.

I went back to Bargain Hunt, the red team had just bought an old milk crate for forty quid, the fuckin' blockheads. If they got a fiver for it at auction, I'd be amazed. There's some proper shite sold in the name of antiques, I know. The doorbell snapped me awake again as I was drifting off.

'For fuck's sake,' I said. 'It's like piccalilli circus today.' I was never going to complete the siesta at this rate. I was getting lazy, and not having to walk Bert was making it worse. I needed him back for both my mind and body. I don't suppose Sally or Warburton were taking him for walks. Fuck me, he'll be like a royal corgi when he finally comes home, both of us as fat as fuck.

'Mr Barratt?' I'd made out the uniform through the opaque glass before I opened the door. It was the visit I'd been expecting. I was relieved it wasn't the nose picker or the young one. This one was a new one, who I hadn't met before, but I'm sure his pals would have told him about the bookies and the porch before they sent him.

'That's me.'

'Do you know Charles Newton?'

'You mean Jimmy Onion, don't you?' I said.

'No, I'm asking about Charles Newton,' said the officer.

'Same bloke,' I said. 'Come in.' I led him into the kitchen and sat him at the table. 'Fancy a beer?'

'I'd love one, but I can't,' he smiled. 'On duty and all that.' He seemed a nice enough lad.

'I've been asking all over about Jimmy's whereabouts,' I said. 'Have you heard anything?' Dogmeat and I had phoned him regularly and left messages. It was the natural thing to do when your mate doesn't turn up at the pub for a couple of sessions and it would all be on record. I'd even been round to his place and put on a show for his neighbours, shouting through the letterbox and looking up at the bedroom window, making sure they saw me.

'I'm afraid not,' the officer replied. 'He hasn't been in to work for a while now.'

'Oh,' I said. Just that.

'We've gained entry to his home, and everything looks to be in place. His neighbours haven't seen him either.'

'He was.' I quickly corrected myself and hoped the officer hadn't noticed the past tense. 'He's a very private person.'

'Apparently so. Can you shed any light?'

'No, not really,' I said. I see him at the Railway on Saturdays, but that's all. We're not in each other's pocket if that's what you think. I assumed he'd gone off somewhere for work. He does now and again you know, but he usually tells us that he'll not be out for a drink the following week. This time, he didn't, but I wasn't too worried. Like I said, he was just a drinking pal.'

'When did you last see him?'

'That would be in the pub, Saturday before last I'd say.'

'And he didn't appear to be different or anything out of the ordinary?'

'He was a bit down,' I said. 'Not his usual self.'

'Depressed, you'd say?'

'Eh?' I said, feigning alarm. 'You don't think he's done something daft do you?'

'We can't rule anything out at this stage,' he said. 'As you say, he's probably gone away and not told anyone. It happens all the time. If you hear anything, you'll give us a call, won't you?' He slid a card onto the table.

'Goes without saying,' I said. 'I'll get him to call you and apologise for being a dickhead. Going away without telling anyone eh?'

90

'Thanks for your time,' the officer said as he left.

'Pleasure,' I said, letting him out. 'That went well,' I thought.

Later, I called Dogmeat and asked him if he'd had a visit from the boys in blue, and if not, to expect one. I reassured him that the officer didn't seem suspicious, but Dogmeat really didn't give a fuck. Good luck to the bobby that went to see him. Mo didn't need to worry, he didn't have the strong links to Jimmy Onion that we had, but I tipped him the wink anyway, just to be sure. I was glad Sally had fucked off, the less she knew, the better. I felt sure that we could get through this if we didn't draw attention to ourselves, that meant keeping the money in the bag for the time being.

Chapter 8

'I know she does Pilates on Tuesday mornings.' We were plotting the release of Bert.

'Should we wear balaclavas?' Mo asked.

'We're not the fuckin' SAS,' said Dogmeat. 'We're only going to rescue a dog, not Prince Charles.'

'He may be only a dog to you,' I said. 'But he's the world to me.'

'I know, Johnboy.' Dogmeat squeezed my lower arm reassuringly. 'Don't worry, we'll have him out, no trouble.'

Walt brought more beer, and we were becoming braver with every swallow. 'Have you heard anything about Jimmy?' he asked.

'Nothing,' I said. 'It's a mystery all right.'

'Rumours are that he topped himself,' Walt said.

'Aye well, he was a bit down in the dumps,' I said. It surprised me how quickly I'd turned into a lying bastard.

'Was he really?' Walt said. 'Didn't see it myself, but you know him better than I do.'

With Walt gone, we returned to the question of Bert.

'Tuesday morning it is then,' Dogmeat said. 'Bring a hammer, Johnboy.'

'What for?' I asked.

'You don't think they're going to leave the fuckin' door open for us, do you?'

'I suppose not,' I said. 'I haven't really thought about it.'

'It needs planning,' said Dogmeat. 'We can't just blunder in there. We need a strategy.'

'We are the SAS,' Mo said.

'Fuck up, Mo, will ya?' said Dogmeat. 'Obviously, I'm not going to get over that wall in the wheelchair, so I'll be waiting in the car.'

'You can ring us if you see someone,' Mo said.

'No phones,' Dogmeat said. 'Phones are electronic tags.'

'I think they're going to know who did it,' I said.

'No phones. If we're going to do it, we're going to do it right. You two will break in and I'll wait in the car, understood?'

'Understood,' I said.

'Right, that's Tuesday sorted, today is Saturday. Let's drink beer,' Dogmeat said.

We returned to the Warburton's on Tuesday morning as agreed. Dogmeat stayed in his car out of sight, whilst Mo and I walked up to the electric gates. The black BMW wasn't there, but there was no mistaking Sally's car, with its redesigned bodywork.

'Do you think she's in?' Mo asked.

'I'm not sure, Mo. Maybe Warburton took her in his car, you wouldn't want to be seen in that motor would you? It's really lowering the tone,' I said, pointing at Sally's car.

'What if she's there, bro?' Mo asked.

'Then I won't have brought this hammer for nothing will I?'

'You can't...'

'Chill, Mo,' I said. 'I'm only kidding.'

An elderly lady approached us with what looked like a brush head on a lead. Its hair was all over its face and eyes, so fuck knows how it saw where it was going.

'Morning,' I said, casually. 'What a lovely dog.' I bent down to pat the hairy canine, but the brush head nearly took my fuckin' finger off.

'He doesn't like strangers,' she said as she walked on. Not a word of apology nor nothing, the ignorant old scrote.

'This wall's a bit tall, Mo,' I said, looking at it. It was a couple of metres high, same as the gates, but the gates had dangerous looking spikes and I didn't fancy one of those up my jacksie.

'Are we going for it then?' Mo asked.

'That's what we're here for.'

The wall had a ledge halfway up and Mo was up and over in no time at all, but he was much younger than me. I threw the hammer over the wall before I attempted the climb.

'Ow,' Mo yelped.

'Sorry, Mo,' I said.

I climbed the best I could, and with much grunting and towing I rolled over the top and dropped on the other side.

'Why didn't you mention the rose bush?' I asked Mo.

'I didn't think it was important,' Mo said.

'Look at my fuckin' arms,' I said, showing him the multiple scratches. 'My DNA is all over that bush now.'

We made our way over the manicured lawn. Warburton must have employed a gardener judging by the condition of the grounds. He was going to be right pissed off when he saw the flattened roses. I couldn't see any cameras on the house, but it didn't matter anyway, you wouldn't need Columbo to know who'd been here. The back of the house wasn't overlooked by any other properties, so we could work unseen. My heart leapt when I looked through the patio door and saw Bert asleep on the settee. Like an idiot, I waved at him, as if my gesture was going to stir him.

'Bert,' I called. 'Bert, wake up boy.' He hadn't moved, so I knocked on the glass. His ears popped up, then his head and he started barking. He jumped off the settee and opened his lungs.

'Fuckin' hell, Bert,' I said. 'Calm down, you're not helping.'

'Do it,' Mo said. 'Break the glass.'

'I don't like it,' I said.

'Just do it, then we can go.'

I hit the glass with the hammer, but it just bounced off. I hit it again, harder. 'Fuck me,' I said. 'This is tough glass.' We went to the side of the house where we'd seen a half-glazed door that led into a utility room. I gave the glass a whack and it shattered easily. Putting my head through the opening, I could see that the key was on the inside of the door. I turned it and pushed open the door. I was unnerved when the alarm went off. Of course, Warburton would have security, why hadn't I thought of that? At least we knew that no one was home. I moved quickly through the house and Bert greeted me with a wagging tail. I'm sure he had a smile on his face.

'Come on, son,' I said. 'We're going home.' Bert followed me as I retraced my steps. I'd be pulling broken glass from his pads for weeks. We ran across the lawn and Mo crouched in front of the wall to create a step up for me. I managed to haul myself up and used the ledge to slowly lower myself down on the other side.

'Pass Bert over,' I said, but Mo didn't reply. 'MO, lift Bert over the wall.' Nothing. 'MO,' I called. 'Mo, are you there?

'I'm here,' he said, walking through the open gates with Bert.

'What the fuck?' I said.

'I pressed a button on the wall by the gate and they opened.'

'I wish I'd have known,' I said. 'I nearly had a fuckin' heart

attack climbing over that wall.'

'Sorry, bro,' said Mo.

'Ah, don't worry about it. Let's go.'

'Get in.' Dogmeat had seen what was happening and was quickly alongside us. We piled in and Dogmeat gunned the engine. The tyres screeched as we moved off. 'Well done, lads, good job,' he said.

In the following days I'd expected Warburton to come after me, but surprisingly we heard nothing and after a while I forgot about him and Sally. It was most likely spite that drove her to take Bert. I suspect they realised he was severely cramping their style. If Warburton had wanted recompense for the damage to his door, I would have paid it, but the cost of a double-glazed replacement wouldn't break the bank and I believed he was happy to let things lie. Bert for Sally, I know who got the best deal there, and he could fuck off when he gave her the elbow, she wasn't coming back here.

After a spread in the local newspaper and a poster campaign, the public eventually forgot about Jimmy Onion. His face had been on every other lamppost, and I was pleased when the posters were taken down or the wind had reduced them to tatters. I was personally responsible for tearing down many of them. The police hadn't bothered us again and it was time to do something with the money.

'I've seen a catering trailer that could be just what we need,' Dogmeat said.

'Oh aye,' I said. 'How much is it?'

'Thirty-five grand.'

'Thirty-five thousand.' I almost choked on a cheese and

onion crisp. 'Did you say thirty-five thousand?' I took a chug on my beer to clear the rogue crisp.

'It's a beauty,' Dogmeat enthused. 'Got the lot, fryer, griddle, potato oven... and one of those bain marie jobbies.'

'We're going to have to sell a lot of burgers to get that back,' I said.

'It's a business, Johnboy. That's how you have to look at it, we're buying a business.'

'It's a bit pricey intit, bro?' said Mo.

'It's almost new Mo, none of your second-hand shite, said Dogmeat. 'It's used, sure enough, but not that much.'

'If it's used, it's second hand,' I said. 'Fuckin' hell, I could nearly buy a house for that.'

'As new,' Dogmeat said. 'Showroom condition.'

'I didn't know they had showrooms for burger vans,' Mo said.

'Not a real showroom, you fuckin' retard, a...' Dogmeat couldn't be arsed to explain. 'If we're going to do it, we're going to do it right or not at all, and we'll still have plenty of change. C'mon, lads, get with the programme, it's a fuckin' goldmine and they'll take cash.'

'Where is it?' I asked.

'Dunstable,' said Dogmeat.

'Where the fuck's that?' I asked.

'Near Luton.'

'Fuckin' Luton,' I said. 'That's down south. How we going to get the fucker back, cos I'm expecting it to be about two hundred yards long for that wedge?'

'We'll have it delivered,' said Dogmeat.

'We'll need to see it first,' I said.

'Of course we will, we're going down next Sunday to have

a look.'

'I've got something on next Sunday,' Mo said.

'I know you have, Mo, you're going to Dunstable,' Dogmeat said.

So we set off for Luton in Dogmeat's car, Mo in the front and me in the back with Bert. It was lashing it down and the spray kicking up from the M1 made it hard to see the road ahead. Every now and again a gust of wind caught the people carrier and shunted us sideways.

'It's fuckin' wild out there,' Dogmeat said.

'Yeah,' I said. 'Lovely day for an outing. We must be off our trollies.'

'One day you'll thank me for this,' said Dogmeat as he wrestled with the steering wheel.

'I'm not feeling it, Dogmeat,' I said.

'You will when you see it,' said Dogmeat.

The weather brightened as we headed further south and stopped off at Leicester Forest services for a coffee and a carpet burger. It was Dogmeat who insisted we have a burger "to sound out the competition". I thought we were getting a little ahead of ourselves, but I went along with it to keep him quiet. I wanted to get fish and chips, but in fairness, the burger was mint and the chips were good too, not those fat greasy things you sometimes get, no these were French fries, lovely.

'It's the gherkins that are doing it for me,' I said.

'Is that what they are, those green jobbies?' Dogmeat said, through a mouthful of burger bun.

'I think so,' I said. 'Are we putting gherkins on our burgers?' I asked.

'I hadn't thought about it,' Dogmeat said. 'It could give us the edge though. Make a note of that, Mo, gherkins.'

'I haven't got a pen, bro,' Mo said.

'You should always carry a pen and paper.'

'Have you got one?' Mo asked Dogmeat.

'No.'

'Why do you think I've got one then?'

'Make a fuckin' mental note then,' Dogmeat said. This was the day Mo became Dogmeat's PA.

'She's a looker,' I said, nudging Dogmeat when a lass sat down at a nearby table.

'Oh aye, not bad at all,' said Dogmeat. 'Eight point five.'

'Nine,' I said.

'Eight,' Mo said.

'You take some pleasing don't you, Mo?' Dogmeat said.

'I'm going to have a drain off before we hit the road again,' I said.

'I'll come with you, bro,' Mo said.

'You're like two women,' said Dogmeat. 'Going to the toilet together. Don't forget your fuckin' handbags.'

We chatted as we washed our hands until someone hit the hand dryer button and drowned out our words. As we left the gents the furore was reverberating around the main hall. Dogmeat was beating the shit out of a vending machine. A security man was trying in vain to stop him.

'What's up now, Dogmeat?' I gasped as I drew nearer.

'I've put my money in, but the fuckin' Mars Bar is still in there looking at me,' he said. 'Fuckin' useless.' *Bang!* 'Fuckin.' *Bang!* 'Thing.'

'C'mon,' I said. 'Let's get on our way.'

'It's only a bar of chocolate,' said the security man.

'Fuck you,' Dogmeat said, as I ushered him away. 'Fuck you all.' He couldn't resist a final volley before he left the building.

I'd lived in smaller places than the trailer we were looking at, and I couldn't help thinking that it was a little over the top for The Railway car park, but it was, as Dogmeat had intimated, "a beauty".

'Build it, and they will come,' Dogmeat had kept saying, and looking at it, I was beginning to believe him. The outside was plain white, ready for our own livery, but internally, the stainless steel gleamed and reflected the ample lighting. In the far corner stood a baked potato oven. Who doesn't like a baked potato, with chilli or baked beans eh? Next to that was a gas hob set into the countertop, then two, yes two, chip fryers. We could turn out no end of fish and chips from those, or fry different things like hash browns or Mars Bars. An extraction canopy was mounted on the wall above the appliances, to keep us from passing out or dying from the products of combustion. Along the same wall was the glass fronted fridge for fizzy drinks and other shit like that, and the all-important tea urn. On the other side, by the hatch which ran the length of the trailer, was the large griddle, so you could fry the burgers in front of the customers, and also, as the seller pointed out, a bain marie so we could keep the frankfurters warm. There was even a freezer and a microwave. The sink was at the very end. I hadn't thought until now, about water and electricity, but were going to need them. We'd have to have a word with Walt about running a lead. Fuck me, Burger Bob would have no chance when we got this baby back home. I was sold. Mo loved it too, and Dogmeat nearly came in his pants. We managed to negotiate the price down a couple of thousand, so we shook hands and left a cash deposit, naturally, we only had cash. Balance to be paid on delivery.

'Let's get something to eat,' I said, 'before we set off back. I'm fuckin' starving.'

'I could use something,' Mo said.

Dogmeat drove us into the centre of Dunstable, where we found a Wetherspoons named "The Gary Cooper". Apparently,

100

he went to school here or something. I wasn't interested enough to investigate properly, I was only concerned with my lunch.

'Every day a school day, eh?' I said.

'Do not forsake me, oh my darling,' Dogmeat said.

'I won't love.' I laughed, hugging Dogmeat.

'Get off me, you fuckin' berk.'

'What are you two on about?' Mo was baffled by our behaviour.'

'That was the song from High Noon,' I explained. 'Gary Cooper was the sheriff, I think.' We were in high spirits.

All three of us had steak and chips with a pint, plenty of salt on the chips for me, got to keep up that blood pressure after all. Mo smothered his in so much red sauce you could hardly see the fuckin' chips.

'You could be eating cardboard there, Mo,' I said, 'with all that sauce on.'

'I like a bit of ketchup on my chips, bro.'

'I can see that,' I said.

'That was bang on,' Dogmeat said, after we'd cleaned the plates. 'Another pint now.'

'Don't forget you're driving, bro,' Mo said.

'Shut the fuck up, will ya? Another one won't hurt.'

'I'm having one if you are,' I said.

'Atta boy.' Dogmeat punched my upper arm, harder than necessary, but I didn't mind.

'I'm not going to be left out,' Mo said, rising to go to the bar.

'That's it, Mo lad,' Dogmeat said. 'Get 'em in.'

So we had another pint, and another, and another, followed by another, until we lost count. Then, because we were feeling bloated with all the ale, we turned to our old friend, Jack Daniel. The hours flew, and by the time we left the pub the sun was dropping. If the giggling didn't give it away, the staggering did. There was no doubt about it, we were pissed, and everyone knew it but us. We thought we were just three blokes walking along the pavement, but we were leathered.

'I'm fucked if I can remember where we left the car,' Dogmeat said.

'It's down here, a couple of streets away,' said Mo.

'How can you remember that?' I asked. 'I wouldn't have a clue.'

'I made a mental note,' Mo said, and we howled. Sure enough, the people carrier was where Mo said it would be.

'Oh, fuck me,' I said. 'I'd forgotten about Bert. Sorry Bert, sorry boy, I forgotten about you, son.' Bert jumped out of the car and made a beeline for the nearest lamp post. He hadn't eaten so I popped into a nearby convenience store. I didn't have a tin opener, so I bought a family size steak and kidney pie. He didn't seem to mind.

With Bert seen to, we set off, in completely the opposite direction than we should have, but none of us realised our mistake until something clicked in Dogmeat's mind.

'Where's that fuckin' motorway?' he asked. 'I'm sure it wasn't this far.'

'No idea,' I said.

It was dark now and we were hurtling down the road, somewhere in the Bedfordshire countryside. I didn't see the sharp bend coming up, and more to the point, neither did Dogmeat. The road went to the right and we went straight on, through some bushes and into a field. We slept there until the early hours of the morning.

Chapter 9

'Can you cook?' It was one thing buying the trailer, but someone had to prepare the food that came from it. I was looking at Mo, hoping that his mum had coached him in the kitchen.

'I can't even boil an egg,' Mo said.

'Just as well we're not going to sell boiled eggs then, intit?' said Dogmeat. 'All you have to do is slap a burger on a hotplate, it's not rocket science.'

'What about the fryer?' said Mo. 'That's more than flipping a burger.'

'All you're doing is chucking a few chips in there.' Dogmeat palmed a few salted peanuts into his mouth. 'I'm not even asking you to peel the fuckin' spuds. They come ready made, peeled and chipped. A fuckin' five-year-old could do it. Look, when the trailer arrives, we'll have a few practice runs, see how we get on. Didn't you ever bang the chip pan on when you got home from the pub?'

'I did,' I said. 'When I was nineteen, I set the house on fire. I put the chip pan on the gas and fell asleep. We had polystyrene tiles on the ceiling in those days and they caught light. Fuckin' 'ell, man, it was raining fire. My dad would've killed me if I hadn't been so sprightly on my feet. I didn't go home for two weeks.'

'Let's not dwell on that,' said Dogmeat. 'You have a bit of history with fires, don't ya? I hope you're not going to reduce the trailer to ashes.'

'When's it landing Dogmeat?' Despite my reservations and my culinary history, I was quite excited about the future. A fresh start was exactly what I needed.

'As soon as they stick a few pictures of burgers and sausages on the side, it'll be with us.'

'I can't wait bro,' Mo said. Even though he knew jack shit about preparing food, he couldn't conceal his excitement. We were going to have to learn on the hoof and hope we didn't poison anyone in the process.

'Have you decided what's on the menu?' I asked Dogmeat.

'Kind of,' Dogmeat said. 'Burgers of course, cheeseburgers, bacon butties, sausage butties, chips…'

'What kind of sausage are we using?' I asked. 'Bratwurst or those saveloy jobbies that you can still taste a month later?'

'Definitely Bratwurst,' Dogmeat enthused. 'I hadn't thought about saveloy. Make a note, Mo.' Now prepared, Mo pulled pen and paper from his pocket and began jotting.

'French fries,' Dogmeat continued. 'Mars bars, I like a Mars bar.'

'A few different kinds of chocolate eh?' I said.

'Yeah, Kit Kat. Write that down, Mo.'

'Kinder Surprise?' suggested Mo.

'What the fuck, Mo? It's not a fuckin' nursery.'

'Just an idea,' Mo said sheepishly.

'Aye, a fuckin' bad one,' said Dogmeat.

'Crisps,' I added. 'Plain, cheese and onion, salt and vinegar.'

'I hate cheese and onion,' Dogmeat protested. 'They stink of sweaty socks.'

'You might dislike them, but lots of people love them,' I said.

'I suppose you're right. Make a note, Mo.'

'Pies.' It was as if I'd had an epiphany.

'Fuckin' pies, yeah.' Evidently, Dogmeat had forgotten about our crusty friends. 'We'll need one of those pie warmers so we can put them on display,' he added.

'I thought that bain marie kept things warm,' Mo said.

'You can't put pies in a bain marie, soft lad.' Dogmeat had suddenly become an authority on bain maries, which considering he hadn't heard of one a few short weeks ago, wasn't bad going. 'Steak and kidney, minced beef.'

'Don't forget meat and taty,' I said.

'Good thinking, log it, Mo.'

'Chicken Balti,' I said.

'Fuckin' curry pies?' Dogmeat said, astonished. 'Are you mad?'

'They're very popular,' I responded. 'The young un's love 'em.'

'He's right, bro,' Mo said. 'I'm quite partial to a Chicken Balti missen.'

'Ah well,' said Dogmeat softening his tone. 'If you say so, we'll get some, but I can't see anyone buying them.'

'Three more pints please, Walt,' I said, as I caught his attention, 'and a bag of cheese and onion crisps.' Just to wind up Dogmeat.

'We have to set prices,' said Dogmeat, ignoring my little joke.

'Not too expensive, not too cheap,' I said. 'We have to pitch it just right. Don't forget, Bob will be at the other end of the car park.'

'He'll not be there for long when people get a taste for our snap.'

'What about adverts?' I asked.

'Oh yeah, of course. We need to let people know we're here.

105

We should get some leaflets printed up and you and Mo can have a day out shoving them through letter boxes locally.' Mo was writing before Dogmeat could tell him.

'Leaflets,' Mo muttered as he worked his pen.

We didn't have to wait long before the big day arrived. Dogmeat, Mo, Walt, Bert and I waited in the car park for the low loader. The building work had almost dried up and my future was about to arrive. Dogmeat had arranged the livery and despite my protests, wouldn't allow Mo and I to have any say on what went on the side of the trailer, but a burger is a burger, so what could go wrong. He had autonomously assumed control of every aspect, despite the fact that we'd had all three of us contribute equally. We could make suggestions, but he would have the final say on prices, food, advertising, and every other aspect of the new business. It's not that I disagreed with his decisions, but it would have been nice to be consulted. Mo would bend any way the wind blew.

'He's five minutes away,' Dogmeat said, flipping his phone closed and dragging on his Woodbine.

'She almost here,' I said, wrapping an arm around Mo's shoulder, who shot me a huge grin. We were like kids waiting for Santa to arrive.

'Shouldn't we have champagne or something fizzy to celebrate the occasion?' Mo said.

'I'll nip in and get something.' Even Walt was feeling the excitement.

And then it swung around the corner and slowly entered the car park. Walt came running across to us with a bottle of prosecco and four glasses, popped the cork and coaxed the oozing liquid into the flutes. Bob was hanging out of his hatch watching the behemoth approach. Then I saw the livery Dogmeat had designed. "Dogmeat Burgers" was the message he'd chosen to promote our business, in large, large letters.

'Fuck me, Dogmeat,' I said. 'You can't put that on the side.'

'What does that say?' Dogmeat pointed at Bob's trailer.

'Bobby Burgers,' I said.

'Well, this is Dogmeat Burgers. Bob runs that trailer and I run this one.'

'I know, but who wants to eat a fuckin' dogmeat burger?'

'Just wait and see,' Dogmeat said.

The driver and his mate eased our new baby off the lorry and placed it in position under the instruction of Dogmeat and Walt, close enough to the pub to easily run an electrical lead. As soon as it was settled, Bert jogged over, cocked a leg and christened the wheel. We all clapped and cheered, making Bert scurry back to my side. I patted him on the head.

'Well done, son,' I said.

'She's been launched,' Mo said.

'It's the beginning of a new era.' I couldn't be sure, but it looked to me like Dogmeat had a tear in his eye.

'What's this?' Bob had appeared at our side.

'Here we go,' I thought. I knew this was going to happen. Bob wasn't going to take it lightly.

'What's it look like?' Dogmeat answered.

'It's not fair.' Bob was looking directly at Walt.

'It's not raining though, is it?' Walt said.

'I thought we had a deal,' Bob pressed on.

'I never said you had exclusive rights.'

'I know, Walt, but this isn't right.'

'Have you noticed how the car showrooms are all in one place these days?' Walt said. 'It doesn't mean that they sell less cars does it? This will probably boost your business… and mine as well. It'll be good for all of us.'

'It's not the same as cars,' Bob pleaded. 'Once you've had a burger, you're not going to buy another one, are you?'

'You're not gonna buy two cars either,' I said.

'Anyway, it is what it is,' said Walt. 'It's here now. I can hardly send it back can I?'

'I'm not having it,' Bob said.

'What you gonna do about it?' Dogmeat asked.

'I don't know yet, but I'm not taking this lying down.' Bob said as he stomped off.

'He's not happy,' said Mo.

'Fuck him,' Dogmeat said.

Over the next few days, we familiarised ourselves with the equipment and stocked the trailer with canned drinks, chocolate and other items that wouldn't perish. The burgers and sausage were kept in a chest freezer we'd installed in Dogmeat's garage. Bob was furious when he saw us unwind the lead. He had to use a generator whilst we had the use of Walt's electricity. He would surely be feeling aggrieved, but business is business, and Dogmeat had negotiated a profit-sharing scheme with Walt, although I didn't expect Dogmeat to declare everything we sold, both to Walt and the taxman. He was even more angry when Dogmeat sent Mo over to copy Bob's price list, which he did, word for word, until some bright spark suggested he take a photo with his phone. We'd become so accustomed to not having our phones at the pub, that we sometimes forgot about them after Dogmeat had ruled that we could bring our phones now Jimmy Onion had gone. Bob's price list was chalk on a blackboard, ours was a back lit affair, like a fuckin' electronic scoreboard. It was mint, once we came to terms with setting it up. We had a trial run, Dogmeat acting as the customer.

'What can I get you, sir?' I asked, awkwardly.

'I'll have a burger with onions and salad and one of those pickled gherkin jobbies. Just pretend with the salad, onions and gherkin for the time being,' he said.

'Coming up,' I said, dropping a burger on the griddle.

'And a cup of tea,' Dogmeat added. Mo dropped a tea bag in a cardboard cup and filled it from the urn.

'And a bag of chips.' I dropped a portion of french fries into the fryer from too great a height.

'Fuck,' I yelled as the fat burnt my arm. That was lesson one.

'Now, now,' Dogmeat said. 'The punters aren't going to like that.'

'Sorry, Dogmeat,' I said.

'Milk in your tea, bro? Mo asked.

'No, black,' Dogmeat said. Mo handed over the tea.

'Sugar is on the end sir,' he said.

'I know it is, I fuckin' put it there.'

The burger was done, so I gave it to Dogmeat in a paper serviette and awaited the verdict.

'Not bad at all,' he said. 'Be even better when we get the onions.' He finished it in a few mouthfuls and screwed up the paper serviette and looked around for somewhere to put it.

'What we need, is a bin,' I said.

'We do,' Dogmeat agreed. 'Make a note, Mo.'

I was both excited and apprehensive when the grand opening came around. Thursday was market day and a good few shoppers dropped into the Railway for a drink on their way home, so we made that our target. Dogmeat brought the food in his people carrier, then went off into town to hand out fifty percent off vouchers. We didn't expect to make much money, but it was a way of making our presence felt. If they didn't know we were here, they would have already eaten in town. Of course, there were some folks who would never entertain the idea of eating out of a trailer, but plenty others would. Whilst Dogmeat was in town, Mo and I busied ourselves by setting up the equipment, plugging in the electrics and stocking the fridge. At the far end of the car park, Bob was doing the same. The only difference was that Bob had to fire up the generator. I waved to him, but the only response I got was a solitary finger. We connected the gas bottles, filled the urn, ignited the appliances and waited. The sauces were ready, the bin was in place and the water was up to temperature in the urn. I fried a sausage, let it cool and gave it to Bert, who was loitering near the door. Dogmeat had insisted we wear the new company aprons complete with the proud logo "Dogmeat Burgers". I had a coffee while we waited.

'It's not bad coffee this, Mo,' I offered.

'We just need someone to buy it,' Mo answered.

Dogmeat had returned and he wasn't best pleased when a van pulled up and three young men got out and stood in front of Bob's. Then more came, ordered their food, and retreated to their vehicles.

'They're all going to Bob,' Mo whined.

'Don't forget,' said Dogmeat, 'he's been going a good few year now. He'll have his regulars. It's up to us to win over those customers.'

'How are we going to do that?' I asked.

'It's only a matter of time. Notice how everyone over there goes back to their van to eat. We are going to get a few tables and chairs. Make a note, Mo.'

A car pulled into the car park and aimed towards Bob's, but he must have seen us at the last minute, because he veered away and made for us. A youngish couple emerged and came to the hatch.

'You new?' the boy asked.

'First day,' I said.

'We usually go to Bob, but I'll give you a whirl.'

'You'll not regret it,' Dogmeat said.

'I'll have a sausage and tomato sandwich,' he said.

'And a bacon and tomato for me,' said the girl. 'And two coffees, one decaff.'

'Oh, sorry,' Mo said. 'We don't have decaff.'

'Make a note, Mo,' Dogmeat called.

'Gimme a Diet Coke then please,' said the girl.

I was shaking as I placed the sausage and bacon on the griddle, but all went well. The rolls were already cut and we decided previously that three pieces of bacon would be about right for a decent sandwich. I spread a portion of hot, tinned tomatoes onto the bread from the bain marie, laid the bacon on top and we were in business.

'Bacon and tomato, sausage and tomato, one tea and a can,' I said. 'That's seven pounds please.'

He gave me a tenner and I handed back three one-pound coins. They ate the food standing under the hatch. Another man had joined us. He studied the menu then said, 'Cheeseburger please.'

'It's on its way,' I said. We were rolling now.

'Three pounds please,' I said.

'I have a voucher.' He passed the voucher through the hatch.

'That makes it one-fifty then.'

'Wait a minute,' said the girl. 'We've paid full price for ours.'

'You didn't have a voucher,' I said.

'You robbing bastards,' said the boy.

'Wait a minute,' Dogmeat intervened. 'Give them back three-fifty and make it half price for everyone today.'

So that's what we did. On top of that, Dogmeat positioned himself near Bob's and told everyone that our food was half price. We only intended to offer half price for the first couple of days. Nevertheless, Bob's fury knew no bounds and the burger wars had begun.

The next session we tried was Friday evening at full price. The lads coming out of the pub would eat anything when they'd got a couple of pints inside them. It was okay until one of them noticed that Bob had reduced his burgers to two pounds twenty-five. He went back into the pub and told all his mates, so Bob won that round. The next time we opened up, our burgers were two quid and they flocked to us. Then Bob reduced his to one-fifty and we couldn't go any lower. It was fuckin' madness.

As things moved on, we still honoured our Saturday get together, even though we could be making money in the trailer. We were of the opinion that we worked to live rather than vice versa. Bob was hard at it though, selling his Saturday burgers at two-fifty.

'What we going to do?' I asked. We were at our regular table. 'We can't continue like this, we'll never make anything.'

'I think we're going to have to talk to him,' said Dogmeat. 'Now he's had his little tantrum, he might be ready to agree prices.'

'What if he doesn't?' I asked.

'We could always let his tyres down,' Mo suggested.

'What good would that do?' Dogmeat said. 'That fuckin' trailer hasn't moved for years.'

112

'His sausages would roll off the hotplate if we just punctured one tyre,' I said.

'You two should work for NASA,' Dogmeat said, shaking his head.

'If we talk to him and agree terms, things will be fine,' I said. 'Now get the beer in, Mo.'

'I'll have a word with him,' Dogmeat said.

'Do you think that's wise?' I asked.

'I thought we just agreed to talk to him.'

'Yes, but I think it would be better if I approached him,' I suggested.

'Fuck off, will you?' Dogmeat's response wasn't unexpected and there was no way I could dissuade him.

'Mo could do it,' I offered.

'I don't mind, bro,' Mo said.

'I'll do it.' Dogmeat was adamant, so we didn't object any further. 'He's out there now, and there's no time like the present.'

We leant on the railings by the ramp and watched Dogmeat wheel across the car park.

'I think we all know where this is heading,' said Mo. We couldn't hear the dialogue clearly, but judging by Bob's flailing arms, we knew it wasn't going well. He almost threw himself out of the hatch with his windmilling. Dogmeat was looking up at him jabbing his finger, then Bob threw a bap at Dogmeat. Luckily it wasn't stale and didn't do any harm. Dogmeat moved around to the rear door, but Bob slammed it shut before he got there.

Back in the pub, Dogmeat wasn't happy.

'That went well then?' I observed.

'I'll kill the bastard,' Dogmeat said.

'We could move to another place,' Mo said.

'We're not moving,' Dogmeat fumed. 'He's going. Mark my

words, he's going.'

'I don't see how we're going to make him move,' I said. 'He's not going to move voluntarily, and he's been here a lot longer than us after all.'

'Leave it to me,' said Dogmeat.

We settled back into our beer and attempted to pull Dogmeat from the depths.

'How's the baby?' I asked Mo.

'Aw, she's lovely,' he said. 'I'm not getting much sleep, but I don't mind.'

'I'll kill the bastard.' Dogmeat's mind was still on Bob.

'C'mon, Dogmeat,' I said. 'Let it go.'

'I'll kill the bastard.' Dogmeat's record was stuck, so Mo and I left him to it and chatted between ourselves.

Thankfully, Bob had shut up shop and gone home when we left the Railway, because Dogmeat was ready to recommence the feud and we had to pass quite close to his trailer on our way out of the car park. Dogmeat didn't have the capacity to contain himself at the best of times, but now he had a few more pints inside him it would have been ugly. Maybe Bob had realised this and made an early exit on this occasion. In Dogmeat's world, discretion was not the better part of valour, but headlocks were definitely up there. I wondered how we were going to overcome this situation in a reasonable manner. In Dogmeat's head, Bob was the enemy, and enemies needed to be eradicated. I vowed to keep a close eye on him in case he did something he would regret.

When I arrived home that afternoon, a shock was in store. My back door was busted in and swinging loose, so I entered the house with some trepidation. Bert went ahead of me, and I wished he was a Pit Bull right now. I wandered through the rooms, and everything looked in place. Apart from the door,

114

nothing was damaged. My wallet and credit cards were where I'd left them in a drawer, and my huge whisky bottle half full of two-pound coins hadn't been touched. Nothing was missing, but I had an inkling why they'd been here. Before I called Dogmeat, I checked in the garden shed to make sure the bag was still there. It was, and it still contained a substantial amount of money. I consulted Dogmeat and we agreed to keep the police out of it.

Chapter 10

We were back in the trailer on Sunday. Bob didn't work Sundays, so our food was back to full price, but it wasn't the cost of burgers that was at the forefront of our minds.

'How can you be so sure they were looking for the bag?' Dogmeat asked, sitting in his car with the window down.

'They didn't take anything,' I said.

'So?' said Dogmeat.

'So, they were looking for something in particular.'

'Might not have been the bag.'

'Of course it was,' I said. 'What else could it be?'

'Do we know who it was?' Mo piped up from the griddle.

'That's the worst thing,' I said. 'I've no idea.'

'Do you think they'll be back?' Mo asked.

'If they were looking for the bag, then almost certainly,' I said. 'I've had to batten up my back door, they've trashed it.'

'And the bag?' Dogmeat asked. 'Are you one hundred percent sure it's safe in the shed?'

'It's well hidden, you can't even see the shed, never mind the bag, so I'm as sure as I can be.'

We were interrupted when an aging lady passed between us to study the menu. 'Do you have soup?' she asked.

'Sorry love,' I said softly. 'No soup.' We'd never thought about soup. 'Make a note of that, Mo.'

'I tell Mo to make notes,' Dogmeat said.

'I just thought it would be a good idea to have soup on the

menu.'

'It could be,' said Dogmeat. 'Make a note, Mo.'

'What's that you say?' The old dear cupped her hand to her ear.

'No soup,' I shouted.

'That's a shame,' she said. 'I can't chew very well you know.'

'I can do you a bacon and tomato sandwich without the bacon.'

'Oh, I don't know.' I could see she was considering the offer.

'Give her a freebie, Johnboy,' said Dogmeat. 'We should look after the old 'uns. No burger though, just tomatoes.'

'What's that you say?' asked the old biddy.

'I said, do you want a sandwich? These bread rolls melt in your mouth, you'll have no trouble at all.' I made the shape of a bap with my hands. If anyone was watching, they would think that I was hearting her.

'How much? I'm a pensioner you know.' As if there was any doubt.

'Never,' I said. 'Do you have ID?'

'What's that you say?'

'I said, you can have one free.'

'Thank you very much, young man,' she said, finally satisfied. I turned my back to retrieve a bap.

'As long as you fuck off as soon as you get it,' I said quietly, so she couldn't hear. Mo laughed. We didn't want to upset her. She took her free bacon and tomato sandwich without bacon and sucked away happily across the car park. She got about ten yards away and turned.

'You can fuck off too,' she cawed, causing Dogmeat to burst out laughing.

'I'm gonna get off now,' Dogmeat said, starting the engine. 'See you after... play nice.'

'Abyssinia,' I called.

'Dubai,' said Dogmeat as he pulled away.

The first wave was beginning to drift out of The Railway now and business was speeding up. Chips and burgers, chips and gravy or a steak pie were always the favourites after a few beers, and I got busy on the fryer while Mo flipped some burgers. The job was becoming a little easier now that we were getting used to the equipment and routine. Mo and I were a good team when we were in the building business, and we were still a good team on the catering front. Good chemistry transfers to any industry. Things were slowly clicking into place, and I was beginning to enjoy it. If we could only sort out the pricing problems, we would be okay.

'Cheeseburger,' said a young buck. 'And don't spare the onions.'

'Bag o' chips,' said another one. 'Plenty of salt and vinegar.'

'One at a time lads,' I said as I scooped chips into a polystyrene container. 'Salt and vinegar are on the end,' I said, handing the chips over to the lad.

'I want you to put it on for me.'

'Put your own fuckin' salt and vinegar on,' I said. Most of the punters were all right, but one or two were arseholes when they'd been drinking.

'It's not the same,' he complained.

'How can it not be the same. It's the same fuckin' salt and it's the same fuckin' vinegar, believe me.'

'Go on,' he smiled. 'Put it on for me.'

'Pass the salt and vinegar up here then.' He held up his chips and for a quiet life, I sprinkled on the salt, then washed it off with the vinegar.

'There you go,' I said, thinking it was a good thing that Dogmeat hadn't seen him, or he'd be eating that salt pot.

'Thanks, boss.' He staggered off to who knows where, his direction of travel a mystery, even to himself. First north-east, then north-west with a little south-west thrown in for good measure.

Cars were pulling up now and we were buzzing. It amazed me how many people would forego Roast beef and Yorkshire puddings in favour of a cheeseburger. It wasn't my idea of a Sunday dinner, but I wasn't complaining, each to their own, eh? The small stacking tables we had put out were proving useful for the punters and the wastepaper bin was filling, even though one or two of the dirty fuckers would insist on either leaving the rubbish on the table, or blatantly throwing it on the floor. It was a nightmare when there was anything more than a gentle breeze. One of us was constantly out in the car park clearing up the litter that had nestled against the low wall. The last thing we wanted to do was cross Walt, who had been pretty good to us up to now.

I was in two minds whether to ignore the ring of my mobile, but I saw that it was Dogmeat, so I wiped my hands on a cloth and answered.

'What you forgot?' I asked. 'Be quick cos we're swamped under here.'

'That's good,' he said. 'But I have to tell you something.'

'Fire away,' I said.

'They've done me as well.'

'Get to the point, Dogmeat, there's a queue round the car park.' It was a huge exaggeration, but it made the point.

'They've done me,' Dogmeat said. 'They've broken into my house as well.'

119

'Oh fuck,' was all I could muster.

'Nothing missing, but they've been in every room, the bastards.'

'Any damage?'

'Only the back window smashed. Fuckin' broken glass all over the kitchen. I wish I could have caught 'em.'

This was worrying. They knew, didn't they? They knew who we were, and they knew we had the money, but we didn't know who *they* were. Fuckin' disaster! We couldn't do anything but wait for their next move. Wait, to be shot, or knifed, or kidnapped, or tortured. It was torment just thinking about it. I worried about Mo and his wife and new daughter, but he assured me that there was always someone home, and he didn't envisage any problems as his parents and brothers lived close by and would keep an eye on things.

'What we going to do, Dogmeat?' I asked.

'What can we do?' he replied, philosophically.

'There's nothing more dangerous than an unseen enemy,' I said. 'They're a U-boat lurking beneath the waves.'

'They'll surface some time,' Dogmeat assured me. 'Then we'll have the bastards.'

'I hope you're right, Dogmeat.' I didn't think it was going to be quite as easy as that.

And a few days later, the culprit did surface. We were just setting up when a black BMW came to a halt in front of the trailer. I was just about to say that we weren't quite ready to open, but a familiar figure emerged from the car.

'I'm glad you're all here.' Warburton grunted. 'I need a word with you.'

'How can we help you?' I sneered.

'You can help me by returning my bag of money.'

'I haven't a fuckin' clue what you're talking about,' I lied, but things were becoming clearer.

'Don't come the innocent with me,' he growled. 'Me and Sally were talking about you the other day.'

'I didn't know you cared,' I said, flippantly.

'She told me the story about you getting into a lather when she dropped some things at the charity shop.'

'So?' I said.

'Fuck knows how you got hold of it, but I believe that bag belongs to me and my colleagues. And what did you do with Wayne?' It took me a moment to realise that Wayne was Bullneck, the guy who was lying at the bottom of the well with Jimmy Onion.

'Fuck off will ya,' Dogmeat railed.

'You've always had a temper, Dave,' said Warburton casually, 'but let's face it, in this instance you don't have a leg to stand on,' Warburton said. 'Well, you do, but they don't work do they?' He laughed at his own waggishness, but no one else found it funny. 'In reality,' he continued, 'this err… burger van is mine. I wondered how you'd raised the cash for it. It's a very impressive set up,' he said, looking it over. 'Sally reckons you haven't a pot to piss in, then bam! All of a sudden you have a top of the range catering facility. How does that figure, Johnboy?'

'We saved up, between us,' I said.

'You must think I'm as green as that cucumber,' said Warburton.

'It's a gherkin,' Mo corrected him.

'Whatever it is, I'm not fuckin' buying it?'

'We don't sell them separately,' Mo was inadvertently tying him up in knots.

'I don't want to buy it, you fuckin' halfwit.' Warburton was losing his cool.

'Was it you who bust my door in?' I asked.

'And my fuckin' kitchen window?' Dogmeat said.

'Only fair,' Warburton replied. 'You caused a lot of damage at my place.'

'We'll take you to the bag,' Dogmeat intervened.

'Wait a minute, Dogmeat,' I protested.

'No,' Dogmeat continued. 'Let's get it settled, but we keep the trailer.'

'It's not my decision alone, but I think that can be arranged. How much did you pay for this?' He scanned the trailer.

'Fifty grand,' Dogmeat said.

'Fuck off, fifty grand,' Warburton chuckled.

'Seriously,' I said. 'You have to admit, it's a beauty.'

'Be here on Saturday morning and we'll take you to the bag. As you know by now, we don't keep it at home. Park your car in town and walk here. We'll meet you behind the pub on the trail about eight o'clock, before it gets busy. No phones.'

'How about now?' Warburton suggested.

'Can't you see we're working?'

'Tomorrow morning then?'

'Can't do tomorrow, we're busy,' Dogmeat said.

'Are you fuckin' around with me? Cos you're pissing off the wrong guy.'

'Are you threatening me?' Dogmeat rolled up closer to Warburton.

'Too right I am, you fuckin' mong.' But Warburton was retreating. Even in his chair, Dogmeat was menacing.

'I've told you, Saturday morning,' Dogmeat growled. 'Take it or leave it.'

122

'Fair enough,' Warburton conceded. 'Don't let me down, or I'm going to be very angry.'

'Just fuck off,' Dogmeat said, and Warburton did.

'What you do that for?' I asked, after Warburton had left.

'Don't worry, Johnboy. Everything is in hand.'

'We're going to be penniless again, bro,' Mo complained.

'We'll be all right, Mo,' said Dogmeat. 'Have I let you down thus far?'

'Don't answer that, Mo,' I quickly chipped in.

'You concentrate on flipping burgers and leave the thinking to me,' said Dogmeat. He pushed away but spun back around to us. 'I've got a better idea. Let's shut up shop and go in for a pint.'

'We've got food in the bain marie,' Mo said.

'It'll keep,' Dogmeat said. 'Most of the punters wouldn't mind if it had been in there a week.'

'I'm up for it,' I said.

We turned off the fryer, and the griddle, but left the bain marie ticking over. Just as we were closing the hatch, a large man was crossing the car park towards us. When I say large, I mean he wasn't very tall. All his mass was on the lateral dimension.

'Get it shut quick before the salad dodger gets here,' Dogmeat said.

'Could be a good sale,' said Mo.

'Fuck him.' Dogmeat had beer on his mind.

'Can I get a foot long hot dog?' the man asked. He looked like he didn't really need it.

'We're closing for lunch mate,' I said. 'Come back in half an hour, forty-five minutes max.'

'A burger van closing for lunch? I've never heard the like of it.'

'It's a catering trailer,' piped up Dogmeat.

'Can't you quickly serve me before you go?'

'No.' Dogmeat was getting annoyed again. 'Get down the Co-op and get something healthy, like an apple or summat.'

'I don't like apples,' he said.

'I can see that,' Dogmeat said.

In The Railway, we were lucky that our table was still free. Walt hadn't been expecting us.

'What are you lads doing in here?' he asked.

'Lunch break,' I replied.

'How can you have a lunch break in a burger van?'

'It's a catering trailer,' said Dogmeat.

'It's a one-off, Walt,' I said. 'We just needed a break. Bring us three pints will you please?'

'Very unusual,' Walt said, as he wandered back to the bar.

'We'll take him to the well and drop him in,' Dogmeat said dispassionately.

'Another one?' I murmured. I had an idea that's what was in Dogmeat's head.

'What else can we do?' Dogmeat was rolling a match between his lips. It wouldn't be too long before he'd be outside, puffing on a cigarette.

'I don't suppose there is any other way,' I said. 'But I'm not comfortable with it.'

'It's your turn, Mo,' said Dogmeat.

'For what, bro?'

'It's your turn. You can dispatch Warburton.'

'Oh no,' fretted Mo, 'I couldn't do that.'

'Me and Johnboy have done one each,' said Dogmeat, 'it's time you chipped in. What you reckon, Johnboy?'

'I'm not sure Mo has it in him,' I said, truthfully.

'Fair's fair,' insisted Dogmeat.

Walt slid three beers onto the table and placed a bowl of water on the floor for Bert.

'Thanks, Walt,' we all said, except for Bert.

'I'm not making much commission at the moment, am I?' Walt complained.

'I don't know what you're griping about, Walt,' said Dogmeat, removing the match from his lips and replacing it with the rim of the pint pot. He took a drink and planted the glass on the dog-eared beermat. 'We're buying your ale aren't we?'

'Suppose so,' said Walt, 'but bear in mind that all the time you're in here, Bob will be reaping the rewards.'

'It's Sunday,' I said. 'He's not here.'

'Why don't you just fuck him off?' Dogmeat said 'He's sapping the profits.'

'I can't do that.'

'Why not?'

'Because it's not right. I'd rather him leave of his own accord.'

'He's not going to do that in a hurry is he?' I added.

'Well, don't make a habit of this,' he said as he left.

'He thinks he's our Gaffer,' said Dogmeat.

'Well, he is, kind of,' Mo said.

We returned to the matter in hand. There was no way I could envisage any scenario where Mo would kill someone, even the obnoxious Warburton. He was such a gentle soul, a true gentleman, but a follower, and I could be leading him into a great deal of trouble. God knows why, but he trusted me implicitly.

'Well Mo?' Dogmeat asked. 'Are you going to do your bit?'

'I'll try,' Mo said meekly.

'Oh, come on, Dogmeat,' I remonstrated.

'We're a partnership, aren't we? All for one and all that shit.' Dogmeat was unyielding and he wouldn't let me step in to save Mo, so it appeared that he was going to have to dig deep and find the courage from somewhere.

'Oh fuck,' I muttered.

'That didn't touch the sides,' said Dogmeat, wringing the last few drops from his glass. 'Get the beer in, Mo.' At this point, Dogmeat was wearing a huge grin. He was loving it. Mo was far too polite to ask Walt to bring the beer, so he went off to the bar.

'Sometimes, Dogmeat,' I said, in the absence of Mo, 'you can be a right bastard.'

'Only sometimes?' Dogmeat chuckled.

'He'll not do it, you know.'

'He has to do it.' Dogmeat had the matchstick back in his mouth, his glass being empty.

After a couple of minutes, Mo returned with the beer. 'Three pints of the finest, bro,' he said, placing one in front of me and handing one to Dogmeat. There's nothing looks finer than a freshly poured pint.

'We better make this the last one.' I raised the amber nectar to my lips. 'Ahh, that's fuckin' lovely man.'

'Should we divvy up the rest of the money after we've got rid of Warburton?' I asked.

'Keep it in your shed, Johnboy. It seems to be safe enough there for the time being,' Dogmeat said.

'It's a big responsibility, a worry, especially now people are sniffing around.'

'Not be much longer, Johnboy,' said Dogmeat. 'Anyway, I think we're going to spend some of it.'

'What on?' Mo asked.

'A big van. That way, we can provide more seating, and use

126

it for storage. It'll be easier for collecting things from the wholesalers as well.'

'We're not making enough money,' I said.

'We will do when Bob leaves the scene,' said Dogmeat.

'I don't think we really need one,' I said.

'Do you think it's fair that I carry on using my car then?'

'I suppose not, but how the fuck are you going to get in a big van.'

'I'll worry about that,' Dogmeat said.

I was ready to get back to the trailer after the second pint, but Dogmeat had other ideas. He reasoned that seeing as there were three of us, it made more sense to have three pints. I couldn't fault his logic, but I pointed out that two of us were driving. He answered with his stock reply.

'Ah, fuck it.'

So we had another pint, and we didn't stop there. I'd got the taste for it and Mo was just going along with it. Dogmeat was waxing lyrical about Sprinter vans, I was thinking about a holiday in the sunshine and Mo was simply chilling. Walt was disgusted with us, but kept the beer flowing nevertheless. The pub was filling up with the lunchtime crowd from the nearby call centre and Walt got busy serving tonic water and non-alcoholic beverages.

'Wankers… don't they have a day off?' Dogmeat said, just loud enough to be heard.

'Come on,' I said. 'Let's get back.' I didn't want Dogmeat to get involved with the office wallahs again.

As we approached the trailer, I could see steam rising from the roof vent. 'OH fuck,' I said. 'We left the bain marie on. Didn't you turn it down low, Mo?'

'I thought I had,' Mo replied.

We opened the back door and peered in. It was like a Swedish sauna, visibility down to zero.

'Somebody get in there and open the hatch.' Dogmeat retreated a few yards to avoid the steam. 'Go on, Mo,' he urged.

Mo disappeared into the mist. 'I can't see anything,' his dismembered voice called.

'You should be able to do it by touch, Mo,' Dogmeat said, unhelpfully.

I was pleased Bob was off duty. He'd have been leaning out of his hatch, laughing like a musketeer by now.

A few seconds later Mo had thrown open the hatch and turned off the bain marie. We let things cool down and inspected the damage. We'd been lucky, it was a lesson learnt. Fuckin' idiots we were, the three of us. We shut up shop and went home.

Chapter 11

Mo and I arrived extra early to prepare for market day, but to our surprise, we saw Dogmeat's people carrier already parked by the trailer. We also noticed a stationary police car at the other end of the car park, next to what used to be Bob's trailer. It wasn't a burger van any more, it was a heap of burnt appliances, plastic and ashes piled up to around three feet tall, the heavy rain rinsing through it. The smouldering scene was taped off with blue police tape. Bob was speaking to a police officer, waving his arms frantically, pointing the finger of suspicion in our direction. Dogmeat wasn't helping our cause by laughing heartily. A small crowd was gathering to take in the scene, film it on their phones and post it on social media. Fortunately, Bob had been afraid of the gas bottles being stolen and was in the habit of removing them after every shift, or we could have been witnessing the first burger van in orbit.

'Get set up quick,' Dogmeat said. 'Those nosy bastards might be hungry.'

The police officer strode purposefully in our direction, with Bob tagging on behind him.

'Here we go,' I said.

'Do you know anything about this, sir?' The policeman was looking at Dogmeat. Evidently, Bob had identified him as the main suspect.

'What are you asking me for?' protested Dogmeat. 'I've only just arrived. You saw me drive into the car park.'

'That doesn't mean he didn't do it,' said Bob, wiping his teary eyes.

'Leave this to me, sir,' said the police officer, easing Bob away.

'I know these bastards did it.' Bob seemed intent on getting at Dogmeat.

'Fuck off, Bob,' Dogmeat shouted. 'You've just had a bit of bad luck, that's all. Nothing to do with us.'

'You lying bastard,' Bob retorted.

'Calm it down, lads,' said the officer, then turning back to Dogmeat. 'Where were you in the early hours of this morning?'

'I was here, torching Bob's van, where the fuck do you think I was? I was in bed.'

'Do you live alone?'

'Sure he does,' said Bob. 'Who'd take him on?'

'Calm down, sir, or I'm going to have to ask you to wait in the police car.' The officer again pushed Bob back a few steps.

'Who the fuck's under arrest here?' asked Bob, indignant at the suggestion that he would be restrained in the car.

'Calm down, sir,' said the officer, 'no one is under arrest.' Once again, he asked Dogmeat, 'Do you have anyone who could verify that you were home all night?'

'I live by myself,' said Dogmeat. 'So, no, no one can vouch for me, but I'm fuckin' telling you that I didn't leave the house.'

'So, no one can verify your whereabouts?' said the officer, writing in his notebook.

'I must remember to ask one of the neighbours to sleep with me.'

'And what about you two,' the officer was looking questioningly at me and Mo now. Both of us offered the same answer as Bob. Mo, the only one of us who had a cast iron alibi.

'Check the CCTV cameras.' Mo was pointing up at the large gable end of The Railway. The officer looked up and you could fair see the penny drop. He played it cool though.

'Yes, we have that in hand,' he lied. He closed his notebook and set off back across the car park.

'Is that it?' Bob said. 'Is that all you're going to do?'

'For the moment, sir, yes.'

This was all too much for Bob. He ran and launched himself headlong at Dogmeat, knocking him backwards onto the concrete, causing him to crack his head and sending Bert scurrying for cover in my truck.

'Hey, watch my dog,' I cried, more concerned about Bert than Dogmeat.

'The policeman joined the fracas and after much scuffling, succeeded in dragging Bob from the fallen body of Dogmeat. Another officer emerged from the police car and ran across the car park. Bob was handcuffed and led away, continuing to shout obscenities and accusations in our direction whilst we righted Dogmeat. Bob was about to become a Facebook star, but a deeper worry for him was that he had gone into Dogmeat's little black book, which was never a good place to be.

'You're fuckin' dead, mate,' shouted Dogmeat, rubbing the back of his head. 'And don't worry, we'll look after your punters.'

'Did you burn his van, Dogmeat?' I asked when the policemen were out of earshot.

'No, I didn't,' he said. 'Get me up in the trailer, I'm getting wet out here.' Mo and I lifted him in and he took up a position in the centre of the hatch, by the griddle.

Now, a man in a suit stepped up to annoy us. He waved the plastic card that swung on the end of his lanyard and declared his interest as a council official.

'Good morning,' he said.

'Fuckin' great morning,' Dogmeat fired back.

'Can I ask you?' the official asked. 'Having seen what has happened over there.' He pointed toward the wreckage of Bob's trailer. 'What steps would you make if your trailer caught fire?'

'Fuckin' big ones,' Dogmeat answered.

'Do you have a fire extinguisher?'

'Course we do,' I said. Mo rummaged around and pulled it from under the counter.

'Fire Blanket?' Again, Mo ducked below the counter and retrieved the fire blanket. The man seemed happy so far and Dogmeat was looking smug.

'Just one more thing,' he went on. 'Can I see your gas safety certificate and your hygiene certificate?'

'He's got us there,' I said.

'We're not on a public road,' Dogmeat objected.

'It maketh no difference,' the bespectacled official said. 'You need them. I'll be back some time in the not-too-distant future to check. Good day.' He strode away, triumphantly.

'It maketh no difference,' Dogmeat scoffed. 'Who the fuck does he think *he* is, fuckin' Shakespeare?'

'Did Bob have these certificates?' Mo asked.

'He did have something on the wall, but I never took any notice,' I said.

'He doesn't need them any more,' Dogmeat smirked.

'How are we going to get the certs?' Mo asked.

'I'll get onto it,' Dogmeat said. 'Maybe I can copy something from the Tinterweb.'

'No,' I said. 'Do it properly, Dogmeat, or it'll come back and bite us in the arse.'

'Okay, okay. I'm only joshing you.' …He wasn't.

A queue of onlookers was beginning to form at the hatch, so we turned our attention to serving the punters. The first one was an American.

'You got on the wrong bus, didn't you?' Dogmeat said, hearing his accent.

'Eh?' The American wasn't understanding Dogmeat's humour.

'He means, you're a bit out of your way,' I offered helpfully.

'Oh yeah,' he said. 'I'm on vacation.'

'In Barnsley?' I said. 'Fuckin' 'ell, the Barnsley tourist board are punching above their weight, aren't they?'

'I'm visiting an old friend. I wanted to see the English market, heard the commotion, and decided to come take a look. Have you guys lived here all your life?'

'Not yet,' Dogmeat said.

'Well, seeing as you're here, what can I get you?' I asked.

'I'll have a chili dog,' he said.

'You'll have to come back in January,' Dogmeat said. Again, the American didn't understand.

'We don't do chili dogs,' I said.

'Aww, just a plain old hot dog then.'

'Bratwurst or rubber cock?' I asked.

'Eh?'

'Never mind.' I threw a few sausages onto the sizzling griddle. One for the Yank and some spares. I kept bumping in to Dogmeat, he was in the way. 'You're going to have to fuck off, Dogmeat, there's not enough room in here. Dogmeat rolled off to the end of the trailer. 'Onions?' I asked.

'Sure.'

'Do you have a gun, bro?' Mo asked the American. He'd

been watching too much TV again.

'Of course he doesn't have a gun,' I said.

'I have one back in the States, but they wouldn't let me bring it to your country. We have the second amendment you know,' the American said, proudly.

'What's that?' Mo asked.

'The right to arm bears,' Dogmeat said.

'Eh?'

'Never mind,' I said. 'Mustard and ketchup on the end there.' I handed over the hot dog and he looked at it as if it was a sample taster.

'It's a foot long,' I said.

'Sure,' said the American disappointedly.

'Next,' I said. Up stepped a tall, rain soaked thirty-something. He shook his bedraggled hair like an English Setter. He considered the menu, his head moving up and down as he read and reread the list.

'What would you like?' I asked. The queue behind him was growing longer.

'Err.' He scratched his wet head.

'Yes?' I asked, impatiently.

'Err…'

'Come on,' someone called from the back of the queue. 'Make your fuckin' mind up. It's raining you know.'

'Decided yet?' I asked.

'Cheeseburger,' he said at long last.

'One cheeseburger coming up,' I said

'No, no, make it a plain hamburger,'

'Good,' I said, reaching for a bap.

'Sorry,' he said. 'Cheeseburger.'

'Are you sure now?' I asked, holding the bap close to my

chest.

'No, hamburger, I'll have a hamburger.'

'Definitely?'

'Yes, I'm sure.' He seemed to have settled on a hamburger.

'Do you want Onions?' I asked.

'Yes please.'

'Cheese?'

'Yes please.' The whole queue applauded as he walked away.

We were having a bumper day. The people just kept coming. Dogmeat had to return home to get more burgers, sausage and chips from the chest freezer in his garage. I wasn't sure how many of the punters were here for the fire, and how many were returning, satisfied customers. It gave me a warm feeling inside to think it might be the latter. Obviously, not as warm as Bob's van, but it was up there. Mo and I occasionally swapped duties to keep things fresh. Half an hour on chip fryer and tea duties, then back to the hatch to face the public. I must admit, Mo was much better at dealing with the great unwashed than I was. Mo looked happy, I was happy and Dogmeat was delighted. The rain wasn't deterring folk either. The only dark cloud on the horizon, the little niggle at the back of my mind, was the forthcoming meeting with Warburton. I'm sure Mo was thinking about it too.

Finally, the queue shortened, custom came in dribs and drabs and ultimately dried up, so we began shutting down and cleaning up. We stowed the tables and chairs in the trailer and locked up. We counted our takings in Dogmeat's car. It had been our best day ever.

'I'm going to have to take five hundred notes from the takings,' Dogmeat announced, 'for expenses.' I wondered what expenses could possibly amount to five hundred pounds.

'What expenses are those?' I asked, puzzled.

'For the lads who burnt Bob's trailer,' he smirked. 'They didn't do it for nothing you know.'

'I knew it was you all along,' I sighed.

'The cameras will prove it wasn't me,' Dogmeat said. 'Anyway, you've felt the benefit haven't you?'

'Yes, but...'

'And don't forget,' Dogmeat cut me short. 'He'll not be here tomorrow, or the day after, or the day after that. It was just a hard-headed business decision, that's all, nothing personal.'

I conceded the point, left the people carrier, and intruded upon Bert's slumbers in my truck, urging him to jump out of the truck and cock his leg. He merely raised his head, looked at me in disgust and went back to sleep. Bert didn't like rain.

Back home, I showered and changed. My immediate challenge was the diminishing stock of socks and undercrackers in the drawers. They'd mostly transferred to the overflowing laundry basket. Instead of facing up to the task, I'd been buying new supplies. It was the same with my tee shirts. My bed linen was running out too and it was becoming clear that I needed to master the art of using the washing machine. Sally had been a pain in the arse, but she had taken control of most household tasks. I'd also neglected the cleaning, and looking around the house with a critical eye, I realised I was living in a tip. It hadn't helped that Bert, desperate for a toilet stop, had given in to his needs, run out into the garden, dumped his load, and darted back into the kitchen, shaking like a rattlesnake, and dispensing water droplets over the kitchen units. Something had to be done.

I decided to start with clothes and advance to bedding later. Baby steps. I'd never given it a thought before, but fuck me, how many buttons and settings does a washing machine really need? I shoved the clothes through the porthole and weighed up my options. Cotton, cotton quick, bulky, quick thirty, baby care, bio care, delicates, and whites. Then on an adjacent list; medic care, pre-wash, intensive and crease care. If that wasn't enough, I could individually set the spin speed and the temperature. After a little soul searching, I slammed the door shut and let the machine make up its own mind. On opening the detergent drawer, I encountered another quandary. The drawer was divided into three separate compartments, with no clue as to where to put the powder. I covered my bases by putting washing powder in all three compartments, that should do it. There's no flies on old Johnboy eh?

The rain had eased a little, so Bert and I decided to go for a walk. I say Bert and I, but I felt as if I was the big instigator here as I had to wake him to impress the idea upon him.

'Come on, son,' I said. 'Get your coat on, we're off out.' His coat was his lead and I waved it in front of him, but he didn't stir. 'Show a bit of enthusiasm, Bert.' In the fullness of time, he dragged himself from his bed and I hooked him up and we were off. As we passed through the back garden, I noticed that the grass needed cutting too. The work was never ending. I put it out of my mind and headed for the trail. We were the only ones daft enough to venture out in this weather, but that suited me fine. I'd had my fill of people today and didn't need to exchange any more inane pleasantries.

We had a long, long walk and returned home for Bert to redesign the kitchen floor, paw prints were in right now. He circled the room a few times, to make sure the pattern was even, slopped water all over whilst he was drinking from his stainless steel bowl, then flopped back down on his bed, closed his heavy eyes and waited for his dinner.

'Don't worry, Bert,' I said. 'I'll clean that up.'

After feeding Bert, my attention turned to my own culinary needs. I stared into the empty box which was my fridge, it was all but bare except for a jar of pickled onions, a jar of olives and some mouldy cheese. It was evident that I needed to add shopping to my "to do" list. Searching the kitchen cupboards, I discovered a tin of hot dog sausages which quickly went, unopened, into the bin.

'I see enough rubber cocks at work,' I muttered to myself. My choice was chicken soup or baked beans, and finding a stale crust in the bread bin, I settled for beans on toast. I was going to have to pull my socks up, big time, but this was going to have to do for now. I detested going to the supermarket, but I was going to have to bite the bullet and face the charging trollies at some point.

The washing machine was beeping, telling me it had finished its cycle. 'That wasn't too difficult,' I thought to myself. I don't know what Sally used to whine about, the machine did all the work. All she'd had to do was put the clothes in and press a button. I placed the washing basket near the appliance door and pulled at the handle. The door didn't open. I pulled again, but it wouldn't budge. I pulled harder, but no joy, then I heard a click and the door opened easily. Patience is indeed, a virtue, especially when it comes to washday.

I couldn't remember loading any pink items, but I was definitely unloading pink clothes. Everything was pink, except my black undercrackers, which were still black, but not as black as when they went in. They also had white powder stripes on them. I was going to look like a skunk. The colour of my underwear didn't particularly bother me, as unfortunately, no one but me would see them. It was the size that was worrying. They went in as large and were now suitable for aged seven to eleven years. It was the same with my favourite, white tee shirt; it was pink, and you'd be hard pressed to get it on a fuckin' doll. I gathered my washing, placed it in a black bin bag and dumped it in the dustbin. It was going to be a trip to Matalan as well. As I'd come outside to throw away my wardrobe, I checked in the garden shed to make sure the bag was still there. It was still tucked away under the bench, but I was going to have to insist that the money was divided, and the bag that had caused so much joy and sadness, could finally be disposed of. I looked forward to the day I could abandon the shed to nature again.

I was beginning to regret the bottle of wine I'd sunk before bedtime. My head was throbbing like a pit head compressor and sleep was elusive that night. The undercrackers, Bob's hot dog trailer, Jimmy Onion, Warburton and the much-needed gas safety certificate jostled for prominence. On the odd occasion I did manage to doze, I was plagued by bad dreams. Bob was bearing down on on me, wearing nothing but tight fitting, pink underpants. I snapped awake before he could bring a giant frankfurter down upon my head. I sat, bolt upright in bed, sweating from every pore, wishing I'd never seen the bag, because all these worries stemmed from the day we found it. I'd become a cheat and a liar, and more to the point, a murderer. I'm not saying I didn't have worries before that day, but they were small change compared to this crock of shit. I gave up and went downstairs, clicked on the kettle and pulled the coffee jar from the cupboard. There was just enough for one cup, so I made a mental note to get coffee when I went shopping. No doubt, I would have forgotten by tomorrow, so I made another mental note to write a list on a piece of paper, but I would forget about that too. Bert was looking at me, worrying that I was going to drag him outside for a walk.

'Don't worry, Bert,' I said. 'You go back to sleep. It's me that's fucked up.' I made the coffee and went off to watch the shopping channel. I managed to blow out a few Zs, woke up about five thirty with a crick in my neck and a mouth that felt like a monkey had slept in it.

Chapter 12

Warburton was already there waiting for us by the time we reached the rear of the pub.

'Morning,' I said.

'Cut the pleasantries and take me to the money,' he replied, churlishly.

A light drizzle was punching above its weight, the type of rain that soaks in, right through the outer garments, through any jumper and directly into the bones, causing your shoulder blades to ache. I circled my head to ease the tension in my neck. Only Mo had been sensible enough to wear a waterproof, hooded jacket. For some inexplicable reason, Warburton had chosen a suit jacket and black tie for the outing. He looked like he was going to a funeral, little did he suspect that it would be his own. The miserable weather meant the trail was deserted, apart from us of course. Even the birds stayed home today. We walked on, heads bowed against the elements. Dogmeat was out front, cracking a pace, negotiating the puddles.

'Come on,' he said. 'Let's get this done. It's fuckin' horrible out here.' We increased our pace and tried to keep up with him. Warburton had his hands tucked in his pockets, his shirt almost see-through now, his highly polished shoes stained with mud and leaves. Because Warburton was with us, I'd left Bert at home, safe and dry. He didn't like being alone, but he wouldn't have enjoyed today.

Warburton grumbled when we asked him to help lift

Dogmeat over the rough ground, but he grudgingly obliged. The unmetalled track had become sticky with the rain and Dogmeat's gloved hands were pushing hard on the wheels, but we knew better than to offer assistance, so progress was slow. It was us that were waiting for him now.

'Where are we going?' Warburton asked.

'You'll see,' said Dogmeat, not willing to divulge any information.

The rain hadn't eased at all as we reached the farm and gathered around the well.

'In there?' Warburton asked, pointing at the steel plate.

'Yes,' Dogmeat said. 'You'll have to help the lads pull it aside.

'Bloody hell,' said Warburton. 'I'd have come in overalls if I'd have known I was in for this.' Nevertheless, he complied and helped us drag the plate away.

'Well done,' Dogmeat said as we stared into the hole.

'What now?' Warburton cautiously leant over and peered down.

'There's a rope there,' I said. 'Pull it up, the bag's on the end of it.'

'I'll dirty my trousers,' Warburton complained. 'Can't one of you do it?'

'If you want the money,' said Dogmeat, 'you'll have to get it yourself. You'll soon have enough money to buy a new pair of kecks.'

'Fuck's sake.' He went down on his knees on the muddy ground, reached in and started to pull at the rope. 'There's nothing on the end of this rope.'

Dogmeat nodded at Mo to urge him to move forward and do the deed, but Mo shuffled forward a couple of steps, then retreated.

'I can't,' said Mo.

'Do it,' Dogmeat insisted.

'Do what?' Warburton had pulled the entire length of the rope out of the well and showed us the end. 'What are you playing at?'

'Mo,' said Dogmeat.

'I can't,' Mo said.

'What's going on?' Warburton asked. It was at this point that Dogmeat pulled the gun from inside his coat and shot Warburton in the head. His eyes were still open, but his soul had departed. For a brash, outspoken man, he died without a whisper, simply slumping forward on to the edge of the well.

'Quality death that was. He didn't deserve it,' Dogmeat said, unperturbed. 'I knew this would come in handy.' Dogmeat stroked the gun as if it was a new kitten.

'Fuck me, Dogmeat.' I was aghast. I'd forgotten about the gun.

'I'd rather not if you don't mind,' said Dogmeat. 'Roll him in then before someone sees us.'

'Sees us?' I said. 'I should think the whole fuckin' town heard us.'

'Look around,' Dogmeat said. 'There's no one here. 'Get him in the well and get the top back on.'

'Okay.' I moved forward but Dogmeat stopped me.

''No,' Dogmeat said. 'You, Mo, you do it. Make up a little bit for a piss poor performance.' Mo reluctantly edged forward and tipped Warburton over the precipice until gravity took over. 'That's a nail out of the boot,' Dogmeat said as Warburton fell. 'No thanks to you two though. I hope you're going to show some minerals in future.'

'Sorry,' said Mo. 'I just couldn't bring myself to do it.'

'It's all right, Mo.' I patted him on the back of the head.

'Right,' Dogmeat said. 'Let's get the plate back on.' Mo and I slid it back into place and Dogmeat pulled two brand new padlocks from his pocket. 'Better put these on, just to be safe.'

We clicked the locks into position and left the scene. Hopefully we'd never have to go back there again.

It was still early, so we elected to return home and meet in the Railway at the usual time. It would give us a chance to dry off and I could pick up Bert too. Better to keep things as normal as possible. If I went to the pub without Bert, Walt would be asking about him and I'd have to lie, maybe say that he was off colour or something, and I wasn't very good at inventing stories. I don't know how a dog can be off colour, perhaps "a dry nose" would have been nearer the mark. My mind was wandering, creating problems and scenarios that didn't exist.

Bert was having ten minutes on the treadmill, walking but imagining he was winning the Greyhound Derby. His lip curled to form a little smile, at least, that's what I thought it meant, maybe he was grimacing and inwardly cursing me. We'd been joined by Jabba, who'd parked himself, without invitation, in a seat he'd pulled from an adjacent table. He'd been known as Jabba ever since he'd sold his semi and moved into a wooden park home, hence, Jabba the Hutt, which became shortened to Jabba the Hut and then simply Jabba as time erased the original meaning, but he seemed happy enough with the name.

'That's your burger van innit?'

'It's a catering trailer,' Dogmeat said wearily.

'It's yours though innit?'

'Yes, it belongs to us,' I said.

144

'What you doing in here then?' Jabba had a habit of laughing at his own words, funny or not.

'We're having a pint with you,' I said.

'And I'm having a pint with you,' he chuckled.

'Don't you have anywhere you need to be?' asked Dogmeat.

'No, I'm all right for a while.' Jabba roared with laughter.

'Are you still in the park?' I enquired.

'I sure am,' he said. 'I love it there. Low overheads, plenty of spare cash left over for this.' He raised his pint, giggling.

'Are you working?' I wondered if he'd gone the whole hog and become a man of pure leisure.

'I still need some income,' he said. 'I've got a right job now though.'

'What you doing?' Mo was intrigued.

'I have a corner office with views over the whole of Sheffield and I drive a vehicle worth over two hundred thousand pounds.'

'You've done well for yourself then, bro?' Mo said.

'I have that,' Jabba said. 'I'm a bus driver.' His mirth was uncontrollable. He leant back and guffawed like a hungry donkey.

'Fuckin' spare us.' Dogmeat said, looking at me, shaking his head. When Jabba came back to Earth, he noticed that we were a man down.

'Where's Jimmy Onion?'

'He died,' Mo said.

'We don't necessarily know that for sure,' I said, kicking Mo's shins under the table.

'Oh... no we don't... we're not sure... not at all,' Mo stuttered.

'What do you mean by that?' These were the first words Jabba had uttered in seriousness.

'He went missing,' I said. 'Nobody knows where he is.'

'What makes you think he's dead then?'

'We don't,' said Mo.

'But you said he was dead,' Jabba countered.

'I don't think that.' Mo had his head down, he was floundering.

'Just shut the fuck up about Jimmy Onion will ya?' Dogmeat said.

'Okay, okay,' Jabba said. 'I'm not that interested. I'll get the beer in, eh?' He laughed again and escaped to the bar, tittering as he went.

'Fuckin' 'ell, Mo,' Dogmeat admonished him. 'You've got a big mouth.'

'Sorry, Dave, I wasn't thinking.'

'You better start thinking,' continued Dogmeat, 'or you're going to land us in deep shit.'

'Sorry, Dave,' Mo said humbly.

'It's all right saying sorry,' Dogmeat pressed on. 'Sorry is only a word.'

'It was just a slip of the tongue,' I interceded on Mo's behalf. 'He's said sorry, just leave it at that.'

'And you can fuck off too.' I allowed Dogmeat the last word as Jabba was returning with a tray of beer.

'Beer up, boys,' Jabba said hysterically. 'You know what's good for you.' Jabba relaxed back into his seat. It looked to me that he was here long term. 'I'm not really a bus driver,' he said.

'I think we've worked that out for ourselves,' Dogmeat said. 'The bottle bottom glasses are a dead giveaway.'

'Any chance of a free burger?' asked Jabba.

'We're closed,' I said.

'Not now,' Jabba chortled. 'I mean when you're open again.

Any chance of a freebie when I'm passing and see you're working?'

'I'll tell you what,' Dogmeat said. 'We'll give you fifty percent off. How's that?'

'It's not as good as one hundred percent, but I'll take it,' said Jabba.

'It's better than no percent at all though intit?' Dogmeat said.

'Beggars can't be choosers.' The intensity of Jabba's convulsions rendered him speechless for a good few minutes. Onlookers were wondering if he'd just heard the world's greatest joke. Bert stopped dead in his tracks, wondering where the racket was coming from, causing him to drop off the back of the treadmill. After a moment, he shook himself down and laid on the carpet.

'Steady on, Jabba,' I said, 'you're going to damage yourself.' But he couldn't hear me inside his cloak of hilarity.

'What a fuckin' jerk off,' Dogmeat said.

The weather was set fair when we were back in the trailer on the Sunday. Just a few light clouds skimmed across an otherwise clear, blue sky. The difference from the previous day was marked. Island life, eh? Dogmeat was in the trailer with us, getting in the way, but he wouldn't be told so we had to put up with it. It was okay until we got busier when he then became a nuisance. His intentions were good, he thought he was helping, but I hadn't the heart to tell him. I got the impression the last time I'd asked him to leave I'd damaged his pride, but he would never admit it. I may have been wrong, but I'd known him long enough to gauge his emotions, despite his hard facade. He was, after all, just a man, flesh and blood and a whole lot of anxiety like the rest of us.

The punters arrived in a steady stream, a burger here, a

sausage there. We were doing all right, the sun was shining and a few of our regulars were sitting at the tables we'd provided. Bert sat just outside the door, waiting for a sausage to be thrown his way. I recognised the next face at the hatch.

'Eyup, Horse, how you keeping?'

'Cinnamon sticks.' Horse had used this phrase to register his wellbeing as long as I could remember.

'Good to hear,' I said. Horse was a big man, and even though his feet were planted on the tarmac, he towered above the counter. He was not only tall, but wide too, filling my field of vision.

'Have you come for your breakfast?' Dogmeat asked. He had always liked Horse, everyone did. He was genuinely a nice guy, despite his forbidding appearance.

'I've come to see you, lads,' he said. 'I heard you were doing this, so I thought I'd come and see you, see how you're getting along like.'

'That's nice of you Horse,' I said. 'You'll have something while you're here though, won't you?'

'Yeah, go then,' Horse said.

'Get some chips on the go for Horse,' I said.

Mo took a portion of frozen french fries from the freezer and tipped them into the fryer.

'We're going to need more than that for Horse,' I said. 'You better double up.'

'I just heard about Jimmy Onion,' said Horse.

'What did you hear?' asked Dogmeat.

'They say he's been murdered.'

'Who's saying that?' Dogmeat's demeanour darkened.

'Just they,' Horse said.

'You haven't by any chance been talking to Jabba have you?'

I asked.

'Yeah, not ten minutes ago. It was him who told me you were here.'

'Thought so,' Dogmeat said.

I piled a mountain of chips along with three bratwurst on to a paper plate. Horse clutched his plastic cutlery and in two strides he was at one of the tables, where he settled himself on a chair. I expected it to collapse at any moment, but it stood up to the task.

'How much do I owe you?' he asked.

'It's on the house, Horse,' Dogmeat and I said simultaneously.

'Aw thanks, lads,' Horse said gratefully. He devoured the food in seconds, thanked us again and left.

'Why is he called Horse?' Mo asked.

'I don't know,' Dogmeat said. 'He's been saddled with that name since his schooldays.'

Then came Jabba, laughing his way across the car park. 'Fifty percent off,' he said before he reached the serving hatch.

'You don't believe in wasting time,' I said.

'I was just passing by, so I thought I'd call in.' Jabba laughed.

'Bollocks,' Dogmeat said. 'You've come especially.'

'No, really. I had to come into town to get... er... some eggs.'

'Don't they sell eggs near you then?' Mo asked.

'Ran out,' he said.

'Come on then,' I said. 'What do you want?'

'Burger please,' said Jabba. 'Lots of onions.' I took a burger from the edge of the hotplate and slid it into a bap with the onions.

'Let me see your money,' Dogmeat said.

'It's here.' Jabba handed a five-pound note to Dogmeat. He did that thing where you don't let go of the money, playing a game of push and pull with an unimpressed Dogmeat. Finally, Jabba had to release the note, mainly to allow himself to recover from his fits of laughter. Dogmeat rummaged in the till and handed Jabba the change.

'You've charged me full price,' Jabba protested, counting the coins.

'So?' said Dogmeat.

'I think we all know where this is heading,' said Mo.

'You promised me fifty percent off.'

'When?'

'In the Railway,' said Jabba. 'Johnboy was there, he'll tell ya.'

'You did, Dogmeat,' I said.

'Fair enough. I'm nothing if not a man of my word.' Dogmeat took a sharp knife, cut the burger clean in two, handed half to Jabba and threw the remainder in the bin. 'There you go, fifty percent off.'

'That's not fair,' Jabba said.

'Life's not fair,' said Dogmeat. 'Now move out of the way, you're hogging the hatch.'

'But you've diddled me.'

'You're lucky I didn't cut *you* in half.' Dogmeat waved the knife at Jabba. 'You might want to keep it zipped, spreading rumours about Jimmy Onion.'

'I've said nothing to anyone.' Jabba pleaded his innocence.

'You haven't been talking to Horse this morning then?'

'I haven't seen Horse for years,' Jabba said.

'You fuckin' lying little prick,' said Dogmeat, pointing the knife directly at Jabba's face. 'Let me out, let me at him.'

'I'm off,' said Jabba. 'Got to be somewhere.' Jabba quickly scurried over the tarmac and exited onto the pavement before we had a chance to unleash Dogmeat. He wasn't laughing now.

'I'll catch up with you later,' Dogmeat shouted. 'And keep your fuckin' mouth shut.'

'Oh, for fuck's sake,' I said.

'What's wrong,' Dogmeat asked.

'He's back.'

'Who's back?'

'That council official bod,' I said. 'He'll be wanting the gas safety certificate. You said you were going to arrange something.'

'I am,' said Dogmeat. 'He hasn't given us much time, has he?'

'Hello gentlemen,' he said amicably. 'It's a beautiful day. Makes you feel good to be alive, eh? The birds are chirping and spreading their wings wide.'

'The bloke's a fuckin' idjit,' Dogmeat hissed through his teeth.

'Yeah, how are you?' I asked.

'I'm fine, just fine thank you.' He sucked in a lungful of summer air.

'We have the gas test in hand,' Dogmeat said. 'The engineer's a bit busy at the minute.'

'I haven't come for that,' Council Man said. 'I rather fancied one of your bratwurst, laid on a bed of caramelised onions and dressed with a pickled gherkin.'

'No problem,' I said. 'We can that sort that for you.'

'It's very old,' Council Man said, 'the bratwurst.'

'I can assure you they're fresh,' I said.

'I don't mean that particular bratwurst. I'm referring to the bratwurst in general.'

'Uh,' grunted Dogmeat.

'Most probably six or seven hundred years old, in actual

fact.'

'Really?' I said, with feigned interest.

'It's been a constant source of bitterness between the good burgers of Franconia and Thuringen, in Germany of course.'

'Burgers?' Mo looked confused.

'It means citizens,' I said.

'Quite right,' continued Council Man. 'Even to this day, both regions claim to be the home of the bratwurst. To us, though, it is but a masterly creation which has stood the test of time.' Council Man lifted his head towards the azure sky and drifted away to another plane.

'Fuckin' 'ell,' Dogmeat said. 'He's getting off on a sausage.'

'Each to their own,' I said, placing the hot dog on the counter, but Council Man wasn't seeing me. 'Are you taking this away with you or are you sitting down.'

'Oh,' Council Man was back with us. 'Is it more expensive to sit here and eat it?'

'It doesn't matter,' I said. 'It's free.'

'Thank you very much,' said Council Man.

'Like fuck it is,' Dogmeat butted in.

'Come on, Dogmeat,' I said. 'Let him have it.'

'I'll fuckin' let him have it all right.'

'Am I paying or not?'

'Yes, you are.'

'No, you're not.'

'He's paying,' Dogmeat insisted.

Council Man slapped the money on the counter. 'It's not worth fighting about,' he said, and stepped away from the hatch. 'I'll be back next week to see the gas safety certificate. I could close you down right now, you know.'

'I realise that,' I said. 'Thank you for your patience.'

'You fuckin' pussy,' Dogmeat said, disgusted with my intervention. 'We can't keep giving food away.'

'We let Horse have a pile of snap that could have come straight from Close Encounters of the Third Kind,' I argued.

'He's a nice lad is Horse. This bloke is a pain in the arse.'

'He might have gone a bit easier on us if we'd given him a hot dog, that's all, a fuckin' hot dog… it's nothing.' I was annoyed with Dogmeat's intransigence.

'He can afford to pay for his own hot dog, the weirdo,' Dogmeat replied.

'That's not the point,' I said. 'You could have made things difficult for us now.'

'What is this?' Dogmeat said. 'A fuckin' protection racket he's running… now there's an idea.'

Chapter 13

I'd been nervous about today ever since the envelope dropped on the mat. I'd tried to play it down, but it was always there in the back of my mind. Both Mo and Dogmeat were going to be there to support me in the Magistrate's Court, even though I'd told them I'd be fine. They wanted to show solidarity, but for now they were sipping coffee in my kitchen, counting out the money from the bag into three separate piles. At last, I needn't worry about the bag in the shed. If I lost the money now it would be just my share.

'What do you think they'll do to me?' I asked.

'Life without parole, for sure,' Dogmeat replied.

I was more annoyed with myself than anything else. I shouldn't have wrecked the old boy's porch, but I was so incensed at the time, blinded by the injustice of it all. Now he would be getting his build for free, just as he would have liked, and maybe a little compensation on top as an added bonus. I'd played right into his hands. What a tool.

We divided the money into three Aldi carrier bags. I took mine upstairs, pushed it into the bottom of the wardrobe amongst a pile of shoes and other bits and bobs and returned to the kitchen where we had a final cup of coffee before leaving for the court. I didn't have an appointment as such, just a time to be there by. It could be hours after that when I was seen, so we would just have to sit and wait. I'd still insisted that we arrive early as I didn't want to make the situation any worse than it already was.

Dogmeat seemed quite jolly about it all, singing and laughing to himself as he guided the people carrier away from my house.

'What's so funny?' I asked.

'You,' he said. 'In trouble with the law.'

'Yeah, it's fuckin' hilarious that I'm in court, going to be fined God knows how much and might end up in jail.'

'It's not that bad, bro.' Mo tried to console me.

'You'll get no more than twenty year.' Dogmeat continued.

'Fuck off will ya?' Dogmeat was becoming really irritating and he knew it.

'It's cushy inside, these days. TV, table tennis, you'll maybe get a job to pass the time.' He kept it up all the way into town. By the time we reached the car park, I was just about ready to tell him to fuck off home. He was supposed to be there to back me up, but it didn't seem like that right now. It was just another laugh for him.

Inside, I checked in with a stern looking lady behind a glass screen. 'Take a seat,' she said without a hint of a smile. Mo and I sat in a corner out of the way and Dogmeat came alongside in his wheelchair. I was trying to keep a low profile, out of the way, to save the embarrassment of being recognised in the court waiting room. I wasn't used to wearing a collar and tie and I fiddled with the knot constantly.

'It's too tight,' I complained. 'I feel like I'm being throttled.'

'Leave it alone will ya?' Dogmeat said. 'It's all right as it is.'

'Sorry,' I said. 'I'm a bit nervous.'

'There's nowt to worry about,' Dogmeat reassured me. At last, he was on my side. 'And you look great.'

'Do I really?'

'Course you do,' said Dogmeat. 'People will think you're

155

wearing a saveloy suit.'

'You mean Savile Row, don't you?' I said.

'I know what I mean.' Dogmeat squeezed my leg just above my knee, so hard that I yelped. He had a vice-like grip. The stern lady looked at me over her glasses.

'Sorry,' I mouthed.

The waiting room was filling up and various officials were approaching the seated people around me. I was beginning to wonder if I should have secured the services of a professional. A particularly pleasant young lady passed through the waiting room clutching a wad of papers.

'I'll give her a nine,' Dogmeat said. 'What about you?'

'Uh,' I said. 'I wasn't concentrating.'

'Give me a score,' Dogmeat snarled.

'Eight then,' I said, to get him off my back.'

'Six,' Mo said.

'Fuckin' six?' Dogmeat asked incredulously.

'Yeah, six,' Mo said. 'She has a face like a robber's hoss.'

'Fuckin' 'ell, Mo,' said Dogmeat. 'Who do you think you are, Matt Damon?'

'That's just my opinion,' Mo said. 'My bar is higher than yours, that's all.'

We waited… and waited… and waited. People were called and new villains took their place in the waiting room.

'I think they've forgotten about you, Johnboy,' Dogmeat said. 'Let's fuck off home.'

'We can't do that,' I said. 'That'll just make things worse.'

A motorcycle officer passed through the room, nonchalantly swinging his helmet. Dogmeat was on him in a flash, blocking his path with his wheelchair before he could get through the door.

'Hey bud,' Dogmeat said. 'How long do we normally have to wait for something to happen?'

The officer, unimpressed by Dogmeat's lack of respect, eyed him with some disdain. 'We're all here because of you, sir. It'll take as long as it takes.'

'Because of me?' Dogmeat raised his voice enough to grab everyone's attention.

'If you can't do the time, don't do the crime,' the officer smiled.

'I haven't done any crime, you fuckin' balloon.'

'Watch your language, sir,' the officer said, pushing past Dogmeat.

'Fuck off, you arrogant...' The officer was gone, and we were no wiser as to how long we'd have to wait.

'Nice work,' I said when Dogmeat rejoined us.

'John Barratt.' The call had come, and I leapt to my feet.

'Steady down, Johnboy,' said Dogmeat. 'They'll wait for you.'

'Sit down please, sir,' said the court usher. 'You're up soon.'

'About time,' Dogmeat said.

'I wanted to make sure you're okay. Do you need a drink?'

'I'll have a double JD with ice please,' said Dogmeat before I could answer.

'Would you like a drink of water, Mr Barratt?'

'No thank you, I'm fine,' I said, lying. I felt terrible, my head was spinning. I wanted it to be over. Considering I was a murderer, I wasn't taking this very well.

The courtroom was a hardwoodfest with polished oak panels on every wall. Three dignified individuals sat at a raised bench.

Behind them was a coat of arms that read "Dieu et mon droit". I'd seen somewhere that droit meant "right", but I didn't know what the rest of it signified. Maybe it was "keep right", but we drove on the left in this country, so I was more than likely wrong. I expected the magistrates to be old, but only the lady sat in the middle had any age about her. The other two, a man and a woman, were more my age. Mo sat in the public gallery with Dogmeat close by in an allotted area with wheelchair access. Mr Dawson was a couple of seats away on the other side. He smiled and nodded when he saw me. I was sat on a hard upright seat behind a brass rail, strangely wishing that Bert was at my side.

'All rise,' said the usher.

'I'd love to,' Dogmeat shouted. He wasn't going to behave himself, was he?

'Apart from you, sir.'

I was charged with criminal damage and pleaded guilty. The magistrates asked if there were any mitigating circumstances and Dogmeat suggested that I was hard of thinking and received a warning about his behaviour. I shamefully recounted the episode and explained my state of mind and state of pocket at the time. Mr Dawson had his say about how traumatised and emotionally distressed he had been by the whole thing, and how his whole world had come crashing down along with the porch. No longer could he enjoy a full night's sleep and he wasn't eating properly either. It was a performance worthy of an Oscar, all designed to optimise his compensation award. He must have been practicing at home in front of the mirror.

The end result was a hefty fine and a huge award for Mr Dawson. I didn't mind the financial losses, I could afford it now. It was the two hundred hours of community service that irritated me. Dogmeat didn't help when he shouted, 'Why don't you just hang him?' This time he was escorted out of the courtroom, chuntering all the way.

'That went well,' he said as we left the building.

'No thanks to you,' I said.

'What's up with you? You're a free man.'

'Two hundred hours of litter picking, that's what's up with me. I'd have probably got one hundred if you hadn't stuck your oar in.'

'It'll fly by, won't it, Mo?' said Dogmeat.

'I suppose so,' Mo said dubiously.

Dogmeat dropped Mo off at home and then went on to mine. I asked him in for a drink, but he declined the offer and left me to slowly wander up my garden path. I put the key in the door, but it was already unlocked. In the fuddle that was going on in my head, I must have left home without locking up. First thing I did was make sure Bert was okay, then I put the kettle on. A shot of caffeine was much needed right now. Sitting at the table cradling my coffee, I heard a noise coming from upstairs, a low thud. "The money," I thought. "Someone's up there looking for the money." Maybe I had locked the door after all. I looked around for a weapon and retrieved a bread knife from the cutlery door and a rolling pin from a drawer. I crept up the stairs gingerly, all the time listening for movement, and sure enough, someone was moving around in the bedroom. Once on the landing, my resolve weakened. What if the bloke in there was a giant, or a boxer, or lunatic, or simply twenty years younger than me? I was ready to turn around, grab Bert and leave him to it, but I remembered the money. I couldn't let him take it, so I would have to do something, but what? Everyone believes they would confront an intruder, but when the moment came, would they really?

Somehow, I mustered up the necessary courage, from where, I couldn't say. I was angry now and I flung open the bedroom door and charged in. Sally looked at me quizzically.

'What are you going to do?' she asked. 'Slice me up or roll me?'

'What are you doing here?'

'I live here.'

'No you don't,' I replied.

'This is my home,' Sally said.

'No it isn't,' I said. 'You left to live with Warburton.'

'Well, I'm back now,' she said.

'Just like that?' I said.

'You sound like Tommy Cooper.'

'You can't live here,' I said. 'You live with Warburton.'

'He's gone,' Sally said, as she removed my clothes from the wardrobe and replaced them with her own.

'Gone where?' I had to be careful what I said.

'Don't know,' she said, continuing to rearrange the wardrobe. 'He's just gone.'

'What are you doing with my clothes?' I asked.

'This was always my part of the wardrobe, and your dirty old working clothes are in here, so they'll have to come out. I can't have my nice things next to these.'

'They're not working clothes, they're my best togs.' I noticed the Aldi carrier bag thrown on the floor by the side of the bed and I quickly retrieved it.

'Too late,' she said. 'I've looked inside it.'

'You can't stay,' I said.

'Fair enough,' she said. 'I'll go to the police and tell them what I've found.' I didn't know what to say, or think. 'By the way,' she said, 'you're in the spare bedroom.'

I retreated to the kitchen, sat at the table and pondered upon my predicament. Sally had got me by the gonads, no mistake. I wondered how long it would take to make the link between the money and Warburton's disappearance. Maybe she wasn't that clever, maybe she didn't care, but she would be wanting her pound of flesh whatever. Dogmeat would hit the ceiling when I told him, and I would have to tell him. There was no way of hiding something like this. Mo would take it in his stride. I thought about ringing Dogmeat there and then, but I decided to wait until he'd had a drink in The Railway and mellowed a little.

'What's for dinner?' Sally had joined me in the kitchen.

'I've no idea,' I said honestly. I never knew what I was going to eat until I'd scoured the cupboards.

'I fancy chilli con carne,' said Sally.

'I've no chilli,' I said, 'and I've no con carne.'

'Don't worry,' she said. 'I brought all the ingredients with me.' She placed a Sainsbury's bag in front of me on the table.

'Crack on then,' I said. 'Do what you want.'

'No love,' she sneered. 'You're making it. I'm going to watch the telly.' She pulled a "Hairy Bikers" cookbook from the shelf, opened it at the relevant page to reveal the recipe, poured a glass of red wine from a bottle and pushed the bottle towards me. I thought she was offering me a drink, but I was mistaken. 'You'll need some of this for the recipe. Shout me when it's ready.'

I didn't have much choice but to do as I was told, so I scanned the recipe. First thing was to chop a couple of onions, and there they were, in the bag. I wasn't entirely convinced it was the onions that were making me cry. I followed the recipe and took the items from the bag in the order they were listed; minced beef, garlic, chilli powder, cumin, coriander, beef stock cube, a tin of tomatoes, a tin of kidney beans, oregano, tomato puree and rice. The table was full, all for one meal. How could this be? I did the best I could but, of course, it wasn't good enough.

'What do you call this?' Sally asked as she took the first mouthful. 'It's slop.'

'I followed the recipe you gave me. I did my best.'

'You're going to have to do a lot better,' she said.

I lost my appetite pretty quickly after that and threw my dinner in the bin.

'You are kidding, aren't you?' Dogmeat said.

Mo knew how it was about to go, because I'd already confided in him, but out of respect for me he didn't sing the song. Bert sat upright at my side, his eyes never leaving mine. He too, using his canine senses, knew how this was about to go. I'd allowed Dogmeat to have a couple of pints, hoping it would place him in a decent mood. How wrong could I be?

'You are fuckin' joking,' he said, as I explained my problem.

'I'm sorry,' I said, meekly.

'What a fuckin' blockhead you are.' Heads turned from the bar area as Dogmeat raised his voice. Becoming aware of the attention he was drawing he turned his head toward the other drinkers. 'Why don't you mind your own fuckin' business?' Most turned away, some mumbled amongst themselves and a few laughed. It was always good sport to witness a falling out amongst others.

'I don't know where we go from here,' Dogmeat said, lowering the decibels. 'You've put us in a right hole.'

'She's even got me cooking and cleaning,' I said. 'It's a living hell. I don't know what to do next?'

'You could try a biryani,' Mo said. 'We have one at least

once a week. I love it, and fish and chips, you can't go wrong with fish and chips.'

'What are you talking about, Mo?' I asked.

'Meal suggestions,' he said. 'I'm giving you some ideas.'

'Thanks,' I said. His heart was in the right place, but sometimes he misplaced his head. 'But that's not exactly what I need just now,' I added.

'We've got a huge problem now,' said Dogmeat. 'Why weren't you more careful?'

'I've said I'm sorry. It's just one of those things, an accident.'

'Some fuckin' accident,' Dogmeat hissed.

'I didn't know she was coming back did I?' I protested. Bert was looking alternately at me and Dogmeat now as we exchanged words. It was almost as if he could understand the conversation, maybe he did.

'Where did you think she would go after Warburton was gone? It was obvious she couldn't stay at his house.'

'It might be obvious now,' I said. 'But you never said anything about it before.'

'Do I have to hold your fuckin' hand now?' Dogmeat drained his glass just as Walt arrived.

'Do you lads have a problem?' he asked.

'Everything's cool, Walt,' I said. 'Isn't it, Dogmeat?'

'Like a frozen cucumber,' Dogmeat said.

'Well, just keep it down a bit will you? You're disturbing the punters.'

'Sorry, Walt,' we said in unison.

'No sweat,' Walt said. 'Can I bring you some more ale?'

'Thanks, Walt,' I said.

What followed was a lecture on meticulous planning, covering your tracks, looking out for each other and generally not being a dickhead. I sucked it all up, understanding that it was pointless to defend my corner against Dogmeat, anyway, he was right. Mo looked embarrassed as I took my medicine. Dogmeat had to get this out of his system before we could move on and find a solution. It seemed to go on forever, but eventually he ran out of steam.

'So, what we gonna do?' I asked.

'I really don't know,' Dogmeat said, rubbing his chin. 'Do you think she'll talk?'

'As long as she's getting what she wants, no, but it'll not take long to move from chilli con carne to new shoes, then a car. I'll be fuckin' skint again before you know it.'

'Does she know that me and Dave are involved?' Mo asked.

'I don't think so, as yet, but when she sees the burger van, she could put two and two together,' I said.

'It's a catering trailer,' Dogmeat said.

'Burger van, catering trailer, call it what you will, but the fact is, when she clocks it, she'll know. She's a cow, but she's not simple. She'll work it out.'

'It's not good is it?' said Dogmeat.

'She keeps asking me where the money is from and I don't know what to say,' I said.

'Has she counted it?' asked Mo.

'Probably,' I said. 'I wouldn't be surprised to find she'd taken some.'

'That makes her an accessory,' Dogmeat said. 'So she can't spill the beans.'

'What about when the money runs out?' I said. 'And it won't be long if she has her way. She might come looking for yours then.'

'She wouldn't do that,' Mo said.

'She fuckin' would,' I said. 'You don't know her like I do. She has a mean streak.'

'Then, we're going to have to do something about it,' Dogmeat said.

Chapter 14

'What's that?' Dogmeat had rolled up to the trailer with a large plastic box on his knee. On top of this box was what can only be described as a "contraption" and two potatoes.

'This,' said Dogmeat, 'is the future.'

'Yeah, but what is it?'

'Let me in, let me in, and I'll show you.' Dogmeat seemed anxious to demonstrate his new toy, so Mo and I helped him into the trailer. He placed the box on the counter, along with the machine and the potatoes. 'Watch and learn,' he said, pushing us aside. He rubbed his hands together in glee, then removed a pack of wooden skewers from the box. 'Is the fryer on, Mo?'

'Yes,' Mo said. 'It'll be up to temperature in a minute or two.'

'Magic this is.' Dogmeat took one of the potatoes and pushed the skewer through its length.

He then mounted it on the machine and turned the handle. Miraculously, the potato spiralled on the skewer corkscrewlike. Dogmeat removed it from the machine and spread it along the length of the skewer. 'That, my friends,' he said, 'is a tornado.'

'A what, bro?' Mo said.

'A tornado, Mo, and it's going to make us a lot of money. Dip this in the batter and fry it for a few minutes.' He handed the potato twister to Mo, who dipped it in the batter and gently slid it into the hot oil. I watched, intrigued as the potato sizzled in the oil, then it was ready to remove from the fryer. Mo shook off the excess oil and handed it back to Dogmeat, who took what looked like a large sugar shaker and sprinkled the contents on to the hot tornado.

'What's that you're putting on it, Dogmeat?' I asked.

'Black pepper, Johnboy, but we can offer loads of flavours. Black pepper, barbecue flavour, cheese, paprika, anything that's available. I tried a paprika one at home, it was fuckin' beautiful man. Try that,' he said, breaking the tornado skewer in half to give Mo and I a taster.

'That's really good,' I said, surprised.

'Bang on,' Mo agreed.

'And you know the best thing about it?' Dogmeat asked.

'What's that?' I said as I enjoyed the new addition to the menu.

'Three quid a pop,' said Dogmeat. 'Cheap ingredients and ready in a flash.'

'Three pounds for one potato?' Mo said.

'I've done my research,' Dogmeat said. 'And that's the going rate.'

'Fuckin' 'ell,' I said. 'That's extortionate.'

'I'm telling you, that's what they go for. I don't just sit on my arse when I'm not here you know. I'm constantly researching the market and evaluating the competition.'

'You're always sat on your arse,' I joked.

'You know what I mean,' Dogmeat said.

'I think they're the dog's,' Mo said, sucking on the skewer.

'We'll add them to the menu then, lads?' asked Dogmeat, even though he'd already made the decision.

'I think so,' I said. 'We can't really go wrong, can we?'

'It's a deffo from me, bro,' Mo said. He was almost as excited as Dogmeat about the tornados.

'We'll give a few free samples away to start with,' said Dogmeat. 'But don't offer them until they've made an order. We're not a charity... Take a note, Mo. Let's create some flavours.'

'I'm on it.' Mo grabbed his ever-ready notepad and pen.

'Cheese, barbecue, smoky paprika... er... help me out here lads,' Dogmeat said.

'Curry,' Mo suggested.

'Nice one, son,' said Dogmeat. 'Make that Chip shop curry and Chinese curry.'

'Is that absolutely necessary?' I asked.

'Variety is the spice of life, Johnboy.'

'Salt and pepper?' I offered.

'Write that down, Mo,' said Dogmeat. 'That's a good one.' Mo knew not to log any words until they'd received Dogmeat's approval.

'Prawn cocktail?' I said.

'They're tornados, not fuckin' crisps,' Dogmeat spat.

'All right, all right,' I said. 'I'm trying.'

'Yes you are,' Dogmeat said.

'Smoky bacon?' Mo had his thinking cap on now.

'I like that, Mo,' Dogmeat said. 'Make a note.'

'That's a crisp flavour,' I complained.

'Yeah,' Dogmeat said. 'It's a good one, yours was shite.'

'Chilli then. Is that any good for you?' I was becoming a tad annoyed by now.

'Now *that*, Johnboy, is a good idea. Now you're thinking clearly.' I felt a little better after Dogmeat's endorsement.

'Chicken,' said Mo.

'On the face of it, that's a good idea, Mo,' said Dogmeat, 'but bear in mind, all these flavours are powders, and if they're

168

not available, we ain't having 'em.'

'Garlic,' I suggested and Dogmeat accepted it. The list went on and on.

A week on, the trials were finished, and the tornado business was up, running and thriving.

The public loved them, especially the salad dodgers. We'd even created a separate dedicated menu to display the myriad of flavours available. I thought we'd gone over the top with it, but Dogmeat was having none of it. We had all the flavoured powders lined up in large plastic tubs. All we had to do was deep fry the potato, dip it in batter and then into the flavoured powder. It was a doddle. We had a spoon in each tub to coat any parts of the tornado that hadn't picked up the powder. One spoon to each tub, after we'd had a complaint of cross contamination. Our customers were very particular. Annoyingly, the most popular choice by a country mile was chip shop curry. Our customers, whilst being particular, also had terrible fuckin' taste.

'What did I say,' Dogmeat gloated. 'One day you'll learn to listen to me.'

'Chip shop fuckin' curry.' I shook my head, more in disappointment than disbelief. 'But what can you expect from folk that eat out of a burger van?'

'It's a catering trailer,' said Dogmeat.

A new punter, one we'd never seen before, materialised at the hatch. I don't know how long he'd been there. I happened to turn around and there he was, a lad of about fourteen or fifteen, in his school uniform. The knot in his tie was pulled to the size of a large pea, fuck knows how he was going to undo that when he got home. The ends of his shirt collar were curled up like dried toast. With leather patches on the elbows of his jacket, he was a real throwback.

'Aren't you supposed to be in school?' I asked.

'Na, it's my break,' he lied.

'Are you sure?'

'Course I'm sure,' the lad said. 'What's it to you anyway? I've got money.'

'I'm worried about the future of our great country,' I said.

'Are you gonna serve me or what, you ballsack?'

'Hey,' I retorted. 'Watch your fuckin' language.'

'If he can pay, serve him,' Dogmeat said.

'What do you want?' I asked.

'Do you do discounts for students?'

'You're only a student if you go to school,' I said. 'Now, what would you like?'

'I want one of them tornado things. My mate says they're awesome.'

'Your mate's right. One tornado,' I called, 'for this young… er… man.' Mo got straight onto it and shortly, the twisted potato emerged, sizzling from the pan. 'What flavour do you want?'

'I want chip shop curry and cheese,' the lad said.

'You can only have one flavour,' I said.

'That's not fair. I want curry and cheese.'

'It's one or the other,' I said. 'Make your mind up.'

'Why can't I have two. I'll pay extra.'

'Because we'll end up with cheese powder in the curry and curry powder in the cheese, so it's make your mind up time.'

'Well, that's just shit,' the lad complained.

'That's how it is,' I said. 'Take or leave it.'

'I'll fuckin' leave it then. I'm going to Maccydees.' With that, he turned and ran across the car park, only turning once to give us the middle finger.

'Little bastard,' I shouted after him. 'I'll remember you.'

'Make a note, Mo,' Dogmeat said. 'Take the money from school kids before you start cooking.'

Apart from the odd incident like that, the new, tornado era had been a great success. I had to hand it to Dogmeat, he'd come up with a winner, but he made sure we never forgot that it was his idea. He was spending more and more time in the trailer with us, generally getting under our feet and doing nothing useful, but naturally, he enjoyed the company, notwithstanding the fact that he would never admit it. 'You love me and Mo, don't you, Dogmeat?' I asked, one day during a quiet period.

'Don't talk so soft.'

'Go on, own up,' I said. 'It's nothing to be ashamed of.'

'Give up will ya?' Dogmeat said. 'You daft twat.' Mo was behind Dogmeat, wiping his hands on a tea towel, smiling, enjoying Dogmeat's embarrassment. After all, it was a rare situation to have Dogmeat on the back foot.

'C'mon Dogmeat,' I pressed on. 'Tell me you love me.'

'Stop it now,' Dogmeat said, but I could see he was blushing, so I persisted.

'Give us a cuddle,' I said, arms akimbo.

'Fuck off,' Dogmeat said, creeping backwards away from me. I advanced, lips puckered. Mo was down on all fours, searching for a clean tea towel from the base of the cupboard.

'Don't be shy,' I said. Dogmeat recognised that I was moving forward with a little more intention and quickly went into reverse, running into Mo. Mo instinctively reacted by grabbing the back of the wheelchair, causing it to topple backwards. Dogmeat's arms went out to grab something to save himself, unfortunately, the first thing he caught hold of was the smoky

171

paprika powder.

Momentarily, it was akin to a Martian dust storm within the trailer. Fine particles of red powder filled the air before settling on every surface. Dogmeat got the worst of it. He looked like he'd fallen asleep on a sunbed.

'Look at the state of you,' I laughed.

'You want to look in a mirror, mate,' Dogmeat answered. Mo, having had his head down appeared to have come out of it well, he was still brown.

'We're never going to get rid of this,' Dogmeat said. 'It's everywhere.' He sneezed violently, sending a cloud of red dust into the air. 'I've swallowed most of it.'

'Bless you,' I laughed out loud.

'It's not funny,' Dogmeat said. 'And it's your fault.'

'How's it my fault?'

'You were fuckin' around. If you'd had your sensible head on, this wouldn't have happened.'

'That's unfair,' I said. 'It was you that grabbed the paprika box.'

'Only because you pushed me backwards.'

'I never touched you,' I grumbled.

'You may not have actually touched me,' Dogmeat said, 'but you caused me to fall.'

'Who'd you think I am, Derren fuckin' Brown?'

'Come on, lads,' Mo stepped in to act as mediator, but was immediately silenced.

'Fuck off, Mo,' Dogmeat snarled, 'this is between me and him.'

'Calm down, Dogmeat,' I said. 'It's not such a big deal.'

'Not a big deal? You've made a right fuckin' mess of my van.'

172

'Your van?' I hissed. 'What about me and Mo's contribution? It's us that does all the work while you ponce around in your car, you ungrateful sod.'

'I ponce around, do I?'

'Come on, lads,' Mo pleaded.

'Fuck off, Mo,' I said. 'This is between me and him.'

'I ponce around, do I?' Dogmeat's face had become even redder now. I could see he was about to blow a fuse, so I tried to calm the situation.

'Let's leave it,' I said, but he was too late. Dogmeat put his wheelchair into turbo mode and launched it at me. The steel foot plates rammed against my shins, making me howl with pain. As my head went forward, he took me in his infamous headlock and squeezed. My arms flailed, knocking over, first the chip shop curry powder, then the cheese powder. The trailer was beginning to take on the appearance of a gay pride meeting. We only stopped when a punter appeared at the hatch.

'Can I help you,' I said as if all was normal.

'What's going on?' A chunky, lady traffic warden looked in at us, puzzlement written all over her face. 'It looks like a Punch and Judy show from out here. All you need is a big nose and a truncheon.'

'Just a bit of ribbing,' I said. 'Nothing to worry about here. Can I get you something love?'

'Double cheeseburger,' she said.

'Salad?' I asked.

'Better do, I'm on a diet,' she said, after a little deliberation.

We cleaned up the best we could, but the trailer was in a proper state. In between customers, we wiped the surfaces, but really, all we were doing was just spreading it around. Now, instead of having white powder here and red powder there, we had pink powder everywhere. All our cleaning cloths were ruined, and we'd almost exhausted our supply of kitchen roll. The griddle had received a coating along with the onions that were sitting, waiting on the hotplate. I ran my finger along the top of the cooling cabinet and that was the same. Dogmeat was none too pleased about the condition of his wheelchair, and his face, at first simply red, was beginning to streak with sweat. I intended to alert him to this situation as I knew he wouldn't take it well, but he could have secured a part in a Michael Jackson Thriller video, no trouble. Mo had been bent over when the paprika was launched and I thought he'd got away with it, but when he turned, I noticed that the back of his head was red.

'You better get undressed in the garden, Mo,' I said, 'or you'll be in trouble when you get home.'

'I will,' he said, untroubled.

I looked into Dogmeat's eyes to gauge his mood. He stared back… and cracked. He began laughing and I joined in.

'Good game, eh?' he said.

'Aye,' I agreed. 'We must do it again soon.'

Our next punters were two teenage girls, with rings through their noses, ears, and lips. I didn't know whether to serve them or weigh them in. Their ripped jeans looked just about ready for the bin.

'Hiya girls,' I said cheerily. Are you all right?' They declined to answer my inquiry, so I asked them what they needed. They didn't seem to notice our dishevelment, probably thinking us quite trendy. 'Hot dog please.'

'Same for me too please.' At least they were polite.

'Bratwurst or rubber cock?' As soon as I said it, I knew I shouldn't have.

'What?'

'German bratwurst sausage or frankfurter style?'

'Frankfurter please.'

'And for me too please.'

'Onions?'

'Yes please.'

'And on mine too please,' said the second girl. It was becoming evident which was the leader and which was the follower. I swished the rubber... er... frankfurters around in the water to clean them up a bit. I made a mental note to replace the water in the bain marie at the first opportunity. I slid the sausages into their respective bread pockets and piled on the fried onions. The first girl took her hot dog, opened it and peered inside.

'These onions are red,' she said.

'Mine are too,' said the follower.

'They're Spanish,' I said. 'Extra flavour... and they look nice too.'

'Cool,' said the first girl, happy with the explanation.

'They were nice girls,' I said as they left.

'Yes,' Mo said. 'You should never judge people by their appearance.'

The next arrival wasn't so welcome. 'Nice little set up you have here,' Sally said. 'But I don't reckon much to your make up. What happened here?'

'Don't you worry about that,' I said. I wanted her to go, not just from the car park, but my life too.

'How are you Dave?' she asked.

'I'm okay,' Dogmeat said reluctantly.

'And you, Mo, are you keeping well?'

'I'm good thanks,' Mo said. 'How are you?' I shot him a

disapproving look.

'I'm lovely,' Sally said. 'Thanks for asking, Mo. At least there's one gentleman on board.'

'What do you want, Sally?' I asked brusquely. 'A burger, a hot dog, a tornado, tea, coffee? Cos if you aren't buying, we haven't time for talking shit.'

'Oooh, you're very brave in front of your mates aren't you John?' Sally mocked.

'What do you want?' I repeated.

'I've come to have a look at my new business,' she said.

'Now wait a minute,' Dogmeat interjected. 'Whatever's going on between you and Johnboy has nothing to do with me and Mo.'

'I think it has,' she said. 'Look, Dave, I have nothing against you personally, in fact I've always had a soft spot for you, but this is purely a business proposition, and twenty five percent doesn't seem a bad deal does it?'

'We're not interested, Sally,' Dogmeat said.

'I'm willing to pull my weight,' she said. 'Do a little bit now and again, not a lot, just a helping hand now and again.'

'There isn't enough money in it for four of us,' I said. 'And we have to pay Walt too.'

'You may have to give up your share then,' she said.

'Don't talk wet,' I said.

'I'm assuming you paid for this with the proceeds of the bag.'

'Aw, for fuck's sake,' Dogmeat said. 'I knew this would happen.'

'It wouldn't be so bad, Dave,' Sally continued. 'Me and you have always gotten on well.'

'Until now,' said Dogmeat.

'I don't see why we can't all get along together swimmingly.'

'It just wouldn't work,' Dogmeat said.

'It's going to have to,' Sally said. 'I keep thinking about that bag and what the police would think if they ever got wind of it.'

'Come on Sally, be reasonable.' I said.

'I consider this proposition to be perfectly reasonable under the circumstances,' she said.

'What circumstances are those then?' Dogmeat said.

'The circumstances that will land you in hot water if you don't accept my offer. Anyway, I'm going to leave it with you. You chaps have a lot to chew over.'

'That's just fuckin' marvellous,' Dogmeat said, as we watched Sally strut across the car park, full of confidence. 'Why weren't you more careful, Johnboy?'

'How was I to know?' I said. 'It's done now. The question is, what are we going to do?'

'Have you still got the padlock keys to the well?' Dogmeat asked.

'I couldn't do that, Dogmeat.'

'You don't have to do anything,' Dogmeat said. 'I'll arrange it.'

Chapter 15

"Glavin is God". My first community payback assignment was to remove graffiti from the Portland stone facade of Barnsley town hall. I had been hoping for something a bit more out of the way, somewhere not so public, but not having a choice, I'd washed up here in the middle of town sporting a high viz jacket and steel toecap boots. Fuckin' steel toecap boots in case I dropped the scrubbing brush on my foot. I wasn't happy about rubbing away the message either, because Ronnie Glavin was God, the greatest player to ever pull on a Barnsley shirt. I had a supervisor with me, who set me at my task before busying herself by sitting on the town hall steps messing with Facebook. She occasionally looked up to see if I'd legged it, but once she was satisfied that I wasn't going anywhere, she pretty much left me to it. After I'd sprayed the area with cleaning solution, I was to wait thirty minutes for it to do its work before I started rubbing. I had strict instructions to only use the scrubbing brush on difficult areas. The town hall was precious. So I was just standing there, waiting, bored senseless. This was only the first hour. If the remaining one hundred and ninety-nine were going to be like this, I couldn't imagine getting through to the end. Now I realised why people with time on their hands smoked cigarettes. It was something to do. We, that's Dogmeat and I, had decided that, rather than do one day a week, I would go full bore at it, knock off the hours so that I could get back to real work, flipping burgers.

To break the ennui, I decided to walk over and take a look at the information board regarding the building. My supervisor saw me leave my post, but she didn't seem at all concerned. All she wanted was a quiet life and anyway, she was probably in the throes of posting pictures of her breakfast. The town hall had been officially opened by the Prince of Wales in late 1933, I read. It had cost almost one hundred and forty-nine thousand pounds, which had apparently annoyed George Orwell who, in his book "The Road to Wigan Pier", had been very critical of the outlay.

'George Orwell wants to mind his own fuckin' business,' I remarked to myself. 'I don't know where he's from, but I'm fairly sure it's not Barnsley.'

'Hey bad boy. Are you talking to yourself?' I didn't need to look up to know that the voice belonged to Dogmeat.

'What are you doing here?'

'I'm here to give you encouragement, love,' he said. 'That's what mates do.'

'If you really want to help me, you'd go home.' Dogmeat's wheelchair was across the pavement, causing people to step into the road to get past him. Strangely, it was me who took the dirty looks.

'Pull yourself over here a bit, Dogmeat,' I said. 'You're blocking the way.'

'Fuck 'em,' was Dogmeat's not unexpected retort.

'Who's looking after the trailer?' I remembered that they would be shorthanded while I was away. 'You haven't left Mo to manage by himself, have you?'

'Course I haven't, Johnboy. Sally is helping out.'

'Tell me that's a joke,' I said.

'Why not?' Dogmeat said. 'We may as well use her.'

'She kept that quiet.' I was a little annoyed. 'She never said anything to me about it.'

'Did you tell her where you were going this morning?'

'I told her I have a building job on,' I said. 'Anyway, we're not really talking.'

'Well, there you are then,' Dogmeat said, as if he'd coordinated it all himself. Then I thought about it, and he had, hadn't he?

'I thought we were going to… err… you know?'

'Nobble her?' Dogmeat offered.

'Yeah,' I uttered.

'We will, Johnboy… at the right time, but I don't want you thinking about that.'

'Uh, what's happening?' Dogmeat exclaimed. A young man, who didn't fancy walking around Dogmeat, had grabbed his chair and pushed him to one side. This was something that happened from time to time, and the outcome was always the same. 'What the fuck do you think you're doing?'

Dogmeat was steaming.

'You were in the way pal. I was…' He didn't have time to finish his explanation. Dogmeat had rammed him into the low wall, and before the lad could finish his protestation, Dogmeat had laid him out on the concrete paving with a perfectly timed, right uppercut, where he lay motionless.

'You've killed him,' I groaned.

'Good,' said Dogmeat.

I turned to see my thirty-something supervisor doing a fair impression of a sprint. Time slowed as her bingo wings waved in synchronised harmony. All that was missing was the theme from "Chariots of Fire". In the fullness of time, she was standing beside me. The young man was just coming round.

'What have you done?' she screamed, surveying the carnage.

I looked around for support from Dogmeat, but he'd gone.

'It wasn't me,' I pleaded.

My first day on community payback could have panned out better.

The following day, I had been placed in a group. Apparently, I'd let myself down and couldn't be trusted with individual jobs even though I'd convinced the police that I hadn't hit the boy.

Problem is, I was there when he was decked and shit sticks. Not wanting to incriminate Dogmeat, I'd claimed that a stranger was the culprit, and I had no idea of his identity, apart from being a wheelchair user. I could tell they didn't believe me. It wasn't until they spoke to the victim that I was in the clear.

Agewise, I was the senior member of the group by a long way, but the thing that really made me stand out amongst the young men and women was my missing tattoos. I had nothing to share with the others, who stood in a huddle comparing artwork. Even the group supervisor, a youngster himself, was in on it. After a while they dispersed, and the leader called me.

'C'mon Grandad.' A titter rippled around the group. 'Grab a paint brush.'

We were in the church hall, tarting it up for free. It crossed my mind that we were putting bona fide decorators out of work, but I didn't say anything, preferring to keep my head down and stay out of trouble. I'd been paired with a young man who I guessed to be in his early twenties, but my estimate was hampered by a mop of curls and a pair of dark glasses. He was pleasant enough though and as the day went on, we got on well.

'What are you in for?' he asked.

'Criminal damage,' I said, proudly. He was so impressed that he relayed the story of the porch to the others. My stock was rising.

'You did right,' he assured me. 'I'd probably have left the porch alone and demolished him.'

'He was an old man,' I said.

'Who gives a fuck?' he said.

'How can you see to paint through those sunglasses?' I asked, changing the subject.

'Who gives a fuck?' Evidently, he didn't.

'How did you end up here?' I enquired.

'Wednesday,' he said.

'How's that?' I was intrigued.

'No, not cricket, football,' he said. 'Sheffield Wednesday at home. I headbutted a Wednesday fan.'

'Oh,' I said. 'I see.'

'He deserved it though.'

'Why?'

'I've just told you, he was a Wednesday fan.'

'Can't fault you then,' I said. I thought I better agree with him in case he head butted me. Apart from being completely blinkered regarding football, he seemed a perfectly reasonable lad. Strange things happen on match days, one being the temporary abandonment of rationality. I expect the abandonment of sobriety plays its part too.

'What's your name?' I asked.

'Ricky, You?'

'Johnboy,' I said, offering a hand, which Ricky shook vigorously.

'Nice to meet you, man,' he said.

'Ricky, you don't mind me asking,' I ventured, 'you're not an idiot. You shouldn't be here with these... err... others. Can't you control yourself?'

'That's just it, Johnboy. I can't. One minute I'm all right, then I do something stupid.'

'That's a shame,' I said. 'Do you have a job?'

'Right now, no, but I've had lots of jobs... mostly dead end. I set off at the bottom of the ladder and worked my way down. It's the way people treat you, man, no respect.'

'What was your last job?' I asked.

'I worked for a plumber. To be fair, the job was quite interesting. And the fella was a decent sort.'

'What went wrong?'

'He dropped me off from work one night and I tripped as I got out the van.'

'He sacked you for that?' I asked with incredulity.

'No, he didn't sack me for that,' Ricky said. 'I dropped my bag and all the copper fittings I'd nicked fell out... so that was that.'

'Did you need the fittings for some spare time work then, a little job on the side?'

'No fuckin' way,' Ricky said. 'I don't work any more than I have to.'

'So, why did you take them?'

'Because they were there, Johnboy, available, because they were there.'

'It makes no sense,' I said.

'Things don't have to make sense. Nothing makes sense, but everything happens for a reason,' Ricky mused. We'd both stopped painting and were giving the conversation our full attention.

'Do you really believe that?' I asked.

'Oh yeah, man... This is the reality I have created for myself, and I have to live in it. These are the problems I've made for myself. You're not really here, Johnboy.'

'I feel like I'm here,' I said. 'Everyone has problems. I have problems.'

'You don't exist,' Ricky said.

'I'm sure I do,' I said.

'You only exist in my reality,' Ricky insisted.

'Honestly Ricky, I exist... look.' I pinched my arm to illustrate my substance.

'When I've gone,' Ricky said. 'You'll cease to exist.'

'You better fuckin' stay here then,' I said, but Ricky ignored my comment.

'That's why it didn't matter when I dropped the nut on the Wednesday fan. He's gone now, he was never there. The only victim is me.'

'If that's true, Ricky,' I asked. 'Why did you create him?'

'A better question, Johnboy, is why did I create Sheffield Wednesday?'

'Come on, you two, snap time.' I jumped as the supervisor loudly interrupted our chat. 'You're not doing anything anyway.'

Some of us congregated around the hatch that opened into the kitchen. Some inside the kitchen making tea and coffee, others had gone outside for a Woodbine.

'Fancy a cuppa?' Ricky asked as he busied himself with the kettle.

'Lovely,' I said.

'Tea or coffee?'

'Coffee please,' I said. 'As long as it's not that cheap stuff that tastes like it's been scraped off the bottom of a budgie cage.'

'Quality stuff, this is.' Ricky held up a jar of Kenco.

'That'll do nicely,' I said. 'Is there no snap?'

'You bring your own sandwiches.' The supervisor chirped

184

up. 'You're not out on a jolly, you know. You wanna think yourself lucky you've got coffee.'

'All right, all right,' I said. 'I just wish someone had told me before I signed up. I'd have made a pack up.'

After an elongated break, the supervisor had managed to drag the smokers back inside, and Ricky and I returned to our corner to discuss world affairs, sex and football. Of particular concern to Ricky was the worry of Barnsley Football Club becoming a yo-yo club, alternately battling relegation, then challenging for promotion.

'We're up and down like a bride's nightie,' Ricky mused. I could see it concerned him a lot. I liked him, he was a good kid, just a little mixed up, that's all. I envisaged, that with a little encouragement, he could make something of himself. I even considered offering him a job in the trailer, but we were overstaffed as it was, and Dogmeat would never have agreed anyway. Still, I hoped he'd find his way in life. Maybe we'd keep in touch, who knows?

At the end of the shift, I offered Ricky a lift, which he accepted with the proviso that I dropped him off in the town centre. It was out of my way, but I didn't mind.

'What you going to do now?' I asked.

'I'm calling in at Bargain Booze for a big bottle of cider, then I'm going to meet some mates.'

'Sounds good to me,' I lied. I worried about him. I didn't ask, but I wondered where he was going to sleep. He may not even have a place to stay, although he looked clean and healthy. He must have sensed my concern because he replied.

'Don't worry about me, Johnboy,' he said. 'I'm sorted.'

We reached a row of shops and he asked me to stop there. As

he left the truck, he paused and put his hand in his pocket.

'No, I don't want anything,' I said, thinking he was going to pay me.

'I haven't got any spare money,' he said, 'but have this.' He withdrew a tin opener and handed it to me.

'What's that?' I asked.

'Don't you know? It's for opening cans.'

'Yes,' I said, 'I can see it's a tin opener, but why?' He shoved it firmly into my hand, so I put it in my jacket pocket.

'It's from the church hall,' he said.

'You stole it?' I asked.

'Borrowed it, long term,' he said.

'But why?'

'Because it was there,' Ricky said. 'You have it, I have loads of them. I'll see you later man, it's been sweet.'

'Okay,' I said. 'Don't be late tomorrow. Thanks for the… err… tin opener.' But he was already gone before I finished the sentence.

Arriving home, I'd almost forgotten that Sally was back. The moment I inserted the key in the lock and realised it was already open, was the moment my heart sank.

'Did you have a good day, love?' she sang, as if the past hadn't happened.

'All right,' I said, but she wasn't listening. She was more interested in telling me about her own goings on.

'I'm working in the burger van… and really enjoying myself.'

'It's a catering trailer,' I said, borrowing a quote from Dogmeat, just to be argumentative.

'Dave comes and goes,' she said, 'but me and Mo get on like

186

a house on fire.'

'Do you now?' For a moment, I was furious with Mo. I planned to have a stiff word with him.

'He's a lovely lad,' Sally said as I ascended the stairs. 'What's for dinner?'

'Make your own,' I said, electing to have a shower and go out. I couldn't stand being in the same house as her.

'I thought we had an agreement,' she shouted.

I never imagined it would happen, but I looked forward to the community hours and meeting Ricky again. In the church hall a few of the white, Formica tables had been lined up, end on end to create a long platform. I looked around and couldn't see Ricky, he was late no doubt, but we did have a couple of young police officers with us this morning to make up the numbers.

'Okay everyone,' the supervisor said. 'It looks like everyone is here who's going to be here.'

'Wait a minute,' I said. 'Someone's missing.'

'There's always someone missing.'

'Yes, but Ricky isn't here,' I protested.

'Who's Ricky?' the supervisor asked.

'The lad I was working with yesterday.'

'I can't remember his name,' the supervisor said, 'but I do know it isn't Ricky. We don't have a Ricky.'

'Well, where is he?'

'Not that it's any of your business, but he's completed his hours.'

'He never said anything,' I griped.

'Like I said.' The supervisor was becoming angry now. 'It's none of your business.'

I let it be and followed the instructions to join the line facing the table. Around fourteen or fifteen of us stood there, waiting to see what was in store for us. I thought we were going to receive one of those motivational speeches or something along those lines, but I'd read the situation wrongly.

One of the police officers stepped forward and addressed the line of ne'er do wells. 'Good morning, ladies and gentlemen,' he said with authority. 'There have been a number of thefts from the church hall whilst the redecoration has been taking place,' he continued. 'So much so that it would almost have been cheaper to employ a decorating firm.'

'That's what they should have done in the first place,' I said. A ripple of approval passed along the line.

'Quiet while the officer speaks,' shouted the supervisor. I was back in my school days.

'Thank you,' said the officer. 'I'm going to ask you who is the offender?'

'We all are,' chipped in a young girl. 'That's why we're here.'

'I'm specifically interested in the thefts from the church hall. Can anyone cast a little light on the situation?' ...Silence... 'No one?' ...Silence... 'No clue at all, anyone?' ...Silence.

'We're not grasses,' someone along the line said.

'Just as I thought,' said the officer.

'Snitches get stitches,' someone else added.

'Well,' said the officer. 'Fancy that, no one did it.' He nodded sagely. 'Now, I realise none of you will have upon your person, the missing microwave, or the shelves from the fridge, or the deep fat fryer, or indeed the toaster, but I'm going to ask you to turn out your pockets onto the table before you... we'll start at the end and work our way along.' He walked over to the first suspect. 'Right, empty your pockets.'

188

'It's not right this,' protested the young man at the end of the table. 'I've done nothing wrong. It's a breach of my civil liberties.' Nevertheless, he complied and proved his innocence. I was the sixth in line and watched with interest as the second person produced six control knobs from the range cooker.

'What's this then?' asked the officer.

'Cooker knobs,' came the answer. 'I've just bought them for my house.'

'Bit of a coincidence that the ones here in the kitchen are missing, isn't it?'

'I don't know anything about that, sir,' he said.

'When did you buy them?' asked the officer.

'The other day,' said the young man. 'I can't remember exactly.'

'You still have the receipt?'

'Lost it, sir.'

'I don't suppose you have a credit card record?'

'Bought them with cash sir.'

'I thought you would have.' The officer gave him a little nod and a knowing smile, just to let him know that he had his card marked. Moving along the line an elusive set of keys came to light before he was standing face to face with me.

'Do I really have to do this?' I asked. 'It's degrading.'

'Are you better than everyone else here?' he said.

'No,' I said.

'Turn 'em out then.'

'Okay,' I said, 'but I'm not happy about it.' I delved into the right pocket and retrieved various odds and ends, a dirty tissue, a couple of pencils, and an old train ticket from way back.

'Now the other one,' said the officer. A soon as my hand entered the pocket, I knew I was in trouble. I could feel the shape of the tin opener that I'd forgotten about. I gently placed it on the table.

The officer's eyes lit up with triumph.

'I can explain,' I said.

Chapter 16

Saturday in The Railway should have been a time to relax and forget about community hours, tin openers and annoying wives, but I hadn't allowed for Dogmeat. He found the tin opener incident hilarious and relayed it to Walt, who by small increments passed the story to the whole pub. People were nodding in my direction, sniggering. Random groups would burst into laughter after one of them had returned from the bar. The way their heads swung in my direction revealed the source of their mirth.

'You didn't have to tell everyone, Dogmeat,' I complained. 'I'm a laughing stock.'

'I only told Walt,' Dogmeat said.

'That's as good as standing on the table and making an announcement. I wouldn't have told you if I'd known you were going to broadcast it.'

'Ah, drink your beer and forget about it,' Dogmeat said.

'I think he's trying to, bro,' Mo said.

'Well said, Mo,' I said. 'I hear you and Sally are hitting it off.'

'Yeah,' Mo said. 'She's all right.'

'I hope you're going to run off with her,' I said. Mo laughed.

'She's a bit too old for me,' he said.

'Don't be getting too familiar,' Dogmeat said. 'She's only temporary until Johnboy finishes his bad boy classes.' A shiver ran through me when Dogmeat said that. I knew what he meant even if Mo hadn't grasped the real meaning.

Walt arrived with three pints and two plates. One held sandwiches and the other mini sausage rolls and growlers.

'Thanks Walt,' I said. 'But we didn't order any snap.'

'On the house, lads,' Walt said. 'They're left over from a do we had upstairs last night.'

'Nice one, Walt,' Dogmeat said.

'Thanks, bro,' Mo added.

'What kind of a do was that then, Walt?' I asked.

'Speed dating,' he answered. 'I could hear them banging around on the wooden floor above. God knows what they were up to. It sounded more like Line Dancing.'

'Lion dancing?' Mo asked, confused.

'Not Lion Dancing, cloth ears, Line Dancing... you know, when all the shit kickers get together for a shindig... you know, cowboy dancing.'

'Oh, right,' Mo said.

'Anyway, it wasn't that it was speed dating,' Walt said. 'They must have enjoyed it cos they've booked it on a regular basis.'

I took a bite of a ham sandwich. It tasted a bit stale and looking at it more closely I noticed that the edges were curling a little. 'Are you sure it was last night?' I asked.

'Might have been Thursday come to think of it. The sandwiches are free though, so I want no complaints,' Walt turned to Dogmeat and said. 'Keep your eye on Johnboy with the plates, Dave. I want them back.' Walt retreated, cackling as he went. I shot an accusatory glance in Dogmeat's direction, but he just shrugged and smiled. I gave the remainder of the ham sandwich to Bert, who had been asleep at my feet. He sniffed at my offering, refused and went back to sleep, so I left the old butty by his nose for when he felt more like tackling it.

No sooner had Walt left than we were joined by Jabba.

'You've got some neck,' Dogmeat spat.

'Aw c'mon, that's all water under the bridge,' Jabba giggled.

'It might be for you, Jabba,' Dogmeat said, 'but I bear grudges.'

'I've just heard about the...' Jabba was struggling to finish the sentence. His laughter was severely impeding his speech. 'I've just heard about...' Again, he failed. 'About the...'

'Fuckin' hurry up, Jabba,' I said. 'We've got things to discuss.'

'I've just heard about the tin opener.' It was too much for him. He was braying like a donkey.

'Fuck off will ya, Jabba?' I said.

Jabba looked at the miniature sausage rolls on the plate and said, 'How far away are those?' Again, he convulsed. Mo laughed with him.

'Don't encourage him, Mo,' I said. 'We'll never get rid of him.'

Dogmeat began moving around the table, and Jabba, seeing this, decided to move away.

'What a fuckin' doll's head,' Dogmeat exclaimed.

'He's gone now,' I said. 'What were we saying?'

'Can't remember,' Mo said, sipping his ale.

'Neither can I,' I said. 'It must be the alcohol.'

'Not to worry,' Dogmeat said. 'What I was going to say is, wouldn't it be nice if we were the only catering trailer in the area?'

'We'd be swamped, Dogmeat,' I replied. 'We've got a lot busier since Bob left the scene.'

'We have,' Dogmeat said. 'Wouldn't it be nice if we got busier still?'

'Oh, I don't know about that,' I said from behind my pint pot.

'Wouldn't it be nice if we could employ that young lass with the big tits?' Dogmeat was acting all dreamy like.

'We've got Sally,' Mo said.

'I've told you once, Mo,' Dogmeat snapped. 'Once Johnboy has finished his stint, she's gone.'

'That young lass with the big tits sounds good to me, Dogmeat,' I said.

'Wouldn't it be nice if we could employ two of 'em?' Dogmeat said.

'I'm assuming she'll have two,' I said.

'Lasses, not tits. I already work with two tits,' said Dogmeat. 'Wouldn't it be nice if we could employ a couple of lasses and sit in here drinking beer?'

'I like selling burgers,' Mo said.

'Well, you can stay in there,' I said. 'You can be Head Chef, nay, Gourmet Chef.'

'More like Gormless Chef,' Dogmeat said.

'I like the sound of that,' said Mo. 'Can I have Michelin stars?'

'No point in that,' Dogmeat said. 'The trailer never moves. Those tyres will last forever.' He laughed at his own joke even though it wasn't funny. 'I'm going to get you a fuck off great chef's hat Mo.'

'I'd like that,' Mo smiled.

'Wouldn't it be nice, eh? How many other burger vans do you know of around here, Johnboy?'

'You mean catering trailers don't you, Dogmeat?'

'Ours is a catering trailer, Johnboy. The others are greasy burger vans. How many do you know of?'

'I know there's a good one in the marketplace,' I said. 'The girl who works in there is lovely.'

'I'm not bothered about the quality of the food or the affability of the staff,' Dogmeat said. 'I just want to know where they are.'

'I just said where it was,' I said. 'In the fuckin' marketplace.'

'Make a note, Mo,' Dogmeat said. Mo pulled out his notebook and scribbled "Market Place".

'One in the B & Q car park,' Mo said.

'Write it down,' Dogmeat said.

'At least two on the by-pass,' I said. 'But what's that got to do with us?'

'Bear with me, Johnboy,' said Dogmeat. 'I've got a plan.'

'Oh dear,' I said.

'There's one on the industrial estate,' Mo said, writing as he spoke.

'You're doing well, Mo.' Dogmeat gave a slow, deep laugh.

'*Fuck me,*' I thought. '*Dogmeat and Mo have turned into Pinky and the Brain.*'

Back in the trailer for the Sunday lunchtime session and Dogmeat was still harping on about the other burger vans in the vicinity. Wouldn't it be nice to do this or that, to have this, that or the other? Why couldn't he be happy with what we had? The weather had turned a little, with a chill wind blowing down from the Pennines, creating little eddies that swirled the litter in the car park. Bert was content to curl up and sleep in the truck, only appearing occasionally to eat a bratwurst. His body clock was finely tuned to rouse him at sausage time. Mercifully, Sally was at home. She'd no doubt be watching some boring cooking programme, arming herself with the bullets to disparage my cooking.

'Cheeseburger and chips please,' said a middle aged man in a flat cap.

'Turned cool, hasn't it?' I had become very adept at small talk, and I chatted away with ease as I prepared the food, took the money, and issued the change.

'I paid less than this last time,' he said, examining the coins I had given him.

'You were lucky then,' I said. 'We'll let you off this time but don't tell anyone.'

'A nice lady served me,' he said. '*She* didn't have an attitude problem.'

'Neither have I,' I said, snatching the food back from the edge of the counter. 'Fuck off and get your dinner somewhere else.'

'Well, that saw him off,' Dogmeat said.

'He was an arsehole,' I said.

'Because Sally looked after him?'

'She's fuckin' haunting me. Even when she's not here, she's here.'

'Wouldn't it be nice,' Dogmeat said, 'if she was gone?'

'Nice?' I said. 'It would be fuckin' marvellous.'

'Wouldn't it be nice if we could pick and choose our customers.'

'I suppose so,' I said.

'Looks like we already do, bro,' Mo said.

'Soon,' Dogmeat said. 'Soon.'

I was in a foul mood when I arrived home and Sally was straight on my case, shouting from the comfort of the settee, wanting to know what was on the menu.

'I'm not cooking for you,' I said. 'That's it, I've done.'

'But…'

'No but's,' I cut in. 'You can see to yourself.' I began to prepare myself a cheese and piccalilli sandwich. Sally was chuntering away, but I'd blocked my ears to her voice. I liked to spread an even coating of piccalilli on the bread before adding the cheese, so I dug deep into the jar and created a thick, yellow base, before swapping the knife for a sharper one in order to cut the cheese into slices of perfect thickness. Around three millimetres was the optimum gauge. I opened the fridge and… the cheese was gone. No cheese!

'Where's the fuckin' cheese?' I shouted. 'It was there this morning.'

'No need to shout.' Sally was standing right behind me.

'Where's the fuckin' cheese?' I hadn't lowered my voice by a single decibel. I was livid.

'Bert finished it. There really wasn't much in there.' Bert heard his name and pricked up his ears.

'Bert has been with me. You've had it haven't you? You knew damn well that the cheese was mine.' I was still shouting, waving the knife in front of her face. Bert was becoming more and more uncomfortable.

'Don't be a baby,' Sally said. 'It's only a bit of cheese.'

'Mature cheddar,' I screamed. 'Mature fuckin' cheddar. What am I supposed do now, you selfish cow, have a piccalilli and piccalilli sandwich?'

'You put that much piccalilli on that it probably wouldn't be any different,' Sally said. 'I'm surprised you can taste the cheese anyway.'

'You fuckin' bitch.' I took a step forward, waving the knife. Bert had seen enough, he leapt up and darted across the kitchen toward the safety of the lounge. Sally had stepped back at the same time as Bert passed behind, tripping her, and causing her to fall backwards. Bert was out of the room before the back of Sally's head cracked against the kitchen table. Her head bounced off the wooden table before she slumped to the floor, motionless. It took me a moment to gather my senses and assess the scene. The knife, tightly gripped in my right hand, had become white hot, so I tossed it into the sink and moved closer to Sally. I bent over her and put my face close to hers, closer than it had been for a long, long time. There was no sign of life. Her accusing, dead eyes were staring at me. I'd killed her, no, Bert had killed her. I don't know, me and Bert had killed her. It didn't matter, she was dead. You didn't need to be a medical expert to see the spirit had left. I was at once, happy and concerned. I would have said "sad", but I wasn't at all sad, however, I had been left with a problem.

I called Dogmeat and explained what had happened.

'It was an accident, wasn't it?' he asked.

'Yes,' I said. 'Pure accident.'

'Then call an ambulance straight away.'

'She's dead. No doubt.'

'Call an ambulance,' Dogmeat insisted. 'Now.'

I did as Dogmeat said, but in explaining the accident I omitted the argument and the knife. After all, I hadn't touched her with the knife and before I called for the paramedics, I'd cleaned it, put it away and thrown the half-made sandwich in the bin. They gave instructions over the phone, designed to revive her, but I knew it would have been a waste of time, so I told them I was carrying out their wishes, but in reality, I couldn't bear to touch her. When assistance arrived, they quickly examined her and drew the same conclusions. Not long after, the police turned up and asked me to run through the story. I blamed Bert, but he couldn't hear me from the lounge. They asked me if there was anywhere I could stay, as the kitchen was a potential crime scene.

'What do you mean?' I asked. 'Crime scene?'

'Normal procedure,' they said. 'Not natural causes, is it?'

'No, but... are you accusing me?'

'Of course not. It's just something we have to do. You can't stay here for a day or two.'

'I'll find somewhere,' I said.

'Don't go anywhere we can't contact you.'

Bert and I stayed with Dogmeat in his bungalow whilst the police did what they had to do. In packing a bag, I made sure I took the money with me in case they carried out an in depth search of the house. I couldn't see why they would, but I was taking no chances.

'Proper result, that was,' Dogmeat said.

'It is if I don't end up in prison because of it,' I said.

'That's not going to happen. It was an accident... well done, Bert lad.' Dogmeat patted Bert on the head as he laid his chin on the settee.

'I hope not.'

'It's saved us a job,' said Dogmeat. 'It's what you call a happy accident. I was all for knocking her on the head and dropping her down the well, but Bert's done it for us. Give him an extra Bonio or whatever he likes.' Dogmeat shuffled himself into a more comfortable position and invited Bert to join him on the settee. 'Come on, my old son, jump up here.' Bert obliged and immediately adopted the curled up sleeping position. 'I've often thought about getting a dog you know.'

'Why don't you,' I said. 'It would be good company for you... and they're a lot more loyal than wives.'

'Mainly because of that.' Dogmeat pointed to his wheelchair parked in the corner of the room.

'You can take the dog for a walk in the wheelchair,' I said. 'You see lots of people doing it.'

'It's not that easy, is it?' Dogmeat said. 'Buying the food, going to the vets, paying for the fuckin' vets, manoeuvring past the fuckin' idiots on the street. It's hard enough just getting the wheelchair through them without a dog. Then there's the dickheads who park on the pavement. No, I don't think it would work.'

'It's a shame you feel like that,' I said. 'I think it would do you a lot of good.'

'And how am I supposed to pick up the dog crap,' Dogmeat added. 'I remember the good old days when your dog could shit anywhere, and nobody batted an eyelid.'

'I'm not sure they were the good old days.' I baulked. 'That street we grew up on was known as "The Street of a Thousand Arses". You really had to watch your step. It was a case of eyes down.'

'Aye,' Dogmeat laughed. 'It was that. And the dogs used to take themselves for a walk.'

'They did, you didn't see many people with dogs on leads.'

'They must have had a set time and place to meet, because they always ended running round in a group, like teenagers,' Dogmeat reminisced. 'But they didn't cause any trouble. They were all mongrels as well, most of them some shade of brown. Not many pedigrees around in those days, at least not roaming the streets.'

'They were as good as gold,' I said. 'They did cause a hell of a mess though.'

'You can't expect them to clean up after themselves though,'

Dogmeat said. 'Did I ever tell you about that time a German Shepherd crapped on our doorstep?'

'I can't recall,' I replied.

'Mi mam went mad,' Dogmeat said. 'She wouldn't have minded, but his dog did too.'

Chapter 17

Weeks went by and the police seemed happy with the circumstances surrounding Sally's death. Things had generally settled down after her cremation and I'd played the grieving husband to good effect. It's not easy pretending to be sad when you're on a real high. After a week or two, the well-wishers left me alone to get on with it, but I was beginning to wonder what "it" was. The euphoria had died, and my spirits slowly dropped along with the autumn sun. The clocks had gone back in preparation for the winter, making the dark evenings stretch longer and longer. Whereas we were once complaining about the heat in the trailer, we now welcomed it, although the novelty of working in there had long worn off.

'Cheer up, Johnboy,' Walt said, placing the ale on the table. 'You've got a face like a slapped arse.'

'Ah, sorry, Walt, I was just thinking.'

'Well, you want to pack that in, it's a mugs game.'

'Walt's right you know,' Dogmeat said. 'You haven't been the same since Sally went. You're not missing her, are you?'

'Fuck no,' I said. 'I just can't seem to get motivated these days. I don't do anything apart from work, come here and take him out.' I gestured towards Bert, sleeping on the motionless treadmill.

'Don't you like coming here, bro?' Mo asked, concerned.

'Course I do... but I don't do anything different. Everything's the same.'

'It's a good same though, isn't it, bro?' Mo asked.

'It's not bad,' I said, 'but it's not different either.'

'What do you want to do?' Dogmeat asked.

'I don't know, I just feel down.'

'You've got nowt to feel down about? Look at me in this fuckin' wheelchair.'

'I know,' I said. 'Leave me be, I'll be all right.'

'No,' Walt said, directing his points at Dogmeat. 'He could be suffering from SAD or something. We need to get him one of those sun lamp jobbies.'

'What you on about, Walt?' Dogmeat asked.

'I hear a lot of things working in this place, mostly drivel, but now and again I pick something up that could be useful, and I'm telling you, there's these lamps that cheer you up.'

'Don't be so fuckin' daft, Walt, reacted Dogmeat sceptically. 'Sometimes you come out with some right tripe.'

'No, he's right,' said Mo. 'My cousin used one for months.'

'And how is he now?'

'He's in heaven, bro,' Mo said sadly. 'Pussy on tap. He killed himself.'

'That's just a one off,' Walt said, seeing my face. 'He was probably beyond help before he got the lamp. If we get one for Johnboy now, we could probably save him.'

'I think we should track one down one of these magic lamps before it's too late,' said Dogmeat, now convinced that this was the solution.

'Can you just stop worrying about me?' I said, but they carried on as if I wasn't there. A young girl wandered into the bar area.

'Eight,' Dogmeat said.

'I'm with you on that, bro,' Mo said. 'It's an eight from me.'

'Johnboy?' Dogmeat needed my score.

'Eight,' I said.

'You didn't even look at her.'

'I did,' I said. 'She's an eight.'

'You fuckin' didn't,' Dogmeat said. 'Fuckin' pull yerself together, man.'

'You can't say that,' Walt said. 'He could be mentally ill.'

'He's a fuckin' wuss, that's what he is.'

'I'm all right,' I said. 'Let it be will you.'

'He needs a girlfriend,' Dogmeat said. 'Someone to snap him out of it, give him a whole new set of problems.'

'That's the last thing I need,' I protested vainly.

'He's not going to get one acting like that is he?' Dogmeat pulled on his pint. 'He needs to give his head a shake.'

'I don't want a girlfriend, and I don't want a fuckin' lamp.'

'Do you know anybody suitable, Mo?'

'No,' Mo said. 'Not in that age bracket.'

'Steady on, Mo,' I said. 'I'm not that old, am I?'

'There you go,' Dogmeat said. 'There's life in the old dog yet.'

'I'm not interested,' I said.

'Why don't you bring him to the next speed dating session?' Walt suggested. 'We do an over forties one now.'

'That's not a bad idea, Walt,' Mo said.

'Am I here?' I asked. 'Do I exist?'

'I'll have a look at the calendar and let you know.' Walt departed, happy in the knowledge that he'd made the world a better place.

'I'm not going,' I said.

'Aw, c'mon, Johnboy,' Dogmeat said. 'It'll do you good, even if nobody wants you.'

'What do you mean, if nobody wants me?'

'Let's face it, Johnboy,' Dogmeat said. 'You're no Brad Pitt are you?'

'I'm not that bad am I? You told me to get a girlfriend and in the next breath you're telling me I'm plug ugly.'

'Take no notice of him, bro,' Mo said. 'He's winding you up, you're lovely.'

The big evening arrived, and I was cajoled into attending. As we gathered in the bar area Dogmeat was giving me advice on how to chat shit. He was animated, looking around at the tables that were populated by women only. I was beginning to realise that it was Dogmeat who was interested in this event, merely using me as an excuse to be here. Mo, being a married man and much younger than us, had decided to take a rain check on this one.

'She doesn't look too bad.' Dogmeat discreetly nodded towards a group of ladies occupying a table near the toilets.

'Which one?' I asked.

'The one in the tight top. What do you think?'

I looked across, and to be fair she was quite tidy for an old 'un. The problem with aging is that as your body starts falling to bits, it neglects to tell your mind. You're still attracted to young fit ones, but reality requires you to lower the bar to just above ground level. 'Aye,' I said, 'let's hope she's going upstairs.'

No one had given a thought as to how Dogmeat was going to arrive upstairs in the function room. The Railway didn't have a lift, so we were going to have to get creative. Luckily, a few lads from the football team were in and offered their assistance, which would have been very kind had they not consumed so much alcohol. The stairway was quite steep and narrow with a right-angled turn at the top.

'Fuckin''ell,' Dogmeat said. 'Half the punters won't make it up here by the look of them.'

The goalkeeper took the front end of the wheelchair whilst a left sided midfielder took the rear and began to ascend the stairs.

'Don't drop me,' Dogmeat said, 'or I'll fuckin' drop you.'

'Don't worry,' said the goalkeeper. 'You're in safe hands.'

'How many goals did you let in last Sunday morning.'

'Only six,' said the goalkeeper.

'I'm worried.'

The goalkeeper, being a tall lad, cracked the back of his head on a piece of wood that crossed the staircase halfway up, but it didn't seem to faze him at all.

'Go steady,' Dogmeat said, having felt the jolt himself.

'Chill, will ya?' said the goalkeeper.

It all went smoothly until they reached the bend in the staircase. The goalkeeper, full of ale, would have had a job on just reversing himself around the bend without the wheelchair. The left-sided midfielder, being short in stature, struggled to hold Dogmeat up above his head.

'Wouldn't it have been better if the tall lad had been at the back?' Dogmeat asked as he held on for dear life.

'Mebbe so,' said the goalkeeper, 'but we're almost there now.'

'Well, fuckin' hurry up. I'm pulling four Gs here.'

Safe ground was reached and Dogmeat was placed safely on the parquet floor. I thanked the lads on Dogmeat's behalf because I could see he wasn't going to do it himself. Looking around, I was quite disappointed with what I saw. I expected a to see a large room, but at some time in the past a wall had been built as a divider and we were in a quite small space. Tables of various shapes and sizes were randomly crammed around the room. The wooden chairs that filled the spaces between the tables looked extremely uncomfortable.

'Fuckin' ell,' Dogmeat said. 'It's not exactly the Tower Ballroom is it?'

'I thought they did line dancing up here,' I said.

'It can only have been one line,' said Dogmeat. 'But it wasn't line dancing, was it? Walt said it just sounded that way.'

'Ah yes,' I said, remembering.

'Come, come.' A middle-aged woman with a pile of black hair heaped on her head clapped her hands to bring us to attention. 'Take your places the best you can. Ladies try to keep to the left and gents to the right. It's a very good turn out tonight, so space is at a premium.'

'You're not kidding there, love,' Dogmeat said.

'Some of you already know me, but for those that don't, my name is Fiona and my job is to bring lonely hearts together. Before we begin though, I'm going to move amongst you collecting subscriptions.'

'Get your wallet out,' Dogmeat said to me.

'Am I paying for you then?' I asked.

'We're here because of you,' Dogmeat said.

You didn't have to come,' I protested.

'You wouldn't be here if I wasn't. Get your hand in your pocket.'

After a lot of rooting in purses, Fiona was satisfied that she hadn't missed anyone and continued with her monologue. 'As I said, the reason we are all here is to find love.'

'Just a shag would do to be going on with,' Dogmeat said rather too loudly.

'You may have noticed that due to a sudden illness we are a lady short, so I will gladly plug that gap. I will be the twelfth

207

man, or lady in this case. To keep things fair, I will be drawing numbers from this bag and issuing them to the ladies. The gentlemen must quickly take their seats opposite a lady, but you must remember her number as you will be moving to the next lady who has the sequential number. That is to say, two comes after one. Is that clear?'

'Not really,' said a bemused-looking bloke sporting a flat cap.

'Good, then we'll begin. We have five minutes with each partner, so use your time wisely.'

Dogmeat and I were sharp out of the blocks and occupied the first two places and the end of the line. I dropped in across from Fiona, number twelve, so my first five minutes would be with her. Dogmeat was next to me opposite a lady with bottle bottom glasses and a number two card.

'Do you come here often?' I asked.

'As a matter of fact, I do,' said Fiona. 'I run the session, remember? You have me at a disadvantage. You already know my name.'

'Oh sorry,' I said. 'I'm Johnboy.' Now I'd got up close and personal with Fiona, I could see that she was a lady who looked after herself. Quite impressive really.

'Have you been alone for a long a while, Johnboy?'

'No, not really,' I said. 'My wife died recently.'

'I'm so sorry,' Fiona reached over and touched my hand. 'Had she been ill?'

'No,' I said. 'It was an accident.'

I couldn't help but overhear the conversation from next door.

'Are you on wheels?' Bottle Bottom asked Dogmeat.

'Yes, I'm upwardly mobile, especially when I'm halfway up Market Hill,' said Dogmeat.

'I couldn't be doing with anyone in a wheelchair,' she said.

'I don't think you're in a position to be fussy,' Dogmeat replied.

'No, no. A spaz would be too much for me. Take too much looking after, wouldn't you?' I expected Dogmeat to blow his top, but I think he felt sorry for her more than anything else.

Fiona was glancing at her watch and the five minutes was soon up. She reached to the floor beside her and produced a school bell. I fancied she used to be a head teacher. 'Time,' she announced. 'Move along.'

Dogmeat's next liaison was with number three, the lady in the tight top. Unfortunately, she was at the far end of the room. A cacophony of shuffling and scraping chairs arose from the wooden floor as Dogmeat fought his way to far end of the table.

'Get out of the fuckin' way, will you?' he cried. 'Let me through.'

Everyone took their new places, but his way was still blocked. I only had to move up a couple of places, so I suggested to Dogmeat that we swap numbers for this one.

'Fuck off, Johnboy. I'm up at the end there with the tasty one.' Dogmeat was ramming chairs indiscriminately, all the time cursing as he went.

'Be careful,' one bloke said. 'I've just had a pulmonary embolism.'

'Then you shouldn't be here should you? What good are you gonna be to a woman? You'd be out of breath before you got your belt undone. I'm surprised you made it up the fuckin' stairs.'

Dogmeat pressed on, banging and crashing, interrupting conversations and generally causing mayhem. I was opposite number two, who hadn't noticed my presence at all, so engrossed in the shenanigans occurring a few feet away, she was. 'My name's Johnboy,' I said.

'Yes,' she said.

'I'm a regular downstairs but I've never been up here before.'

'Yes,' she said again. She was with me, but she wasn't.

'I murdered my wife not long ago,' I said, 'well kind of, it was an accident really. The dog did it.'

'Yes.'

'I've also been involved in the murders of a few other people as well.'

'Yes,' she said. 'Lovely.' Still, she hadn't looked at me.

'I found a bag with a lot of cash in it and it's changed my life big time.'

Eventually Dogmeat reached his hard-fought-for destination and everyone's attention returned to the matter in hand and number two smiled across at me.

'You were saying, sweetheart?' she said.

There was no time to answer. Fiona had rung the bell again.

'For fuck's sake.' Dogmeat was kicking off again. 'I've only been here thirty seconds. Who designed this system?'

'It may be better if we allow the gentleman in the wheelchair to take his place first,' Fiona called out, in an effort to avert a repeat of the chaos. I was now entertaining a dishevelled-looking creature. A solitary tear ran down her cheek.

'What's wrong, love?' I asked, concerned.

'My husband left me.'

'Oh, I'm sorry to hear that,' I commiserated.

'He went off with another woman.' More tears emerged from her sad eyes. 'A younger woman. A better-looking woman.'

'You'll get over it, love. I can see it's still raw, but time heals everything. You'll get over it.'

'We'd been together eighteen years.'

'You'll be fine.' I lied. I could see that she wasn't going to be fine. 'What's your name, love?'

'Cathy. He said he'd love me forever, but he lied.'

'People say things,' I said. 'And I'm sure he meant it at the time.'

'He lied to me.' Now the dam had well and truly burst, and the tears flowed unchecked. 'I'm so lonely.'

'Believe me, Cathy,' I said, holding her hand. 'You'll get over it. Things will get better. How long since he left?'

'Twelve years,' she said.

As the session moved to a close, I reflected on who I'd met and decided it hadn't been a complete waste of time. Some of the ladies were quite interesting, the most impressive being Fiona. The one in the tight top had turned out to be the female version of Shallow Hal. Rather than ask any questions, she filled the five minutes with verbal diarrhoea, extolling the virtues of herself and her extended family. A real let down, and she didn't even ask my name. Five minutes had been four minutes too many.

At last, amid much jibbering and jabbering, the punters shuffled off downstairs to the bar to enjoy half a lager. I left Dogmeat with Fiona, assuring him that I would find some hardy volunteers to carry him down.

'Don't ask those fuckin' dopey footballers,' he said.

I didn't struggle to find willing helpers. Most people are more than happy to assist someone in need. This time, the two young men I found were sober and carried out the task with care and precision.

'It's like riding on air,' Dogmeat said. 'Thanks very much, lads.'

We decided to have a drink at our usual table. I'd left Bert at home, so there was no treadmill exercise for him tonight.

'How do you think that went?' Dogmeat asked.

'It was all right I suppose,' I replied.

'Only all right? I thought it was quality.'

'I thought you'd got the face on cos you couldn't get near the tidy one?'

'No, I'm fine with it,' said Dogmeat.

'You didn't miss much anyway. She was an arsehole. There wasn't a lot to pick from though was there?'

'Oh, I don't know,' mused Dogmeat. 'The older generation have had time to develop a bit of character, you know, they are what life has made them.'

'Aye,' I said. 'Some of them are right fuckin' headcases.'

'How'd it go, lads?' Walt had come over for feedback.

'It was all right,' I said.

'Don't listen to him, Walt,' Dogmeat said. 'It was bang on. We enjoyed it.'

'You made enough noise,' said Walt. We couldn't hear ourselves think down here for banging and scraping. I thought the line dancers were loud, but you've gone one step beyond tonight.'

'You haven't had any line dancers, Walt,' I said.

'Oh,' said Walt. 'Haven't I? I'll take your word for it. But you were definitely louder than the line dancers that I didn't have.'

'You can blame Dogmeat for that,' I said.

'Now be fair,' Dogmeat protested. 'That room isn't really fit for purpose, is it?'

'It used to be one large room,' Walt said. 'But at some time in the past, long before I came here, it was split into three for some reason.'

212

'Have you ever thought about getting an elevator?' Dogmeat said.

'Who needs a lift when we've got a football team?'

'Those fuckin' halfwits? I'm surprised they can stand up long enough to kick a ball.'

'I must admit, they're not very good,' Walt said. 'In fact, they're bottom of the league.'

'Why do you bother?' I asked.

'They buy beer,' Walt said. 'Anyway, tell me, did you pull?'

'No,' I said. 'They weren't really my type.'

'What about you, Dave?'

'Aye, I did all right,' said Dogmeat.

'Ah bollocks,' I said. 'You spent most of the time crashing chairs around.'

'I'm telling you,' Dogmeat insisted. 'I did all right.'

'Tell us more.' Walt was all ears now.

'I've arranged to take someone out.'

'He's lying,' I said.

'Why would I lie?' Dogmeat asked.

'To stroke your own ego mebbe?'

'Please yourself what you think,' Dogmeat said. 'But I'm going for dinner next week with a nice lady.' I swear I saw Dogmeat's chest puff out.

'Which one?' I said. 'There were no nice ladies up there.'

'Fiona,' Dogmeat finally announced.

'Fiona?' I exclaimed. 'I fancied her.'

'I thought you said they were all munters,' said Dogmeat.

'They were, most of 'em, but Fiona was all right.'

'You should have said something to her then,' Dogmeat said.

'You sneaky bastard,' I complained.

'Hey, Johnboy. All's fair in love and war.'

'I know, but you were supposed to be fixing me up.'

'You said you weren't bothered,' said Dogmeat.

'I'll leave you lads to it,' Walt said, sensing the mood change.

Chapter 18

I left Mo to open the hatch and fire up the appliances whilst I sat outside at one of the tables with Dogmeat. When the urn had reached a suitable temperature, he brought out a couple of steaming, cardboard cups. We thanked him for the coffee before he returned to preparing the trailer for the day's business. He was a good lad, never a moan or a complaint. An absolute diamond was Mo. It was Friday, so I'd called off at the newsagent for a copy of the Barnsley Chronicle, or the Chronic Barnacle as we affectionately called it. I scanned the back page for the football news as I spoke to Dogmeat. Bert sat at my feet, gazing up at me in the hope a few scraps of food would fall his way even though the table was empty.

'How are you getting on with Fiona?' I asked.

'I've given her the elbow,' Dogmeat replied.

'I thought you liked her.'

'I did at first, but it was getting a bit intense.'

'In what way?' I asked.

'Well, to start with, she kept asking to come round my place.'

'What's wrong with that?'

'It's my place, not hers or anyone else's. If I want to leave dirty undercrackers on the floor, I can.'

'You don't do that do you?'

'No, I don't,' Dogmeat said. 'What kind of dirty fucker do you think I am?'

'But you just said…'

'What I'm saying is that if I want to leave dirty undercrackers on the floor, I can. I didn't say I was going to.'

'You've fuckin' lost me.'

'The point is, I don't want a woman in there rearranging things and filling the place with pink shit.'

I flipped the newspaper to the front page and read the headline, "Police Investigating Burger Van Fires". I read on, "In the early hours of Sunday morning, two burger vans at two different sites were razed to the ground."

'Is this anything to do with you?' I brandished the newspaper at Dogmeat.

'Me?' Dogmeat's smile told me all I needed to know. 'How could I do a thing like that? Look at me.' He looked down at his wheelchair.

'You got the lads to do it didn't you? You can't do that. You can't just do what you fuckin' like you know.' I was outraged.

'Why not?' Dogmeat asked, clearly befuddled by my reaction.

'Because... because there are laws.'

'So?'

'So, there are some things you simply don't do,' I explained.

'Like giving a hedgehog a balloon for its birthday?'

'No,' I said. 'Like burning burger vans.'

'It's okay to kill people then?'

'No,' I said, looking around in case anyone was listening, 'it's not, but we didn't have a choice, did we?'

'Of course we had a choice,' Dogmeat said. 'And we chose to do it. You chose to do it, so get down off your ivory tower. What I have just done is eliminate the competition, which will in turn drive more custom to us, which will mean more money in your pocket, which will mean the young lass with the big tits will

216

arrive sooner. It's a no-brainer, a pure and simple business decision. You'll thank me for it.'

Dogmeat had a point about the killings, and I didn't have an answer, so I rose and joined Mo in the trailer.

The morning was bright and crisp with a cloudless sky, apart from a few interlopers lurking on the horizon.

'Nice day, bro,' Mo said.

'Lovely,' I said. 'Have you seen what Dogmeat has done?'

'Yeah,' said Mo.

'And what do you think about it?' I asked.

'Not bothered either way,' Mo said.

I looked over to the tables, at Dogmeat casually reading the newspaper, then at Mo who was standing over the hotplate whistling a merry tune. Nobody was bothered, so I went along with it. No good trying to swim against the tide. Fuck it.

A carload of youngsters pulled up too close to the tables and chairs for comfort. 'Gis a hot dog will ya, garcon?' said the driver. He didn't look old enough to have a driving licence, and thinking about it, he probably didn't.

'Do I look French?' I asked.

'What ya mean?' he asked as the three other lads gathered around him.

'Garcon,' I said, 'it's French.'

'I didn't know that,' said the driver. 'Did you know that, Danny?'

'No, I dint,' grunted one of the lads.

'We all want hot dogs,' said the driver. 'Four hot dogs with onions and mustard.'

'I don't want onions,' said a tall lad.

'Four hot dogs,' said the driver, chewing gum. 'One without onions.'

217

'I don't want mustard.' A black lad in a hoodie piped up. 'I don't like it.'

'Four hot dogs, one without onions and one without mustard.'

'I don't want a hot dog,' said Danny. 'I want a burger.'

'For fuck's sake.' The driver was agitated now. 'I'm getting you a free hot dog, blud. Can't you be satisfied with that?'

'Free?' I blurted. 'I don't think so, son.'

'Look here, pal,' said the driver. 'We ain't got money, so you're going to give us hot dogs.'

'And a burger,' Danny said.

'Shut up, Danny. I'm negotiating.'

'Sorry, Bronco.'

'Fuckin' 'ell, Danny. How many times have I told you not to say my name in public?'

'Sorry, Bronco... er... sorry... sorry.'

'You fuckin' retard,' said the driver. 'Anyway, back to business.'

'There is no business 'til I see the colour of your money,' I said.

'I'll give you five pence and you'll be sorry you crossed me. I like hot dogs. I want one. I'll take one off your hands... four... I'll take four off your hands.'

'Three and a burger,' said Danny.

'Fuck up, Danny.'

'Yeah, be quiet, Danny,' I said. 'What is this anyway? Dreadlock holiday in Barnsley?'

'You're going to give me four hot dogs... three hot dogs.'

'And a...'

'Shut up, Danny,' I said before he could finish. 'Why on earth do you think for one moment that I'm going to give free food to a fuckin' article like you?'

'Because of this,' said the driver, pulling an eight-inch blade from his clothing. Both Mo and I took a step back when we realised what he was brandishing.

'How about this?' Dogmeat, who had been looking on from his table, lowered the Chronic Barnacle to reveal the pistol he'd kept just for moments like this.

'Woah,' said the driver. 'We were only having a laugh.'

'You're not laughing now though, are you?' Dogmeat said gleefully.

'Who wants the first bullet?' I hoped Dogmeat was bluffing.

'No need for that,' said the driver. 'We'll be on our way.'

'Leave the knife,' Dogmeat said.

'Sure.' The driver placed the blade on the counter and began to back off toward the car. 'Come on, lads, let's get out of here.'

'Don't come back,' Dogmeat said. 'I know who you are... Bronco.'

'Fuckin' 'ell, Danny,' the driver said. 'What did I tell you?'

'Bye,' I said, waving as they piled into the car.

'What about my burger?' I heard Danny ask before they sped off.

'How long have you been packing that thing?' I asked.

'Only recently, Johnboy. When I thought things might be hotting up,' Dogmeat replied.

'What if they tell the police?'

'Don't be daft, Johnboy, they're telling nobody.'

'Well, you wanna be careful, that's all I'm saying.'

'I am being careful,' said Dogmeat. 'That's why I'm carrying this.' He kissed the barrel of the pistol.

'For fuck's sake, put it away before someone sees it,' I said.

'Stop being a pussy,' Dogmeat said. 'I'm off to get some gear now, so play nice, you two, see you later.'

'Come on, Mo,' I said, turning away from Dogmeat. 'Steady away today, eh? Shouldn't be too busy.'

'Yeah, bro,' Mo said. 'I'll make us another brew.'

Dogmeat left the car park, so I put the crazy fucker out of my mind and settled down to my shift. My spirits lifted as the morning wore on. 'Do you know what I'd like to do one day, Mo?'

'What's that, bro?'

'I'd like to tour Europe in a motorhome.'

'Sounds like a plan to me.' Mo nodded.

'A breakfast of churros and chocolate, the sun glistening on the med. Senoritas strolling by, taking the morning air.'

'Do you think it's really like that?' Mo asked.

'It is in my head.'

'Do it then, bro,' said Mo. 'Don't just talk about it, do it.'

'While ever it's in my head, Mo, it's perfect. Reality spoils things.'

'You have the money,' said Mo. 'Make it happen.'

'Would you come with me?'

'I have a family,' said Mo, 'but you know I would if I could.'

'I do, Mo,' I said. 'You're a good 'un.' I squeezed his shoulder as a mark of my trust and friendship. Thinking about sea, sand and sunshine made me feel warm inside.

'A bag of chips please,' said a young salad dodger.

'Coming up, young man,' I said, tipping a portion of chips into the fryer. 'Ah fuck it, I'll put you a few extra in, eh?'

'Aw, thanks, mister,' said the youth appreciatively.

I sang as I fried, happy to feel the hot fat stinging my skin.

A couple of minutes later and the young man was filling his face with my cuisine. 'Thanks, mister,' he said between mouthfuls.

'My pleasure entirely,' I said. 'Go careful, they're hot.' He ignored me and sucked in the chips like noodles. Evidently, he didn't need my advice on how to eat chips. He was a master, and at such a tender age too.

My good mood continued throughout the morning. It's surprising how a little sunshine lifts the spirits. I was still singing to myself as I watched as a lady walked across the car park. She power dressed and she power walked. She was probably from the nearby office block, but her slim figure made her an unlikely customer. However, her determined walk and arrow-like direction made it clear she was heading right for the hatch. 'Good morning,' she said.

'Good morning, love,' I said.

'I'm not your love, and there's no prospect of me ever being so.'

'Sorry,' I said. 'I'm just trying to be friendly.

'I don't want you to be friendly. I want you to take my order.'

'Fair enough,' I said. 'What can I do for you?'

'This,' she said, handing me a sheet of A4 paper. I looked at the list in horror; twelve times fish and chips, fourteen cheeseburgers, nine hamburgers, seven hot dogs and four minced beef pies.

'You're hungry, aren't you?' I said.

'Now, some want onions, and some don't,' she said, 'so I suggest you do a separate bag of onions, and we can distribute them ourselves. We have our own condiments and hot drinks. As quick as you can please. The CEO is visiting and he doesn't like to wait.'

'So when the CEO visits, you all have to eat what he eats?' I asked.

'It's only for one day,' she said. It was the first time I'd made a chink in her armour of confidence.

'It's a big order,' I said.

'Can you handle it or not?' she asked brusquely.

'Of course we can,' I said. 'But you'll have to give us a bit of time.'

'I'll wait,' she said.

'Take a seat over there,' I pointed at the tables and chairs.

'I don't think so,' she said, looking down her nose at our furniture.

'Right, Mo let's get cracking. And we did. Mo took care of the burgers and hot dogs while I did the frying. The fryer wasn't big enough to take all the order, so I had to do it in batches, earnestly trying to keep the food fresh and hot. Sweat dripped from my forehead and was swallowed up by the hot oil. I saw out of the corner of my eye that Mo's arms were moving like windmill sails as he flipped, pressed, and slid onions off to the side. It was hot, sticky work, but it was a decent order and if we got it right, maybe they'd be back.

'How long will it take?' asked the lady in frustration.

'We're going as quick as we can.' A queue was beginning to form now. 'Sorry,' I called, 'we'll be with you shortly.' But a couple at the end of the line couldn't wait and left.

'We only get thirty minutes break,' they said as they walked away disappointed. We were winning customers and losing them at the same time. I began to wonder if we'd done the right thing, but a tattooed bloke with close cropped hair waited patiently for his turn.

'It'll not be long now, mate,' I said to him.

'No problem, squire,' he said. 'I've got all day.'

'You'll probably need it,' said the sour-faced office worker.

'No need for that,' I said. 'We're doing our best.'

'I don't doubt that you are,' she said. 'Problem is, your best isn't quite good enough is it?'

'There's only two of us,' I said.

One way or another, we reached the end and ended up with a mountain of white paper bags.

'At last,' she said.

'Good things come to those who wait.' Mo smiled.

'That's just nonsense,' she said grimly.

I wondered if she ever cracked a smile at home. Was this her work persona which gave way to a kind, considerate person once she'd crossed the threshold of her own home? I suspected she was a miserable bastard wherever she was, whatever time it was.

'Would you like a bag, sweetheart?' I said, to annoy her.

'Yes,' she answered with a stony expression.

'You're going to have to make do with this Iceland bag,' I said, pulling it from beneath the counter. 'We're right out of Sainsbury's.'

'That'll do,' she said. 'But turn it inside out before you fill it.'

I filled the bag, and she was on her way without a word of thanks. 'Pleasure,' I said as she left. I turned my attention to the bloke who'd waited so patiently. 'Sorry about the delay. We don't usually get that busy.'

'Like I said. I have all day.'

'What can I get you?' I asked, mopping my brow with a tea towel.

'I'd like a bag too,' he said.

'Iceland or Aldi?' I joked.

'A black leather one about this long.' He held his palms apart to indicate the length of the bag. My heart jumped, then began to race.

'I'm not with you,' I lied.

'I think you know exactly what I mean,' he said.

'No, no,' I stuttered. 'I don't understand.'

'I also know that you're the chaps who've been setting bonfires.' I just looked at him, speechless. 'Yes, Johnboy, I've been doing a bit of research and I know all about you and your pals. I'm not going to mess around. I need the bag back, that's if you haven't spent it all, and if you have, you're going to be sorry. Hand over the bag and I'll turn a blind eye to the fires.'

'I don't have it,' I said.

'You better had. I'll leave you to ponder on it, but I'll be coming to see you soon... to collect what belongs to me.' He turned and left.

When he had cleared the car park, I got on the blower to Dogmeat. It went to voicemail after several rings, so I left a message; 'Call me as soon as you hear this,' I said in a panic. I waited a minute or so and tried again, with the same result, so I tried again... and again... and again. 'For fuck's sake, pick up,' I hissed, but he didn't. 'He's not answering,' I said to Mo.

'Leave it for a while,' Mo said. 'There's no emergency. We're okay right now, aren't we?'

He was right of course, there was no immediate danger, and I was overreacting. 'Breathe,' I said to myself. I took a few deep breaths and lowered my heart rate.

'That's it, bro, chill.' It was evident that Mo wasn't suffering any stress at all. I don't think he had it in him. My phone rang and I answered it in an instant.

'What the fuck's wrong now, Johnboy?' Dogmeat said. 'Are you low on fish?'

'We are as a matter of fact, but...'

'Chips?'

'Yes, chips as well, but that's…'

'Burgers?'

'Yes,' I shouted. 'Everything. We had a big order, but that's not…'

'Don't worry, Johnboy. I'm outside the suppliers now.'

'That's not why I rang,' I screamed.

'Steady on, Johnboy. You're gonna bust a fuckin' blood vessel if you're not careful.'

'Just listen will ya?' I relayed the series of events to Dogmeat.

'I'll be back soon,' Dogmeat said.

'Don't forget the fish,' Mo shouted before I hung up.

'Fuck the fish,' I said.

'What did he look like?' Dogmeat asked when he returned.

'Just a bloke,' I said

'That narrows it down,' said Dogmeat sarcastically.

'He had very short hair, tattoos and a crooked nose,' Mo said.

'Very observant,' Dogmeat said.

'What struck me was his tee shirt,' Mo continued.

'Go on,' Dogmeat said.

'It said "Firestarter" on it,' Mo explained.

'So what?' Dogmeat said.

'You're the Firestarter,' said Mo.

'Why don't you broadcast it to the fuckin' nation, Mo?' said Dogmeat, annoyed.

'He knew about the burger van fires,' I said.

'What else was he wearing?' asked Dogmeat.

'I don't know,' I said.

'Blue jeans and dark glasses,' said Mo.

225

'Fuckin' 'ell, Mo,' I said. 'You're a proper Poirot.' I turned to Dogmeat. 'Well, do you know him?'

'How the fuck would I know him?'

'Why are you asking then?' I said.

'I'm only trying to get to the bottom of it all,' Dogmeat said. 'No need to be arsey about it.'

'I'm not being arsey,' I said. 'I'm worried, that's all.'

'There's nothing to worry about, Johnboy. Are you worried, Mo?'

'Not particularly,' Mo said.

'There you go, Johnboy. Why don't you take a leaf out of Mo's book?'

'It's a serious problem this, Dogmeat,' I said, trying to impress the gravity of the situation upon him.

'I know, I know, Johnboy, but we've dealt with all the obstacles that have been put in our way so far haven't we?'

'I can't take much more,' I said. 'My nerves are in tatters.'

'Heads up, lads,' Dogmeat said. 'Punters ahoy.' A couple of building workers had pulled up in a pickup and were heading for the hatch.'

'I hope they don't want fish,' Mo said.

Chapter 19

Bert was back on the treadmill, Dogmeat was flicking peanuts in the air and occasionally catching one in his mouth, Mo was chilling, I was worrying, and Jabba was talking shite again. Par for the course then. The weather was atrocious this Saturday morning. The rain was coming in bucketfuls as the wind caught it and banged it against the large windows in swathes. 'At least they'll get a clean,' I thought to myself. I'd picked up Mo and driven in, as had Dogmeat. No one in their right mind would walk in this lot. I'd intended to go easy on the beer, but I was already on to my third pint. I could always leave the pickup here and walk, but I knew in my heart of hearts I'd be driving home, and Bert wouldn't thank me for walking him home in these conditions. I looked down at his face, void of expression as he got his steps in. 'Good lad,' I said and patted him on his head reassuringly.

'You know what happened to me,' said Jabba. No one responded, but he ploughed on regardless. 'I bought one of those stick deodorant jobbies and it said on the instructions to remove cap and shove up the bottom.' Again, no one took any notice of him. 'I can hardly walk,' he said, 'but when I fart the room smells lovely.' And away he went, roaring and rocking like the laughing policeman. Dogmeat fired a peanut that caught Jabba square on the forehead, dead central between his eyes, which only served to stop the laughter for a brief moment. 'You're a one, Dave,' he said, before the hilarity continued.

'You know something, Jabba?' Dogmeat said.

'What's that, Dave?'

'You're a fuckin' bell end. Why don't you go and sit somewhere else?'

'I like to sit with you lads,' said Jabba, still chuckling.

'No one invited you though, did they?'

'I was just about to get the beer in,' Jabba said. 'Anybody want one?'

'Aye, go on then,' Dogmeat said. 'Mine's a pint.' The fickle hand of John Smith had swung Dogmeat's view quicker than you could say "Free Beer".

'I'm all right,' Mo said, not wishing to take advantage of Jabba's need for friendship.

'He'll have a pint as well,' Dogmeat cut in.

'No, really,' Mo said.

'You're having a pint,' Dogmeat said.

'What about you?' Jabba asked me.

'That's very kind of you Jabba,' I said. 'I'll have a pint of Guinness.'

'He might not have a lot of money,' I said, whilst Jabba was at the bar.

'He shouldn't fuckin' come out then, should he?' said Dogmeat unsympathetically.

'Anyhow, we need to talk about that guy.'

'What guy's that, Johnboy?' asked Dogmeat.

'The guy that wants his money back. You know, the big fuckin' threatening one?'

'Ah, that guy,' Dogmeat said. 'I wouldn't worry about it. He'll be all bluster.'

'He's not all bluster, Dogmeat. You have to take this seriously. He won't just go away.'

'What do you want me to do?' Dogmeat asked.

'I don't know,' I said.

'Exactly,' said Dogmeat. 'We can't do anything right now. We can't give the money back, cos we've spent most of it.'

'Eh, Hombre,' Mexican Miguel had just entered the building. 'I just waved to you.'

'What you talking about, Miguel?' I asked.

'In el coche negro.'

'What?' I asked.

'El coche negro.' Miguel turned an invisible steering wheel, and I immediately knew what he meant.

'My truck,' I screamed. We all ran out into the car park just in time to see my truck leaving through the gap in the wall.

'Did you get his number?' Jabba blurted breathlessly.

'What the fuck you talking about, Jabba,' I said. 'It's my truck, I know the fuckin' registration.'

'Bastardos,' shouted Miguel after my truck.

'You're not kidding there,' Dogmeat said.

'Ah, tis only a coche,' Miguel sighed.

'Yes,' I said. 'But it's my fuckin' coche.'

'Que sera,' said Miguel. 'I need cerveza.' He turned and went back inside The Railway, as did everyone else when they realised there was nothing more to be done, but drink beer and debate the issue.

My pickup was found ten days later in the woods, burned beyond recognition and to cap it all, I received a bill for the clean-up and a stiff letter about polluting the local environment, which annoyed me greatly, but my main emotion was one of relief that I hadn't left Bert in the truck. I don't think they'd have thought twice about... I couldn't even contemplate it. I was now temporarily using an aging Vauxhall Corsa which had been loaned to me by the insurance company. Perhaps if I hadn't taken Bert with me to collect my courtesy car, I would have got a better spec. Anyhow, Bert wasn't impressed with it. In the truck, he'd poke his head through the open window and have a good look round before he'd fall asleep on the bench seat. The seat in the Corsa was neither big enough nor high enough for him. He spent most of the time turning in circles before settling into it.

What we thought would be a run of the mill day in the trailer turned out to be anything but. It started as every other day did with a brew before Mo and I prepared the equipment while Dogmeat remained outside by the tables, giving us a pep talk. Christmas was just around the corner and the weak sun was trying in vain to warm the car park. It hadn't seemed two minutes ago that the tarmac was bouncing with heat, but the world had turned, and we were blowing in our hands and rubbing them together, thanking our lucky stars that we weren't brass monkeys.

'Cannon balls,' said Dogmeat.

'Sorry?' I asked.

'Brass monkeys, it's something to do with cannon balls.'

'Really?' I asked. 'Tell me more.'

'Fuckin' google it,' Dogmeat said.

'I'm glad you cleared that up,' I said.

Under Mo's expert supervision, the griddle was up to temperature and the bain marie was simmering away happily. We didn't have to wait long until the first punters began to arrive. We'd learnt that if we opened just a little earlier, many of the shop workers would grab an unhealthy breakfast before going into work. These were mostly young, sausage-fingered men who didn't really care what they shoved down their throats. Only later in life would they realise their folly, the illusion of immortality and eternal good health being widespread amongst the young.

'The early bird catches the worm,' I said to Mo as I attended to the fryer.

'That's right, bro,' said Mo, 'but the second mouse gets the cheese.' Mo was very diligent in his work, but no one was going to rush him or change his philosophy. Things were moving along smoothly, until *he* arrived, yes him. Dogmeat was straight on the attack.

'Look, mate, you may as well fuck off,' he said. 'You can have the bag back, but it's empty. We've spent the money so there's no point keep coming round here.'

'It's not quite as simple as that,' the man said. 'There are others involved. Others who aren't quite as forgiving as me. They will need recompense.'

'I've already told you,' Dogmeat said. 'We don't have the money.'

'I've come today to give you a chance, please don't waste it.' He spoke to Dogmeat, but he was looking straight into my eyes. He knew weakness when he saw it. 'There's also the question of our missing friends, but we're willing to overlook that if you play nicely.'

'Dave's telling the truth,' I said. 'The money's gone.'

'Is this your burger van?'

'It's a catering trailer,' said Dogmeat, annoyed.

'We'll have this to start with.' The thug ran his hand along the counter as if he was stroking a Rolls Royce.

'No way,' Dogmeat said.

'You're going to have to pay one way or another and believe me, the other way isn't very pleasant. It's kind of terminal if you know what I mean.'

'You're not scaring us,' said Dogmeat.

'*Speak for yourself,*' I thought.

'Is that your final word?' asked the man.

'Our last and final offer is an empty leather bag and cheeseburger,' Dogmeat said.

'So be it. It's your necks on the line.' The man turned and left.

'He's not going to let it go,' Mo said.

'He'll get tired,' Dogmeat said. 'I wouldn't worry.'

'I do though,' I said. 'I lay awake at night thinking about it. I sometimes wish we'd never found that bag.'

'Christ on a bike,' Dogmeat suddenly blurted.

'No need to blaspheme,' I said, despite not really caring.

'No, really,' said Dogmeat. 'Look, it's Christ on a bike.'

Well, lick my larynx, sure enough, coming across the car park was Christ... on a mountain bike. He dismounted and leant his bicycle against the trailer.

'Hey,' shouted Dogmeat. 'Watch the paintwork.'

'Rustle us up a quick cheeseburger will ya?' Jesus was in a hurry. 'I want to pop in the bookies before rehearsals.'

'What rehearsals are them like?' asked Mo.

'Nativity play,' said Jesus. 'Onions please... Amateur Dramatics.'

'Aren't you a bit old for the nativity?' I asked.

'I kept saying that, but this director has funny ideas. I keep bobbing on the stage now and again, hands clasped in prayer, chipping in with the odd sage remark.' Jesus was shaking his head now. 'It's fuckin' mental, man. Poor show all round. We can't have a live baby, but we couldn't even find a whole doll. All we've got is the head. I can't wait until the infant child's head falls out of the blanket and goes rolling across the stage, but hey, man, I'm not the boss.' He sighed. 'There's not even anywhere to change. It's a right shithole in there. Needs a lot of work, but the theatre group are brassick, man. We're on the lookout for sponsors if you're interested.' He slid a cigarette from a packet and casually lit it.

I couldn't help thinking that this Jesus looked vaguely familiar. 'Where are you based,' I asked with genuine interest.

'Over the road, man. We could do with your help. We've got Twelfth Night coming up after this.'

'I don't mind a bit of Shakespeare,' I lied. 'I'll pencil it in; 2b or not 2b?'

The tiny theatre was opposite the car park, but I don't think anyone realised it had been acquired by the Thespians. Last time I took any heed of it, it was being used as a carpet warehouse. It was an unimposing stone building under a slate roof, that most people walked by without a second glance, or a first one come to that. In its first incarnation, it had been a Methodist Church, but as organised religion went out of fashion, it had at different times been adapted to sell various items, such as fishing tackle, bicycles, and the aforementioned carpets. Apart from friends, family, and school groups, I couldn't imagine anyone going to the play as there wasn't a sign of adverting outside the theatre, not even any signage to indicate its present use.

'I know you, don't I?' I'd heard his voice before, but I couldn't quite put my finger on it.

'Mmm,' he said, focusing on my face, trying to put a name to it. 'I may have seen you somewhere before.' He was quite obviously being careful.

'And I've seen you somewhere before too,' I said.

'I've got it.' He clicked his fingers as the realisation hit him. 'You're the guy that stole the tin opener from the church hall...

Johnboy. My mates told me all about it.'

'Ricky,' I said. 'I didn't recognise you in that get up. And it it was you who stole the tin opener. I just got the blame for it.'

'Technicalities, Johnboy, mere technicalities.'

'Is this your mam?' I asked, pointing behind Jesus to a young lady emerging from a car. He turned to look.

'Aye,' he said, quickly stubbing out the cigarette. 'That's Mary.' He leant into the hatch and spoke quietly. 'I'll let you into a secret, I can't stand amateur dramatics, it's full of dickheads, but she's fuckin' hot man, I'll tell yer. I've been trying to get into her pants since we started, but she's taking the play a bit too seriously, thinks it's relevant and all that shit.'

'Is she a bit of God botherer then?' asked Dogmeat.

'Almost fanatical,' said Ricky

'Then you've no chance,' I said.

'I'm going to have a good go at it. I really like her.'

'You need to have a word with your dad,' I said pointing up at the sky. 'See if he can't help you.'

'Morning,' said Mary. Ricky wasn't wrong, she was everything he said she would be.

'Ten,' shouted Dogmeat.

'Ten,' echoed Mo.

'What can I get you, love?' I asked.

'Just a coffee please. Ricky said your coffee was good.'

'Ricky as in Jesus?' I asked.

'Yes,' she smiled. 'Jesus.'

'*He must be psychic then,*' I thought, because he's never been here before, but then again, he was Jesus.

Ricky waved me to the end of the counter. 'Skip the burger will ya?' he whispered in my ear. He had hoped to get the burger down his neck before Mary arrived, probably telling her he was a vegetarian or something. 'I'll just have coffee.'

'Fair enough,' I said. The burger hadn't hit the hotplate, so it was no trouble. Jesus sidled up alongside Mary.

'I'll get these,' he said, digging into his trouser pocket beneath his tunic. He was trying hard, and I hoped our coffee wasn't going to let him down.

'Mary and Joseph had no luck at all looking for digs, did they?' said Dogmeat.

'It was a difficult time for them,' Mary said. 'But the Innkeeper was kind enough to let them use the stable.'

'Aye,' said Dogmeat, 'he worra right bloke. He must have seen that Mary was up the duff, but he still shoved them in with the goats.'

'It was better than nothing,' Mary replied.

'I suppose so, but it was their own fault.'

'Why do you say that?'

'They should have known that everywhere is rammed at Christmas,' Dogmeat laughed.

'That's not funny,' Mary complained.

'I thought it was,' said Mo.

'It was a good 'un, Mo,' Dogmeat agreed. 'Make a note of it. I'll use it again.'

'Here's your coffee,' I said. 'Enjoy.' I winked at Jesus. 'Take a seat.' Jesus and his mother retired to the seating area.

'These chairs are freezing,' said Mary.

'I wouldn't worry,' said Dogmeat. 'You'll be sleeping in the straw on Christmas Eve.'

'I've had enough of this,' Mary said, exasperated. She stormed off across the car park clutching her cardboard coffee cup, swiftly followed by Ricky, pushing his bike.

'Hey,' I called. 'Bring some tickets over and we'll try and

235

sell a few for you.'

'We need some seats first, man,' Jesus replied as they made their way to the carpet warehouse... er... theatre. 'God bless,' was his parting shot.

Next at the hatch were a group of woolly creatures carrying their heads under their arms. They came in all shapes, sizes and ages, from a mere slip of a lad who couldn't have been more than nine or ten years old, to a sizeable, aging lady who would have been more suited to playing the ugly duckling, judging by the way she waddled towards us.

'What you supposed to be?' Dogmeat said.

'We're the animals in the stable,' said a middle-aged lady.

'Put your head on then,' Dogmeat said. 'Let's have a look at you.'

'Hold that,' said the lady, passing her handbag to her friend. I could see by her demeanour that she was proud to have been selected as a sheep for this year's production. She pulled the head over her face and turned directly to Dogmeat.

'What's that supposed to be?' Dogmeat asked.

'I'm a sheep,' said the lady, pleased with herself.

'You look more like a Bedlington Terrier,' said Dogmeat.

'Take no notice of him,' I said. 'You look great. Right, what do you want?'

They got their heads together to decide what they would be eating, that is, their real heads and not the sheep heads they were holding.

'Six hot dogs and six cups of Rosie Lee,' said a balding man.

'Everyone wants the same then?' I checked.

'That's right,' said the man.

'Your casting director did a great job didn't he?' Dogmeat said.

236

'Following blindly isn't confined to sheep, bro,' Mo said.

'When you've quite finished,' said the large lady, 'could we have our breakfast please?'

'I'm on it, love,' I shot back. 'Bratwurst or Frankfurter?'

'Frankfurter,' she said without consulting the others.

'What's them Tornados, mister?' asked the youngest member of the flock.

'A potato spiral, deep fried and flavoured as your whim takes you,' I said.

'I want one of those,' he said.

'You'll have what you're given,' said the balding man. 'And like it.'

'You can't make me like it,' the child protested. 'I'm gunna tell my mam.'

'Is your mam here?' The balding man bent down and was right in the child's face.

'No,' said the child meekly.

'It's a hot dog then, and think yourself lucky.'

'I'm not lucky,' said the child, rallying again. 'My mam gave you the money for my breakfast.'

The balding man's face was dangerously red, and he raised a hand as if to strike the young lad.

'Lay a finger on him,' Dogmeat said, 'and you'll be wearing the sheep's head and carrying your real one.'

'I fuckin' hate Christmas,' Dogmeat said between peanuts.

'It's what you make it,' said Mo, philosophically.

'I didn't think you'd celebrate Christmas,' said Dogmeat.

'Course I do, bro. I like a mince pie as much as the next man. Why don't you like Christmas, Dave?'

'It's just another day intit? Only worse.' Dogmeat downed a

third of his pint in one gulp. 'I'll be sat by myself, nowhere to go and no one to go with.'

'I'll be on my own this year as well I suppose,' I said.

It was the last weekend before the big day and the decorations in The Railway had been up that long, they were beginning to look a bit sad, like Dogmeat... and me. The pub was extra busy with people professing their undying love for mankind in general. Another week or two and they'd be at each other's throats again.

'There you go, lads.' Walt dropped a plate of food in front of us. 'Merry Christmas.'

'There's nowt merry about it,' said Dogmeat.

'Cheer up, Dave,' said Walt. 'It'll soon be over.'

Jabba had got himself a pint at the bar and headed over to sit with us.

'For fuck's sake,' Dogmeat said when he saw him approaching.

'Happy Yuletide,' Jabba laughed.

'Fuck off, Jabba,' Dogmeat said, but Jabba ignored him and took a seat beside me. I threw a sausage roll to Bert, who had been licking his bollocks on the stationary treadmill.

'I wish I could do that,' Jabba said.

'Give him a biscuit and he'll let you,' said Dogmeat. Jabba was away again, immersed in his own world of joviality. When his guffawing subsided, he had a question for us.

'What's the difference between an Indian and an African elephant?'

'I don't know, and I don't care,' said Dogmeat with a hint of ennui.

'Ears,' Mo offered.

'No,' said Jabba. 'One's an elephant.' And off he went again, as if it had been the first time he had heard it himself.

'I've got an idea,' Dogmeat said to me, disregarding Jabba. 'Why don't you and Bert come and stay with me for a couple of days over Christmas?'

'I don't know, Dogmeat,' I said.

'Come on, Johnboy,' Dogmeat continued. 'We could come down The Railway then go back and have a Christmas dinner, with crackers and the lot, you know, a traditional Christmas day, like everyone else.'

'Who's going to cook that then?' I asked.

'We'll manage, Johnboy. It'll be a good crack... and it's got to be better than both of us sitting by ourselves, I know.'

'I think it's a great idea,' said Mo.

'It is intit, Mo?' Dogmeat enthused. 'What do you say, Johnboy?'

'Aw, go on then. What could go wrong?'

Chapter 20

Christmas Eve found Bert and I round at Dogmeat's, and I'll give him his due, he'd made the effort. As I settled back on the sofa with my third Irish whiskey and a bowl of mixed nuts, a sense of wellbeing overcame me. The Christmas tree lights twinkled and "Carols from King's" filled the air. Two places were set at the table in readiness for the big day, each having a cracker precisely positioned alongside the cutlery. Bert was curled up in a new Christmas themed dog bed that Dogmeat had bought him for the occasion.

'You haven't done all this for us, have you?' I asked.

'I have a tree every year, Johnboy.'

'I had no idea, Dogmeat, you big softy.'

'I like the idea of Christmas,' said Dogmeat, 'I always have done, but it's the only time of the year I don't like being alone. I love living by myself, but I really feel the solitude at this time of the year. There's been times when I've heard next door partying and it's fuckin' torture. These walls are paper thin you know.'

'Fuckin' 'ell, Dogmeat,' I said. 'All those years... you should have said something. You could have come round to ours, Sally wouldn't have minded, in fact she'd have been delighted. She would have had someone to talk to.'

'I've had invites, but I know they just feel sorry for me,' said Dogmeat. 'Fuck that, I still have some dignity.'

'I don't know what I'd have done with myself if I'd been by missen,' I said.

'Aye, the first one is the worst,' Dogmeat lamented. 'Fuckin' soul destroying, but you can't let it get to you. You have to soldier on.'

'Well, I'd just like to say thank you,' I said.

'For what?'

'For this. For asking me round.' The whiskey was kicking in now. 'You're a good pal, Dogmeat.'

'Aw, fuck off will ya?' said Dogmeat. 'You'll be telling me you really, really love me next.'

'I do though, Dogmeat,' I slurred.

'Stop right there,' said Dogmeat abruptly. 'Have a top up.' He took my glass and replenished it from the bottles at the side of the sofa. 'Have that and fall asleep, you daft sod.'

I had a bit of a thick head on Christmas morning having slightly overdone it on the whiskey, but it wasn't anything that wouldn't pass quickly with a little hydration. Bert had spent the night with Dogmeat in his bedroom. I felt vaguely betrayed but consoled myself with the knowledge that if anything ever happened to me, my canine friend would be looked after. Now he was back in his own bed, which Dogmeat had pulled into the kitchen so he could be with us. Bert didn't give me a second glance when I walked into the kitchen. He had never been very demonstrative, so I didn't take it personally. The beautiful aroma of bacon and eggs was beginning to permeate the air, making Bert's nose twitch a little, and mine.

'Bert will need to go for a walk,' I said.

'He's been out in the garden with me,' said Dogmeat. 'I needed a Woodbine, so we went out together.' Dogmeat never liked to smoke indoors. 'I've fed him as well, so he's set fair.'

'He wants more exercise than that,' I said.

241

'Does he look like he wants to go anywhere?' Dogmeat asked.

'I suppose not,' I said, looking at Bert who seemed quite content in his bed.

'It's Christmas, leave him be,' Dogmeat said.

Dogmeat expertly prepared and served a breakfast of bacon, sausage, eggs, mushrooms, and tinned tomatoes. We enjoyed it in the kitchen on the dropleaf table, with salt, pepper, and sauce of both persuasions. Bert received more than his fair share of sausage, with it being a special day. This really was the life. What more could a man ask for? I silently thanked myself for accepting Dogmeat's invitation.

After breakfast, I helped Dogmeat wash up and we retired to the front room to open presents. I'd previously noticed the two parcels neatly wrapped beneath the tree.

'This is for you,' said Dogmeat, passing one to me and placing the other in front of Bert, who looked at it questioningly.

'You shouldn't have,' I said.

'I know I shouldn't, but I have done, so open it.'

'I have something for you too,' I said, handing over the gift which I'd secreted behind a cushion.

'Thanks,' said Dogmeat. 'I didn't expect anything.'

'Neither did I,' I confessed. Bert had torn away the wrapping paper on his present to reveal a hide chew shaped like a shoe. 'He'll love that, thanks, Dogmeat.' I was beginning to feel a bit teary. Dogmeat and I simultaneously opened our packages and burst into laughter. We'd got each other identical gifts of a socks and underpants set. Matalan was just down the road from The Railway and this gift set was in your face as soon as you entered the place. Evidently, we'd both had the same idea of quickly grabbing something and getting out.

'You can never have enough undercrackers,' chuckled Dogmeat.

Before we set off to The Railway, we prepared the lunch. I peeled the potatoes and par-boiled them ready for roasting whilst Dogmeat tackled the sprouts and carrots. There was only two of us, so we guessed a small, stuffed turkey crown would be sufficient, and it would only take an hour or so in the oven. We sang carols and sipped sherry as we worked.

'*We three kings of Orient are,*' I belted out.

'*One in a taxi, one in a car,*' Dogmeat continued.

'*One on a scooter, blowing his hooter,*' I sang.

'*Following yonder star,*' we both sang.

'I'm fuckin' loving this, Johnboy,' Dogmeat professed.

'Me too,' I agreed. 'What about this one?' I cleared my throat because I wanted as near as perfect delivery of the first line. '*While shepherds washed their socks by night.*'

Dogmeat was quick to join in. '*And hung them on the line.*'

'*The Angel of the Lord came down, and said, those socks are mine.*'

We were already half cut by the time we took our seats in the pub. The Christmas day atmosphere was magical, everyone appeared in high spirits. Mo, the family man, was missing of course, but a lot of the regulars were there, including Jabba and Mexican Miguel who were propping up the bar. When they saw us, they ambled over and joined us. Remarkably, Dogmeat didn't complain.

'How yer doin', Jabba?' Dogmeat asked. 'My old mucker.'

'I'm good, Dave,' Jabba said, confused.

'And you, Miguel, are you good as well?'

'Si, Dave, canela en ramas.' Which translates as "Cinnamon

Sticks". We'd no idea what he was saying, but we grasped the meaning. He was all right.

'What you having for Christmas dinner, Miguel?' I asked. 'Chicken with chocolate?'

'No, hombre, I'm having the pavo, the turkey, with the sprouts. My wife make it now. I come here because her mother is with us.'

'Fair play, Miguel,' Dogmeat said, raising a glass.

'What about you, Jabba?' I asked.

'I'll find something in the cupboard.' For once, Jabba wasn't laughing. He was facing a miserable Christmas alone. 'I'm not really bothered about Christmas.'

'Are you going to be by yourself, Jabba?'

'Yeah, but like I said, Christmas doesn't bother me,' he lied.

'Have you no family?' Dogmeat asked.

'No, not really.' I looked at Dogmeat, who looked at me. We communicated without words, and we knew what we must do.

'You're coming with us, Jabba, there's only me and Johnboy,' Dogmeat said. At that moment I was so proud of my friend.

'I couldn't,' said Jabba.

'Why not?' I asked.

'Well, I'm… I'm busy.'

'No, you're not,' Dogmeat said. 'Look, Jabba, even though you grate a bit, we're not leaving you alone on Christmas day. No arguments, okay?'

'If you're sure you don't mind.'

'That's settled then,' said Dogmeat, sealing the deal. 'Now get the beer in.'

The three of us weaved our way back, with Dogmeat leading the way on his wheels. So far, the day had been brilliant. Whereas I was expecting a melancholy day alone, as we all were, I now had good company and a nice Christmas dinner to look forward to. I felt lifted, loved, and wanted, although even through the fog of alcohol, I was experiencing pangs of regret for not giving a thought to Dogmeat in previous years. The same went for Jabba too, even though he wasn't such a close friend he didn't deserve to be alone. I wondered how many folk were feeling the intense isolation of the festive period right now. I was determined to put my mind to it in future.

We arrived back at Dogmeat's, cracked a few cans of ale, and turned on the oven.

'That'll not take long to warm up,' said Dogmeat. 'Let's watch a bit of telly.' We retreated to the front room and lined up on the sofa in front of the TV. We watched "Scrooge", the original and best version in black and white. Alastair Sim played the miserable bastard, then Dogmeat remembered the oven.

'Time to put the turkey in,' he said.

'I'll do it I said,' not wanting to put Dogmeat to the trouble of climbing into his wheelchair. I slid the baking tray containing turkey, potatoes and parsnips onto the shelf and mulled over whether to turn on the sprouts, but in the end decided it was too early.

'Grab three more beers, Johnboy,' called Dogmeat.

'Will do,' I said, diving into the American fridge.

'This is really good of you,' said Jabba as I squeezed back onto the settee and handed out the beer.

'That's what friends are for,' Dogmeat said as he pulled the ring on his can.

'I think we should do this every year,' I suggested. 'Next year you can come round mine.'

'Am I included in that?' Jabba enquired.

'Course you are, love.' I gave Jabba a little cuddle, causing him to burst into laughter again. This time, Dogmeat and I joined in. Marley rattled his chains and put the fear of God into Scrooge. 'I'd shit my pants if that happened to me,' I said when the laughter had subsided.

'Ah,' said Dogmeat, 'it's just bollocks.'

'I think there's something in it,' I said.

'Are you telling me?' asked Dogmeat, 'that you believe in ghosts?'

'I keep an open mind,' I said.

'My dad once told me,' said Jabba, 'that he once saw his friend's dead mother walk across the room.'

'And you believed him?' Dogmeat scoffed.

'Of course I believed him. He was my dad.'

'No disrespect, Jabba,' said Dogmeat, 'but I'm just not buying it.'

'You know, years ago?' said Jabba. 'When I got a job on the renovation of the old rectory.'

'Before you decided work didn't suit you?' I added.

'Yeah,' Jabba agreed. 'There were rumours that it was haunted. We never saw a ghost, but we did find a skeleton behind a wall.'

'Really?' I said, all ears.

'We were knocking some walls down between rooms and it turned out there was a void between them, and there it was, a skeleton, stood up there like it didn't have a care in the world.'

'Get away,' said Dogmeat. 'You're having us on.'

'True as I'm sat here now,' Jabba said. 'It had a huge, round medallion hung around its neck with a gold chain. The medallion was gold too, with an inscription etched into it. I can still see it as clear as day.'

'What did it say on the medallion, Jabba?' I asked.

'South Yorkshire Hide and Seek Champion, 1842.' That was the cue for Jabba to lose it again. They could probably hear us laughing next door. The tables had been turned.

'You soft get,' Dogmeat said.

Then we fell asleep, Jabba with his head on my shoulder, Dogmeat with his head on Jabba's shoulder. All three of us with our mouths open, blowing Zs. It must have sounded like a sawmill in there. How Bert slept through it all was a minor miracle in itself.

We woke to the piercing screech of the smoke alarm.

'Fuckin' 'ell,' I said as I leapt into action, 'the turkey.' I sprinted into the kitchen, yanked open the oven door and was met by a cloud of acrid smoke. I opened the outside door to clear the smoke and went to inspect our dinner. The turkey was as black as a black thing in a coal cellar with a busted light bulb. I grabbed the oven gloves and pulled it out. I cut through it and it was black inside. It was truly black… and unquestionably inedible, as were the potatoes that sat beside it like so many pieces of anthracite. Thank goodness I hadn't put the sprouts on.

'Oh dear,' said Jabba, who had come to see the damage.

'Wowee,' said Dogmeat as he wheeled into the kitchen. 'Bit foggy in here intit?'

'Woof,' said Bert, who had finally roused himself.

'The turkey's had it,' I said, poking at it with a fork. 'Looks like sprouts and peas for Christmas dinner.'

'It's still better than the oxtail soup I was planning,' said Jabba.

'Tell you what,' Dogmeat said. 'I've got some burgers in the freezer. If we put plenty of gravy on, you'll not know the difference.'

'Have you got frozen chips?' I asked.

'I sure have,' said Dogmeat.

'Good,' I said. 'They'll replace the roasted spuds.'

'Where there's a will, there's a death, hey, Jabba?'

'Great idea,' Jabba said, smiling from head to foot.

We put the veg on and began to assemble a Christmas dinner with a difference and by the time we sat down at the table, we had sunk another couple of cans. However, there was still room for a bottle of bubbly, which Dogmeat popped open and almost took out Jabba's eye with the cork. I felt a deep sense of comradeship as I tucked into my burger and chips with sprouts, peas, carrots and stuffing, all concealed within a thick gravy covering. I couldn't grumble, it was mint, but when you've had a skinful even carpet burgers are good.

'What you reckon, Jabba?' I asked through a mouthful of chips.

'My compliments to the chef,' he replied.

'It's not three bad, is it?' said Dogmeat.

'I think we've stumbled upon a new Christmas recipe here,' I said.

'Happy Christmas,' Dogmeat said, raising his glass.

'And a merry new year,' I said, joining him in the toast.

'Thank you,' said Jabba.

'Oh,' said Dogmeat, 'I nearly forgot the crackers.' He reached over to the sideboard and retrieved an extra cracker for Jabba. Dogmeat slid the drawer shut and we pulled the crackers simultaneously, hands crossed in a circle. The contents fell out onto the table, a cheap, plastic whistle, a keyring and some kind of puzzle that no one could make head nor tail of. We each placed a paper crown on our heads and began to read the jokes.

'How does Good King Wenceslas like his pizza?' asked Jabba.

'Deep pan, crisp and even,' I said. Of course, we'd heard them all before, but that didn't keep us from howling. 'My turn,' I jumped in. 'What do you get if you cross a snowman with a vampire?'

'Frostbite,' said Dogmeat. 'Here's mine,' he said, trying to focus on the tiny piece of paper. 'How does Darth Vader like his turkey?' No one had an answer, so Dogmeat carried on, 'On the dark side, a bit like ours eh?' The jokes were bad, nay, they were terrible, but we laughed anyway.

After three microwave puddings and more beer, we did a bit of washing up and retreated to the sofa, stuffed full of ten bob burgers and sprouts. Bert was back slumbering in his bed, having enjoyed a couple of burgers himself. We settled down to watch a film, but all any of us saw of it was "DreamWorks". This time we were sure that everything was turned off. It was a good sleep, but boy did we wake up with bad heads.

Bert and I ended up staying through to the new year, the three of us making frequent visits to The Railway where we were invariably joined by Jabba who had become a fixture at our regular table. Mo managed to get away from the family and make a couple of appearances too. The only problem with Jabba being with us was that we couldn't quietly discuss the bag, and more to the point, the consequences of finding the bag. We still had to deal with the man, or men, whom I knew weren't going to leave us be just because we'd told them that the money was gone. When I broached the subject in the privacy of Dogmeat's home, he wouldn't take my worries seriously, or he didn't want to think about it, preferring, in my opinion, to bury his head in the sand. I knew they'd be back, and the thought was always there, lurking in the shadows at the back of my mind.

For us, the new year slipped in almost unnoticed. Dogmeat and I were too tired to stay up and see it in properly. We weren't too bothered, we'd seen plenty of them before and we made a conscious decision not to go near The Railway, or any other public house on that particular evening. Drunken idiots ruled the roost for one night only. Walt once told me that he loved the profits but hated the punters. It was a night for plastic glasses, because without doubt the evening would end up with a punch up that would spill out into the car park. We had considered opening up the van for the evening. We would certainly have made quite a bit of money but it just wasn't worth it, so we opted to have a quiet night in with Bert. We had intended to watch Jools Holland's Hootenanny, but the festivities had taken their toll. We bid each other a good night a couple of hours short of midnight. I wished Bert a happy new year and gave him a big sloppy kiss before he sloped off to sleep with Dogmeat. I went to my own bed and fell into a deep sleep almost before my head had hit the pillow. It had been an exhausting, but enjoyable, festive period; probably one of the best I'd experienced. A fresh, new year lay ahead, a clean sheet ready for me to stain.

'Ah well,' said the soul. 'Arsehole,' said the well.

Chapter 21

January days are over in a flash, it's the nights that linger on. Bert and I were back home and Dogmeat was flying solo again. I was tired as I rolled up at work in my Corsa, which I had now bought because the courtesy car period had come to an end and the insurance company were dragging their feet with the settlement. I needed some wheels and the vehicle I had was doing the job, so I kept hold of it. Mo and Dogmeat had already opened the serving hatch and were setting up. When I offered morning pleasantries, Dogmeat grunted back at me. Evidently, he wasn't too happy about being back at work either. Mo, on the other hand was full of joy, as he always was.

'That's all over for another year,' I said.

'I enjoyed it,' said Mo.

'So did I,' I said. 'I'm not happy about being here though this morning.'

'What about you, Dave?' Mo asked. 'How was your Christmas?'

'Fuck off will ya.' The Dogmeat we knew and loved was back.

That morning, everyone that came to the hatch was fuckin' miserable and it made me even more depressed than I previously had been, if that was possible. It was cold and the air stung as I drew it into my lungs, so I was pleased when the appliances came up to temperature.

'Tea please,' said a man hidden behind a scarf and woolly

hat.

'Morning,' I said.

'Uhh,' he replied, so I didn't engage any further. He took his drink and left. I turned to thinking that somewhere in the world, someone was walking on a beach beneath a golden sun. If the sun came out here, the police would be inundated with reports of a UFO. The car park was icy and when a dark BMW pulled up near the van it skidded on a little. Someone in a balaclava emerged from the passenger side and approached the van. I kind of knew that he wasn't wearing the balaclava because of the weather, but by the time I'd got myself off the beach it had happened, literally in a flash. Mercifully, Mo had left the trailer to deliver Dogmeat his habitual morning coffee. I was old enough and wise enough to recognise a Molotov Cocktail when I saw one. They were popular back in the day and featured regularly on the ten o'clock news, so I was already diving to the floor as he lit the wick. The flames exploded on the back wall and the last thing I remembered was the close proximity of the floor to my face as I travelled across it. Bizarrely, a fleeting thought alerted me to the fact that the floor could do with a serious clean instead of the mop around that we usually carried out. Shortly, I was in an ambulance, but in my mind, I was floating horizontally, facing the tarmac at a height of around two feet, much like Maximus Decimus Meridius. Music from the Gladiator movie was playing in the background as I gently hovered across the car park above a bed of bratwurst, burgers, pies, and chips.

'Mr Barratt, can you hear me? Can you hear me, Mr Barratt?'

'Where am I?' I asked.

'You're in hospital, Mr Barratt. You've banged your head.' The doctor was peering into my eyes to see if anyone was home.

She took my hand and reassured me that everything was okay, and I was in the best place. 'You've had bit of a shock.'

'Hospital?' I asked groggily.

'Yes, but don't worry, we'll look after you now.' I tried to turn my head but was constrained by a neck brace, so I looked up at the ceiling of the small cubicle they'd put me in. From the corner of my eye, I could see a chair and a sink with a soap dispenser above. 'Try and keep still,' the doctor said. 'It seems someone doesn't like you.'

I began to recall the moment when the man stepped out of the car with the bottle, but not much after that. 'Am I burnt?' I asked.

'No,' the doctor reassured me. 'You don't appear to have any burns, but you do have a pretty big lump on your head. We're going to keep you under observation for a day or two, to make sure you're okay.'

'I can't go home?' I said, alarmed.

'Not yet, until we know you don't have any lasting damage.'

'But I have to get back for Bert.'

'Who's Bert,' asked the doctor.

'He's my dog. I need to be home to look after him.'

'Relax,' she said. 'I'll find out about... Bert.' She smiled. 'I'm sure he's being taken care of. By the way, there's a policeman here saying he wants a word with you. Do you feel up to it?'

'Yes, send him in,' I said, deciding it was better to get it over with rather than have it hanging over me. The doctor left and a moment later the curtain was pulled back to allow the entry of not one, but two, police officers. I told them almost nothing, nothing about the car, the man, the petrol bomb, nothing. The less they knew, the better. I didn't want them digging and finding something incriminating, so I claimed that I couldn't remember anything at all about the attack, it was all a blank, and they believed me. I was reassured that they wouldn't bother me again, after all, I was the victim in this case.

After interminable hours of prodding, poking, x-rays and scans, I was moved to a ward. It was light and airy, having windows along two of the walls which formed the corner of the building. There were six beds and, fortunately, I had one at the end. I didn't fancy sleeping between two strangers. There was no television or radio, just a button to call for assistance and a control on the end of a wire which enabled me to alter the angle of the bed if I wanted to sit up. A stack of what looked like cardboard party hats sat on the windowsill alongside a few cardboard piss pots. I'd only have to get up for a shit by the looks of it. I soon worked out that the party hats were for being sick in, and hopefully I wouldn't be needing them. After the porter had transferred me from the wheelchair to the bed, he bid a cheery farewell and left me to it. I surveyed my surroundings and got myself settled. Maybe it wouldn't be too bad in here. I wouldn't be here long so I may as well make the most of it. After a while I got chatting with Steve, the bloke across from me, who seemed like a decent type. He told me that he'd been in that bed for a couple of weeks now and appeared resigned to his lot. Little was I to know that he was the only sane one in here. The guy in the next bed had been asleep when I arrived, but when he woke, he came over to my bed and leant over me. I thought he was going to introduce himself, but he simply produced an imaginary tape measure and extended it from my head to my toes.

'Six feet,' he said. 'Around fifteen stones.' He recorded his findings in an imaginary notebook.

'Who the fuck are you?' I asked. 'The local undertaker?' He

bent over and put his face close to mine. 'Fuck off out of it you lunatic. Get your face out of mine. Who knows what you've got?' But he just carried on measuring and making notes, scratching his chin as he made decisions about my physique.

'Fuck off,' I said. 'Or you'll be measuring your own coffin.' I know that didn't make sense, but it was all I could come up with at short notice.

'Get back in your own bed, Colin.' A nurse came to my rescue and returned Colin to his bed. 'He's not quite with it,' she said for my ears only. 'The lift doesn't go all the way to the top floor, if you know what I mean.'

After a few days in the bed, it became apparent that no one was going anywhere. Various doctors had seen me, but I'd had to retell my story to each different one. None of them appeared to know why I was there, which made sense when one of them admitted to me that they'd lost my notes.

'Don't worry,' he said. 'They'll turn up,' which was all well and good. I had no doubt that they'd get on top of my case, but in the meantime, I was rotting in this bed.

'I think I'd be better off at home,' I suggested.

'Don't worry, Mr... er.'

'Barratt,' I offered.

'Don't worry, Mr Barratt, we'll soon have you out of here.'

The meals were good, but Colin was an awkward fucker. For breakfast he wanted two slices of toast. One with marmalade and one with raspberry jam. You needed the patience of a communion of saints to work on a ward. He frequently left his dinner because he was constantly munching on the crisps that people brought him. Then he'd fall asleep, only to wake at bedtime. He paced the ward all night long, one end to the other, all the time talking to himself.

'Got to keep fit, got to keep fit, got to get my steps in,' he'd say during his nocturnal march. He'd reach the limit of the ward, then spin, squeaking the soles of his slippers on the polished floor.

'Shut the fuck up, Colin,' I'd call, 'and get back in bed.'

'I need the exercise,' he'd reply. By the time the sun came up everyone was exhausted, except Old Jack in the middle bed opposite, who wasn't quite stone deaf, but deaf enough to get a good night's sleep. Colin would have his toast, then have a power nap to recharge his batteries in readiness to annoy us again.

'God, you look awful, Johnboy,' Dogmeat said during his first visit. 'Worse than when you came in.'

'I'm shattered,' I said.

'You should be getting a good rest,' he said. 'Nice bed, good food. What more could you ask for?'

'A good night's sleep,' I said.

'Are you not sleeping well?'

'I can't because of that idiot,' I said, jabbing my thumb towards Colin in the next bed.

'Do you want me to have a word with him, Johnboy?'

'It'd do no good,' I replied. 'He's fuckin' nuts. Anyway, how's Bert?'

'I'm looking after him, he's happy enough.'

'Thanks Dogmeat.' It was a load off my mind to know that Bert was being taken care of. 'And the burger van?' I enquired.

'It's a catering trailer,' Dogmeat said. 'Or, should I say, it was a catering trailer. It's gone, Johnboy, burnt to a crisp, finito.'

'Gone? I didn't realise it was that bad.'

'You're lucky you're not gone too, Johnboy,' Dogmeat

added. 'It's a good thing you jumped when you did, or you'd be toast.'

'What we going to do?' I asked.

'What can we do?' Dogmeat mused. 'It's gone and that's it.'

'Is it repairable?' I asked.

'Fraid not, it's gone,' said Dogmeat sadly.

'Are we getting another one?'

'I don't know, Johnboy. We'll think about that when you get out of here.'

'If ever,' I said. 'They've forgotten about me you know.'

'Things take time,' Dogmeat said. 'Why don't you just relax and enjoy the free food? It's like a five-star hotel in here. Breakfast in bed eh!'

'Have you contacted the insurance company?' We'd discussed insurance early on in the purchase and I'd left it to Dogmeat to organise.

'Ah,' said Dogmeat. 'I meant to talk to you about that.'

In the bed by the window, next to Old Jack, was Percy, a retired science teacher who mumbled nonsense during most of his waking hours. He'd quietly utter things like 'The black cat's the furthest one away,' and 'There are three boxes in a room,' or 'The whites need to be separate from the colours.' He was clearly mad, but when called upon, would come up with any answer you wanted. On one occasion, Steve and I were discussing American presidents. From nowhere, Percy would pipe up.

'There were four presidents assassinated in office. Abraham Lincoln 1865, James Garfield 1881, William McKinley 1901, and John F Kennedy 1963. In addition, Theodore Roosevelt 1912 and Ronald Reagan 1981 were injured during attempted assassinations.' Then he'd go back to mumbling about oven gloves or something.

'I have to get out of here, Steve,' I said, during one of our long conversations.

'So do I,' Colin exclaimed.

'Shut the fuck up, Colin,' I said. 'I'm not talking to you.'

'But I want to go home,' he said.

'I've had enough as well,' said Archie in the bed next to Colin.

'I'm happy where I am,' Steve said. 'My wife hates me. My home life's a torture.'

'Does anyone ever leave here or is it the Hotel California?' I asked Steve.

'Not many get out alive,' he said.

'Well I've had enough and I'm going home,' Archie said as he pressed the buzzer for the nurse.

Old Jack could see all our lips moving but had no idea what was going on. His head was turning from one to the other, sensing that something was in the offing.

'Fold the eggs in,' Percy said. 'Don't beat the mixture.'

Adam, the nurse, arrived and explained to Archie that he couldn't go home just yet, besides he had a catheter fitted and it was in his best interest to stay where he was.

'Take it out,' Archie shouted, becoming more agitated.

'Calm down, Archie, you can't go home yet.'

'I'm going,' Archie said adamantly. After much persuasion, Adam appeared to pacify Archie, but I wasn't convinced, he still had that mad look in his eye, that Billy Goat look. Steve saw it as well and flashed a knowing smile to me.

'Looks like we all want to go home,' I said. 'Except Steve of course, who has a good reason to stay.'

'We should form an escape committee,' suggested Archie.

'We could dig a tunnel,' said the fuckin' idiot that was Colin.

'Great idea, Colin,' I said. 'Only problem is that we are on the fourth floor.'

'The first man,' said Percy, 'to escape from Colditz was Lieutenant Alain le Rey on April eleventh, 1941. He eventually reached neutral Switzerland. Another notable escapee was Airey Neave who made his bid for freedom on January fifth, 1942.'

'Thanks for that, Percy,' I said.

'You're welcome... six eggs in half a dozen.'

Later that morning a physiotherapist brought a walking frame for Archie. It had wheels at the front and he made great progress during his practice run. It couldn't have arrived at a better time for Archie, as this was to be his getaway vehicle. He asked the physiotherapist, without success, to remove the catheter. Archie had plans.

Colin, between naps, was becoming more and more anxious about the situation, until he finally broke. Old Jack's eyes were on stalks as Colin jumped out of bed and stripped off his pyjama top. He knelt at the entrance to the ward, where all the nursing staff could see him. Spreading his arms out horizontally, he looked like he'd just slid there after scoring a goal.

'Look,' he cried. 'No concealed weapons. I am unarmed, I just want to go home.'

'Well done, Colin,' I said mischievously.

'Go back to your bed, Colin,' someone shouted from outside the ward.

'Dear Jesus.' Colin had now brought his hands together in prayer. 'Please give me the strength to burst out of this place. Get me out of here.' A nurse appeared, pulled him to his feet and led him to his bed. 'Bring me a piece of paper and a pen,' he continued. 'I need to write my last will and testament.'

'We're very busy, Colin. I don't really have time for this, so behave yourself.' Suitably chastised, Colin climbed meekly into his bed. His protest was over.

It was Friday, so I chose fish and chips for lunch and went for the traditional mushy peas to accompany them. Old Jack couldn't hear the choices and ended up with goulash after the person taking the orders gave up after the third time of shouting out the choices and decided that Jack looked like a goulash man. He looked surprised when the meals arrived, and everyone had fish and chips except him.

'I'd have had fish and chips if they'd asked me,' he complained. He slammed his hand down on the overbed table and flipped the plate into the air, which floated like a flying saucer before hitting the floor, dispensing its contents in a cowpat-like pile, but the plate kept on spinning and spinning.

'Fuckin' 'ell,' Steve said. 'He must be Greek.' I was tempted to throw my plate in with it, but I didn't want to waste the fish and chips. Old Jack, realising that he'd lost his dinner, pulled back the bed sheets and stepped out of bed. I tried to warn him, but he didn't hear my cries as he planted his foot square in the goulash cowpat.

A few minutes later Archie, fully dressed, was making his way down the ward on his walking frame towards the exit.

'I'm out of here,' he said as he moved at full speed across the floor. Full speed being around two hundred yards an hour.

'Go for it, Archie,' Colin said.

'Send us a card from Switzerland,' Percy called.

'Go on, son,' Steve encouraged.

'Are you sure you're doing the right thing, Archie?' I asked, knowing full well that I'd planted the seed.

'Too right I am. I've had enough of this.'

He didn't get far. The nursing staff clocked his attempt to run for freedom and gently turned him round so he was heading towards his own corner of the ward again.

'You can't go, Archie,' said one of the two nurses. 'You have a catheter fitted.'

'No, I don't,' Archie said.

'Yes, you have.'

'No, I fuckin' haven't,' Archie said. 'It's there,' he said, pointing over at the bed where the severed catheter tube lay. Archie had used mealtime and in particular his fish and chip knife to hack through the tube. He must have been plotting this all day. If we were to form an escape committee, Archie would definitely be chairperson. I was relieved when he was back on his bed, having felt a little responsible for what had happened. When they pulled the curtain around his bed, all sorts of gasps and sighs emanated as they tried to retrieve the remainder of the catheter.

'You've made a right mess here, Archie.'

'You should have listened to me,' Archie said, over and over again.

It was a great relief when Dogmeat and Mo collected me after a week or so in the hospital. Apparently, there was no lasting damage, and I was good to go, but what would the future hold now we'd lost the van? We would never afford another one like the one we'd lost, but maybe we could begin again on a smaller scale. When I got home I intended to count what money I had left. Dogmeat shamefully admitted that the bookmakers had the bulk of his and Mo had already passed what surplus he had on to his greater family. But at least I was out of the nut house.

Chapter 22

Mo held me steady as he led me up the garden path towards my door.

'Let go, Mo,' I said. 'I'm fine.'

'You don't look fine, bro,' Mo said, refusing to release his grip.

'Yeah, Johnboy,' Dogmeat added. 'You look like shit.' He was always the one to come forward with constructive criticism. The truth was that I didn't feel fine. I was tired and weak, but I was trying in vain not to show it. I shook Mo's hand away ungraciously.

'It's just lack of sleep.' I insisted. 'I'll be right as a bobbin when I've had a couple of nights without that fuckin' lunatic pacing up and down.' I reached the door under my own steam with Bert loping ahead. 'Oh for fuck's sake,' I spat. The door was slightly ajar. As we entered the kitchen, I saw the devastation. Every drawer had been pulled out and the contents scattered on the floor. All the worktop appliances had been ripped from their sockets and cast aside. The table was turned over and the chairs smashed, and to add insult to injury, red and brown sauce had been squirted everywhere, up the walls, on the ceiling, everywhere. We cleared a path for Dogmeat's wheelchair and moved through the hall into the lounge, where the scene was replicated. They'd even gone to the trouble of opening cans of baked beans, soup, canned tomatoes, and anything else they could lay their grubby hands on, in order to redecorate the room.

The curtains were stained and ripped, as was the sofa. The carpet looked beyond saving and the light fittings were smashed.

'Don't step in that,' Dogmeat said, pointing at a pile of human excrement in the centre of the room.

'The dirty bastards,' I said, almost in tears. The smell was rank. I covered my nose and mouth with my hand to try and block it.

'You'll have to come back to mine,' Dogmeat said. 'You can't stay here.'

'The money,' I said, running up the stairs, hoping against hope. I knew every bedroom would have been trashed, but I headed straight for the wardrobe. Just as I thought, the money was missing.

'It's gone,' I said, when I went back downstairs.

'Are you going to phone the police?' Mo asked.

'No,' I said. 'I don't think so. I think it's best if I bite the bullet on this occasion.'

'But,' Mo said, 'you can't let them get away with this, bro.'

'Johnboy's right,' Dogmeat said. 'We're better not involving the police.'

'How are you going to put everything right again with no money?' Mo asked.

'I have a little bit in the bank,' I said. 'Not much, but enough to tidy up the place. Nothing fancy mind, just basic stuff.'

'I'll help you, Johnboy,' Dogmeat said.

'Thanks, Dogmeat.' I knew I could rely on him.

'Yeah,' Mo said. 'I'll do what I can as well.'

'You're good mates,' I said, putting my arm around Mo's shoulders.

Jabba, having secured a regular seat at our table in The Railway seemed at peace with himself, in contrast to the disquietude I was experiencing. Zero to hero and back to zero was my story. How could I have been so stupid? Everything was there for me, and I blew it. Conversely, Mo didn't look to be perturbed at all.

'I still have my shovel, bro,' he said dispassionately. 'Have shovel, will travel, eh?'

'Aren't you at all worried, Mo?' I asked.

'Nah,' he said. 'Things happen for a reason. Something will turn up and we can always go back on the tools if the worst comes to the worst.'

'That's exactly what it would be,' I said, 'the worst.'

'Don't worry, Johnboy,' Dogmeat said. 'When one door closes, the next one is locked.' He flicked a peanut into the air and nearly caught it in his mouth. 'Fuck,' he said.

Walt arrived with a tray of beer and snacks. 'I see you've got your feet under the table, Jabba.'

'We've always been good pals,' Jabba laughed.

'What you going to do now the burger van's gone?' Walt asked.

'It's a catering... aw, fuck it,' said Dogmeat. 'It doesn't really matter any more.'

We'd spent ten minutes in the car park, inspecting the remains of the trailer, and what we had left was... a chassis. The scorched tea urn was lying nearby, but most of the items which had any scrap value, including the large griddle, had long gone. Even the stainless-steel sink had been liberated. Anything plastic had been burnt beyond recognition and the wooden cupboards were now nothing more than ashes. It had been good while it lasted, but that game was now over. They'd taken the trailer, my money, and wrecked my house and my furniture so there was no point in them returning. The cupboard was bare.

'No idea,' I said, replying to Walt's question.

'You could always get a job,' Walt suggested.

'Work for someone else? You are kidding, aren't you?' I said. I'd always been self-employed and was determined to remain so, no matter what. 'I'd rather shit in my hands and clap.'

Walt laughed and retreated. The pub wasn't overly busy that morning and Bert was getting in some quality snoozing time. I spared him the treadmill as he looked a bit tired. He was probably picking up the vibes from the humans around him, however it was nothing he was going to lose sleep over. With the help of Dogmeat, Mo and Jabba, my house was back into some kind of shape, filled with cheap furniture from charity shops and contributions from various benefactors. Dogmeat bought a new bed for Bert, and they were both delighted with it. Jabba, it turned out, was a dab hand at wallpapering. Who'd have known? When the chips were down, my mates had come to the fore, although no one volunteered to remove the shit from my living room carpet. I had to do that myself. When Sally died, my small mortgage had been settled, so that was one less thing to worry about. Well done, Sally. However, I was going to have to generate some income in some way or another. It was good that my friends had helped me, but I couldn't rely on them forever. The small amount of money I had in the bank wouldn't last very long, so I was going to have to do some serious thinking.

'Have we got enough money for another van?' I asked.

'I don't think so, Johnboy,' Dogmeat said.

'I haven't got much left, bro,' Mo said.

'I have a little bit of money,' Jabba said. 'You're welcome to it if it will help.'

'Tell you what, Jabba,' said Dogmeat, 'you're nothing less than a fuckin' diamond, but you keep your money.'

265

'I don't mind at all,' Jabba said, then burst into laughter for no apparent reason.

'He's not right in my head,' said Dogmeat, shaking his head. He was smiling though. Dogmeat and Jabba were bonding.

'What about ice cream?' said Dogmeat.

'What about it?' I enquired.

'We could get an ice cream van,' Dogmeat went on. 'There's some money in ice cream... just sayin' like, cos I can get by financially... just. We could sell other stuff under the counter as well.'

'Like what?' Mo asked.

'Oh, I don't know,' said Dogmeat. 'Vodka for instance, and cider. We could have done that in the trailer, we missed a trick there, lads.'

'Oh, that would've been magic,' I said. 'The six-year-olds asking for an ice pop and a bottle of White Lightning.'

'I used to buy cider from the ice cream man,' Jabba said. 'It was common in the old days.'

'Getaway,' I said.

'I did, when I was a teenager, living at home,' Jabba mused. 'When mi mam heard the chimes, after mi dad had left, cos he was a right bastard, she would send me to the van. When me and mi brothers were very young, mi dad used to turn the TV up really loud to drown out the chimes. It was years before I realised that he wasn't hard of hearing. After he'd gone and we could hear the chime again, I became friendly with the ice cream man and found out that he sold booze under the counter. I'll give him his due though, he wouldn't sell to anyone under twelve even if they did look thirteen.'

'Bully for him,' I said. 'A model citizen if I ever saw one.'

'I'd go out to the van, quick like,' Jabba went on, 'and be the first there and get a bottle of cider and a 396.'

'What's a 396?' Mo asked.

'Four 99s innit,' Jabba said.

'You soft...' Dogmeat said.

'I don't fancy being an ice cream man,' I said. 'One thing I realised selling burgers, is that I don't like kids and an ice cream van is going to attract an awful lot of them.'

'There must be something we can do, bro,' Mo said, 'that doesn't involve kids.'

'What about a sex shop?' Jabba suggested.

'Are you some kind of expert on the subject, Jabba?' asked Dogmeat.

'Not really,' he said. 'I meant for you three.'

'Don't ask me,' I said. 'I've forgotten all about it.'

'I don't think my missus would be very pleased if I did that,' Mo said.

'I have an idea,' I said.

'What's that, Johnboy?' Dogmeat asked.

'Why don't we get more beer and think about it?'

'Great idea, Johnboy,' said Dogmeat, flicking another peanut... and missing.

We stayed longer than we usually did, mainly because we had nothing better to do. Walt, bless him, kept bringing the ale and we kept on supping it. Strangely enough, I didn't feel any more intoxicated, I just felt numb. I suppose something would turn up sooner or later, but it was going to be more difficult without money. A group of young lasses entered the pub, but we didn't bother marking them. It didn't seem important any more. The chatter from the rest of the drinkers became more noticeable as we retreated into our shells. The correlation between noise and alcohol consumption became evident as the afternoon wore on.

People two feet apart were shouting at each other to make themselves heard, and the noisier the pub became, the louder they had to shout. We simply sat and listened until Mo declared that it would be best if he headed home. The din didn't seem to have affected Bert at all. It made me feel happy to see him slumbering, without a care in the world. Ultimately, I had to rouse him and bid farewell to Jabba and Dogmeat. Bert and I were going to take a steady walk home.

On the way we walked past the path that led to the farm. I gave it little thought. It seemed like a lifetime ago, no, it felt like someone else's life. We wandered on and Bert squatted for a dump right in the middle of the path. I didn't have any bags, so I left it where it fell. Some unfortunate soul would probably come along and plant their foot in it, but I had other things to worry about. We took our time along the trail, not wanting to be anywhere but here. My home invoked feelings, mostly bad, but here under the open skies the world felt a better place. Bert kept running ahead, then returning to look up at me questioningly as I sauntered on. Truth is, he wanted his dinner. His life was about sleeping, eating and shitting. I envied the simplicity. A curtain of darkness was dropping when we finally reached home. I turned the key and swung the door open, allowing Bert to make a beeline for his water bowl. Having tanked up, he laid with his head on the edge of the bed, his eyes following me, waiting until I made a move towards the place I kept his food. I wondered if he was ever aware of the mess I'd made of my life, or was he simply living in blissful ignorance? I found a small piece of cheese, stuffed it between two slices of bread to create the semblance of a sandwich. No butter, I couldn't be arsed. It looked like a sandwich, but the reality told a different story. When we'd finished eating Bert joined me on the sofa and slept along with me through the news, of which I caught the first five minutes before drifting off to my safe place. It was the same news as yesterday and the day before, and probably tomorrow as well.

I woke up with a stiff neck, a dry mouth and a dull ache in my head. The TV was showing some panel game in which the celebrity contestants were vying to be the loudest and cleverest, talking over each other and laughing at their own jokes. Bert had moved into one of the armchairs, probably disturbed by my snoring or shuffling. I made my way into the kitchen to prepare what I hoped would be a recuperative cup of coffee. Just as I'd filled the kettle and pressed the switch down, I heard my phone ringing, so I went back into the lounge to answer it.

'Hello,' I said, groggily.

'Hello, Mr Dawson here.' I was in a fug, yes that was it, a fug. So much so that I thought the person on the end of the line was the bloke whose porch I had demolished some months earlier.

'Who? What? Sorry, I'm er…'

'Mr Dawson,' he repeated. 'You know, Sycamore Rise.'

'What do you want?' Surely, he wasn't after more from me. 'I don't have any money, I'm skint.'

'Steady on, lad,' he said. 'I don't want any money from you. That's all settled now, water under the bridge. Let bygones be bygones, eh?'

'I don't understand why you have called me.'

Well,' he said. 'I've heard that you are at a loose end, and I need someone to rebuild my porch and bearing in mind what a good job you did, I wondered if you'd like to come and do the job for me?'

'You are kidding?' I asked incredulously.

'No, John, I'm very serious.'

269

'For nothing? You've already had the costs.'

'Not for nothing,' he said. 'No, you'll be paid for your services, just as before.'

'That's the problem isn't it, Mr Dawson? You didn't pay. How do I know you'll pay me this time?'

'Of course I'll pay you. I'll give you a deposit this time, to put your mind at ease.'

'Can't you get someone else to do it?' I asked. After his last showing, I'd tipped off as many local builders as I knew about him. Maybe he'd rang a few and got the cold shoulder, or more likely he'd collected a few prices and didn't like what he saw. Now he was realising what a great deal he had with us.

'I like your work, John,' said Mr Dawson. 'Not so much the demolition, but the building side of things are spot on.'

'I don't know,' I mused. We needed the work, that was for sure, but I'd look a right Judas to the other tradesmen, wouldn't I?

'Same price as before,' added Mr Dawson.

'Fifty percent up front,' I insisted.

'No problem for me that, lad.' No it fuckin' wouldn't be because in reality he was paying for it with my money.

'And the full balance the moment we finish?' I said. 'Not the day after or the week after, but the full payment on the day?'

'That's fine with me,' he said. 'Do we have a deal?'

'We'll be round next Monday,' I said and hung up. We'd come full circle and still, we didn't know the depth of the well.